S...

*Three friends must end their military careers
to become peers of the realm!*

Lieutenants Hartley Edmenton, Rafe Tynesley
and Charles Marsdon are three friends who bonded
while on campaign in Spain and Portugal
in the Napoleonic Wars...

All have different family backgrounds, but through
unexpected events, they've inherited titles!
Now they must confront all the responsibilities
of the noble elite—run vast estates, attend
parliament—and marry to continue the family line!

Don't miss any of this wonderful new
miniseries from Julia Justiss:

Book 1: *The Unexpected Duke*

And look for the next titles coming soon:

Book 2, Rafe's story: *The New Earl's Convenient Wife*

Book 3, Charles's story: *The Marquess's Forbidden Bride*

Author Note

Sometimes a gift that most people view as wonderful is seen by its recipient as more burden than blessing Such is the case with Lieutenant Hartley Edmenton. His father scorned for marrying the daughter of a Scottish landholder, and treated with disdain himself on his few visits to his uncle's ducal estate, Hart is appalled when his cousin's unexpected death forces him to abandon his army career and return home—to become an English duke.

With the widowed young duchess still recovering from a miscarriage, her sister, Claire Hambleden, resents the rough Scottish interloper who arrives to take possession of Steynling Cross. Since the death of her own soldier husband two years ago, Claire has cared for her often-ailing sister, gradually assuming management of the estate and the upbringing of her son and her sister's daughter. She knows her duty is to groom the newcomer into becoming a worthy duke, even as she worries about where she will go once he takes over—and resents his replacing the man she once secretly loved.

Both are disgruntled by the inconvenient, annoying attraction that pulls them together from the first.

I hope you will enjoy Claire and Hart's story.

THE UNEXPECTED DUKE

JULIA JUSTISS

HISTORICAL

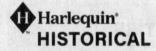

Harlequin® HISTORICAL

Recycling programs for this product may not exist in your area.

ISBN-13: 978-1-335-53999-1

The Unexpected Duke

 Harlequin Enterprises ULC
22 Adelaide St. West, 41st Floor
Toronto, Ontario M5H 4E3, Canada
www.Harlequin.com

Printed in U.S.A.

Julia Justiss wrote her own ideas for Nancy Drew stories in her third-grade notebook and has been writing ever since. After publishing poetry at university, she turned to novels. Her historical Regency romances have won or placed in contests by the Romance Writers of America, *RT Book Reviews*, National Readers' Choice and the Daphne du Maurier Award. She lives with her husband in Texas. For news and contests, visit juliajustiss.com.

Books by Julia Justiss

Harlequin Historical

Least Likely to Wed

A Season of Flirtation
The Wallflower's Last Chance Season
A Season with Her Forbidden Earl

Heirs in Waiting

The Bluestocking Duchess
The Railway Countess
The Explorer Baroness

The Cinderella Spinsters

The Awakening of Miss Henley
The Tempting of the Governess
The Enticing of Miss Standish

Sisters of Scandal

A Most Unsuitable Match
The Earl's Inconvenient Wife

Visit the Author Profile page
at Harlequin.com for more titles.

To Jane Austen, trailblazing Regency author whose dry wit, incisive eye and deep insight into the joys and tragedies of love have made her beloved by readers from the first publication of *Sense and Sensibility—by a Lady* in 1811. She launched a genre that continues to inspire, right up to Julia Quinn's smash hit Netflix series, *Bridgerton*. Thank you, Jane!

Chapter One

Steynling Cross, Hampshire—March 1813

Lieutenant Hartley Charles Edmenton, late of His Majesty's First Royal Dragoons, pulled his horse to a halt and gazed down the long, tree-lined avenue leading up to Steynling Hall. As his gaze swept over the palatial central Palladian mansion flanked by its two neoclassical wings, bristling with marble columns and carved pediments, a bitter taste filled his mouth and brought a frown to his face.

His batman gave a low whistle. 'Aye, it's an impressive pile there, Lieutenant. Or is it Yer Grace I should be sayin'?'

'Stifle it, MacInnes,' Hart retorted. Finding himself unable to move forward, he abruptly dismounted and led his horse back into the shelter of the Home Woods through which they'd just ridden.

There was no escaping the imperative to finish his long journey from Portugal and take up his responsibilities here, he knew. Everyone from his friends to Colonel Richardson, his commanding officer, had been urging it since he'd received notice of his cousin's untimely death just after the Battle of Salamanca last July.

'It's a dukedom, man,' Richardson had rebuked him sharply after word of his alteration in rank was brought to the commander's attention. 'And you the only direct male heir?'

'My late cousin was young, and the widowed Duchess is even younger. It's not been that long since his passing. There might still be the possibility of a son.'

'Indeed, but if there is not? The welfare of scores of tenants and dependents at multiple properties count upon the estate being carefully managed. Not to mention the well-being of the widowed Duchess and the rest of your family. Such a task can't be left in abeyance. You've been a fine soldier. You know where your duty lies.'

And so he did. Nor had he ever been one to shirk it, no matter how unpleasant, from covering the attack of the Forlorn Hope at Badajoz to serving with the rear guard on the bitter retreat from Burgos. He didn't mean to start now. But he couldn't help wanting to linger in the friendly shade of the woods and savour his last few breaths of freedom.

As he knew well from his few previous visits to Steynling Hall, nothing but aggravation and conflict lay ahead.

Finally, knowing he could put it off no longer, Hart took a deep breath, remounted his horse and urged Midnight back on to the carriage way.

All too soon, they arrived at the double rise of stairs leading to a massive front door behind which, he felt sure, the butler was lurking. Before he could pull up his horse, two liveried footmen sprang out from unseen positions beneath the stairs to catch his bridle and help him dismount.

Brushing aside the proffered hands, he jumped from the saddle. He'd been expected, he knew. The poor footmen had probably been posted on lookout duty beneath the steps every day since he reluctantly sent the message from London that he'd returned, at last, from the Peninsula and would be making his way to Steynling.

After glancing at the immaculate garb of the lackey now holding his own horse's bridle, his batman looked at Hart, amusement in his eyes. 'Should have stopped at the inn in the village, as I advised, Lieutenant,' MacInnes murmured. 'Yon uniforms look better than your one.'

His regimentals were rather threadbare. But he'd stifled the impulse to purchase new garments when he reported to Horse Guards before resuming his journey. The inhabitants of Steynling could take him as he was, as battle worn as his uniform.

If the widow and her family were anything like his late cousin, they would do so reluctantly and with scorn.

Well, he was about to find out.

With ever greater reticence, Hart mounted the stairs.

As he'd suspected, the entry door opened soundlessly before he could knock. A tall, thin man he vaguely recognised as the butler bowed deeply. 'Welcome back to Steynling Hall, Your Grace. I hope you had a pleasant journey?'

He caught the man's flicker of distaste as he took in Hart's road-weary appearance. 'I'll have Thomas show you to your rooms so you may...refresh yourself, if you like, before you greet the family. Michelson, the late Duke's valet, is ready to serve you until you make your own choice. The Duchess is still not leaving her rooms, but her sister will be waiting to greet you.'

A sister? Hart wondered what her role was. Travel-weary or not, he'd rather get the inevitable greetings over with as soon as possible, so he might relax.

As much as he'd ever be able to in this cavernous, echoing marble tomb.

'Thank you... Tompkins, isn't it?'

'Good of Your Grace to remember,' the butler replied, bowing again.

His memories of Steynling were too painfully acute to

forget any detail, Hart thought ruefully. 'I'd prefer to proceed with greetings immediately. It would be impolite to keep the…lady waiting any longer than necessary. I'll go to my rooms afterwards.'

To his rooms. His cousin Fitzhugh's rooms, really. Probably furnished with elegant fabrics dripping gold thread and emblazoned with the ducal crest. A far cry from the tent and simple camp bed in which he'd lived most of the past four years, since Wellesley, as he was then, first led troops into Portugal.

His lips creased in a smile as he imagined the household's reaction if he ordered them to remove all the elaborate furnishings and install his camp bed. He *would* have the rooms redone, however, if he found they contained too many gilded cherubs grinning at him from the ceiling.

'Richards will show your man to the servants' wing,' Tompkins continued.

Hart turned to MacInnes with wry smile. 'We've ridden hard. You can use some rest, too. Until later, then.'

'Summon me when ye like—Yer Grace,' MacInnes said, giving him an exaggerated bow instead of the usual salute.

'Off wi' ye, scurvy lad,' Hart tossed over his shoulder in the Scottish brogue of his youth as the butler led him away, his batman chuckling.

He followed the butler through the vast entry towards the door to what must be a grand reception room. Where on the threshold, a tall lady appeared, giving him a look that would have iced over the Douro in July.

'The Duke of Fenniston, ma'am,' the butler said. 'Your Grace, may I present Mrs Hambleden, sister to the widowed Duchess.'

He had only that fleeting glimpse at the woman's expression before she dipped her head and dropped into a deep curtsy. 'Welcome home to Steynling, Your Grace,' she murmured. 'Thank you, Tompkins. I'll take charge now. No need for tea. I expect H-His Grace will prefer to have it—or something stronger—in his rooms.'

'As you wish,' the butler said, bowing himself away.

So the sister was managing, Hart noted with some amusement. She was a tall woman, slender, but with a figure that verged on the statuesque, well-rounded in all the places a man would want it to be, but garbed in a modest high-waisted style, long sleeves concealing her arms and the fichu covering her from neck to bodice. The garment's midnight-blue colour signalled half-mourning, appropriate to her position as a near relation of the widow.

The hue flattered her pale skin, the dark hair braided and tucked under a cap, and the eyes he remembered from her brief glance as a piercing blue.

Only then did it strike him that the widowed Duchess was still not receiving, nearly nine months after her husband's death. Had the sister been running the household all that time, as, evidenced by her order to the butler, she was now? Might that chilly glance represent her fear that his arrival meant her imminent loss of control?

'Please, do have a seat, Your Grace,' she said, gesturing him into the room without looking again into his face. 'You are obviously weary after your long journey. My sister's late husband often mentioned you and your... Scottish legacy. I hope you won't find our English ways too foreign.'

His first thought was if Fitzhugh had indeed mentioned him, the reference wouldn't have been complimentary. His second thought was, with the hall such a large, echoing space, as she approached the anteroom's threshold, she could well have heard him call his Scottish-accented farewell to MacInnes.

She expected a rough Scottish country bumpkin did she? Maybe he'd give her one.

'Should I tug me forelock to you, ma'am, or should I say m'lady?'' he asked, as if ignorant of the rules that placed him above her on the social ladder.

She looked straight at him and Hart caught his breath. The dark hair brushed back under her cap, a few glossy blue-black curls escaping to frame her face, emphasised the porcelain fineness of her skin. High cheekbones defined her face beside an imperious nose. Eyes blue as the Mediterranean under sunlight skies mesmerised over plump lips so eminently kissable he felt an unwelcome stir of desire.

That tempting mouth twisted briefly with distaste before she smoothed her expression. Ah, so she did expect a bumpkin.

'You must become accustomed to having men tug their forelocks to you, Your Grace,' she replied. 'As is due your station. And it's a simple "Mrs" Hambleden.'

Letting that recommendation pass, he replied, 'And when should I be meeting Mr Hambleden, the lucky lad?'

'Not soon enough, I'm afraid. He died of wounds sustained at Fuentes de Oñoro.'

After the instant it took him to grasp she'd just hinted at a desire for his demise, he almost smiled. She might display the same arrogant sense of superiority all Fitzhugh's family possessed—but she was unexpectedly quick-witted.

And her husband had been a soldier. Hart didn't recognise the surname, but if Hambleden had been a good trooper, he could only respect that.

''Tis sorry I am for yer loss. A double loss, husband and brother-in-law.'

At the mention of loss, she swept a pointed glance over his ragged uniform. A raise of her eyebrows indicated she noted with disapproval that he'd not put off the military dress he no longer needed and donned more appropriate black garments. But after a pause, she refrained from whatever comment she'd seemed poised to make.

'Do you wish to dine downstairs tonight? Or would you prefer a tray in your room, so you might recover from your long travels?'

'Will the Duchess be comin' down? If so, I should appear an' present my condolences. I didn't want to call at her rooms and intrude. It cannot be but a…difficult time fer her.'

She tilted her head, as if silently reflecting, then nodded. 'I believe I could persuade her to come down. She simply couldn't face meeting you this afternoon, but she must acknowledge you at some point. Delaying will not make the task any easier.'

'Dinna do so fer me,' Hart said feelingly.

She gave him a searching look at that, but once again made no comment. 'I shall see you at dinner, then. I'll send Michelson up to assist you.'

'No need to bother aboot that, ma'am. Me batman will do fer me. He has been these last four years.'

Again, a quick expression of exasperation appeared before she smoothed her features. 'Your uniform will do for this evening, I suppose. A batman as valet is all well and good for a soldier on campaign, but it simply won't do for a duke's establishment.'

She shook her head with a sigh. 'Obviously our ways seem strange to you, but I will do my best to help you adjust, as I promised my sister. You are the Duke now, and you must look—and act—the part. It's not important what I think, but it is very important that you create the correct impression on the staff, tenants and the many visitors you will receive.'

'And ye dinna think much of me, I ken?' Hart said, unable to resist tweaking her again to see if he could incite another flash of the temper he suspected lurked beneath the calm veneer.

He provoked a dangerous sparkle in those excellent blue eyes, but after pressing her lips together firmly for a moment, she replied 'Fitzhugh—the late Duke, that is—said you were the most annoying person he'd ever met. I'm inclined to accept that assessment. None the less, for him and my sister, I must still do all I can to assist your becoming a worthy successor.'

Hart bit back his reply that it shouldn't take much to be more worthy of the position than Fitzhugh, if all he'd heard of his cousin's drinking, wenching and gambling were true. Added to the fact that he'd met his untimely demise in a fall from the phaeton he'd been racing on a wager down a dangerous dark stretch of road on a moonless night.

His arrogant, self-indulgent cousin had never appeared to him anything like the concerned, involved landowner his commander had stressed a dukedom needed.

Hart suppressed a sigh. As a boy, Fitzhugh had delighted in knowing he would one day be Duke and far outrank his country cousin, his arrogant attitude part of the reason Hart had always been glad he'd never hold high rank. The annoyance it caused his pretentious cousin was also the reason he'd persisted in calling him, 'Fitzhugh', his given name, even though everyone else referred to him as 'Barkley', the courtesy title of Marquess he'd held from birth until he became 'Fenniston' upon his father's death.

Hart had been as appalled to discover he was to become the Duke as his cousin had revelled in expecting to be.

Mrs Hambleden had evidently respected Fitzhugh— or at least, his rank. Had she harboured warmer feelings than respect towards him? His cousin had prided himself on charming all the women around him—at least, the ones he felt it worthwhile to charm.

Could her mourning be more personal than grief at her sister's loss of husband? That would help explain her obvious animosity. But if there had been affection there, how had that impacted her relationship with her sister, the Duke's wife?

The situation here might be more complex than he'd anticipated.

Making her a bow, Hart turned to leave, following the footman and fighting a deepening depression. Despite the presence of the lovely Mrs Hambleden, who looked to be a worthy adversary, returning to Steynling Cross promised to be as unpleasant and problematic as he'd expected.

Claire Hambleden watched the new Duke walk out, his return reviving the tumultuous emotions she'd spent the last nine months trying to bury for good. But the instinctive resentment she'd felt at the appearance of this rough, ill-clad and ill-behaved replacement for the late Duke proved she'd not yet completely purged her heart of the hopeless love she'd always felt for Fitzhugh. The handsome, teasing, beguiling one-time suitor who had dazzled the young debutante she'd been…before going on the following Season to marry her far more beautiful younger sister.

She thought she'd hidden it well over the years, that never quite extinguished passion. That she'd fully expunged it after learning how he'd met his death in that ridiculous midnight carriage race—the more ignominious details of which she'd kept from sister—coming so closely on the heels of his reprehensible request. A request she still couldn't believe her sister had seconded. Making it all worse, the guilt she still felt over how tempted she'd been to agree. If it hadn't been for Alex…

As always, she submerged guilt, grief and uncertainty under the wave of quiet joy thinking about her son evoked.

Focus on Alex and how best to make a life for him, and she'd weather this latest challenge.

She'd continue to care for her son and her floundering sister, adding to those tasks her duty to help the interloper— who looked and sounded every bit the crude, uncouth Scot her sister's late husband had described.

Still, to be fair, as the Duke's estranged cousin, he'd never thought to inherit. It was unrealistic to expect he'd be prepared for the task. He'd spent years as a soldier instead, and if he were clinging to that familiar role in the midst of vast change, one should hardly fault him.

He might be rude and uncouth, but her careful enqui- ries revealed that Lieutenant Hartley Charles Edmenton had been an exemplary soldier, one of the heroes assist- ing the Forlorn Hope's successful breaching of the walls during the siege of Badajoz, a man mentioned in the dis- patches by Wellington himself. Under his unfinished ex- terior lurked a man of proven character. She'd just have to try to polish it up.

And after that—what? Her sister Liliana was unlikely to let go of her any time soon, not since she now ran her household so efficiently. When Claire had accepted her sis- ter's invitation to take refuge at Steynling Cross after her own husband's death, as time went on, she'd just naturally resumed the role she'd played since their childhood, moth- ering her younger sister.

Sighing, she walked to the window, gazing out at the manicured topiaries in the side garden, their pristine ap- pearance reflective of her care for the estate. The assump- tion of responsibilities had happened so gradually, she'd scarcely noticed it at first.

With Mother as usual occupied with Father in London, assisting as he went about his duties as private secretary to a cabinet minister, everyone in the family had approved having her retreat with her young son to Steynling. It would give her a home—as she had no other, her late husband being a younger son of few resources—and enable her to look after her recovering sister, who'd suffered a miscarriage all too soon after the difficult delivery of her daughter, Arabella.

In the course of caring for her sister, Claire had taken over one household task, then another, then another, until the staff began to look to her rather than their mistress for direction. When Mr Evans, the estate manager, suffered a serious illness, she'd taken on most of his duties as well.

Though the ducal establishment was much larger than any household she'd lived in before, after having in her teen years assumed charge of their country manor during her parents' frequent absences to London and then managed for her husband while following the drum in Portugal, by now, the direction of a diverse staff and multiple duties was second nature to her.

Would she move with Liliana to the Dower House after the new Duke settled in? Would Liliana want to go to London and consider marrying again once she was out of mourning? Claire had no idea. Her sister needed to be looked after. She thrived on attention and flattery, especially from attractive men, and had loved being Duchess. But a widowed duchess was another matter entirely. Liliana was far too young and beautiful to spend the rest of her life wearing black, sitting among the dowagers.

As she had no answer to the troubling question of where she might end up next, Claire focused back on the present. Since the new Duke didn't wish for a tray in his room, she'd consult Cook to make sure all was in train for dinner in the Green Room, the smaller space used when they took meals *en famille*.

Not the vast state dining room, though as annoying as the man was, it would serve him right if she had his meal

presented on the thirty-foot table where he'd have to practically shout to be heard from his place at the head by her
sister holding court at the other end.

Which would probably not be a problem, though. Despite the thick Scottish brogue, one couldn't miss the commanding tone in his voice—the timbre such that his words
would travel even over that distance. A useful attribute in
a battlefield soldier, she imagined.

Despite his somewhat ragged appearance, she had to un-
willingly concede that he cut an impressive physical figure,
too. Though she was tall for a woman, he was taller still, the
broad shoulders and muscled arms filling out the sleeves of
his frayed uniform doubtless the result of years of wield-
ing a dragoon's heavy cutlass in battle. His legs were well
muscled too, speaking to countless hours on horseback.

Though she'd limited her glances straight at him, she
couldn't help noticing a face most would deem handsome—
a high forehead over which a lock of dark hair curled, pen-
etrating grey eyes, strong chin and firm lips that curved
into a beguiling smile, crease lines by his eyes a testament
to skin weathered by many years' exposure to the glaring
Peninsular sun.

Arresting in his ragged regimentals, he should at least
look the part in proper ducal dress. As she reviewed his
physical attributes through her mind's eye, she felt an unexpected and highly unwelcome stirring of sensual awareness.

Irritated, she squelched it. His physical attractiveness
was a positive attribute in a duke. However compelling he
might be, she had reasons enough not to be susceptible, she
informed her rebellious senses. Armed with his pedigree,
proper clothing and after some coaching in manners, which
she hoped he would accept without fighting it too much, she
could take him to London, find him a suitable duchess and
her duty to her sister complete, be through with the man.

Time to return to household matters, she told herself, dismissing further thoughts of the ill-garbed Lieutenant-turned-Duke. Dismissing, as well, a niggling sense that she'd eventually part from the new master of Steynling Cross with more regret than she now assured herself she would feel.

Chapter Two

'Are you certain I must go down?' Liliana asked. Stubbornly attired in a lacy dressing gown, the Duchess tarried before her mirror while Claire brushed her golden locks, despite Claire having informed her that dinner would be imminent. 'You know I've still not fully recovered.'

She knew her sister played on her delicate health when it suited her, Claire thought, trying to stifle the uncharitable observation. Her sister had always been fragile, subject to frequent ailments of the lung. And to be fair, the widowed Duchess had struggled to recover her strength after the second miscarriage she'd suffered a year ago, compounded so soon afterwards by the death of her husband. Her return to full strength had been hampered, Claire thought, by the melancholy that kept her inactive, shut up in her rooms brooding despite her sister's efforts to coax her out.

'I know it's difficult,' Claire replied, putting a soothing note in her voice. 'Delaying the meeting won't make it easier. It's desperately unfortunate for all of us, but your Fenniston is gone, and nothing can bring him back. As we both know, there's no chance of an heir who could displace Lieutenant Edmenton. You shall have to recognise him eventually. At least he gave us almost nine months to adjust to our…changed circumstances.'

'If you'd agreed, it might never have come to this,' her sister muttered, giving her a dark look.

'I thought *we* agreed never to discuss the matter again,' Claire snapped back. 'The idea was unworthy of you and him.' Though, after what she'd learned over this last year, such a request was apparently not unworthy of the man who'd once stolen her girlish heart. Did one always end up disillusioned by the love of one's youth?

'I know, Claire, but…what's to become of us? When I try to think it through, I just keep going round and round in circles, everything beyond the present so great a muddle of pain, uncertainty and grief that I can scarcely face leaving my bed.'

That comment was too bleakly true for Claire not to feel another wave of sympathy. Liliana had always been able to manage that, her sweetness of temper and generally docile manner disarming the anger and resentment her self-absorption sometimes aroused in Claire. She was ever the beautiful, golden child who'd never truly grown strong enough to shoulder adult burdens. How much of that lack was Claire's fault, for cosseting her all during their growing up?

She squeezed her sister's shoulder. 'We'll be all right. You and Bella are amply provided for—Father's solicitors set up the settlements to ensure you'll never want for anything. You can remain here or in the Dower House if the new Duke prefers. Or engage a house in town.'

When her sister shook her head with a groan, Claire hastened to continue, 'When you feel strong enough, of course. No need to do anything or make any decisions yet. The Lieutenant might be…somewhat rough-edged, but he seems to be a kind man. Didn't I tell you, he wished to see you at dinner so as not to have to invade your private rooms to make his introductions? He possesses some sensibility, it seems. I doubt he'll push you to take any steps about your future immediately.'

'I hope not, for I cannot do it. Not yet. I can still hardly believe Fenniston—*my* Fenniston—is gone.'

Claire wasn't sure what her sister really thought of her late husband—if she'd become as disillusioned at the end with the dazzling, handsome but utterly selfish man as Claire had. She hadn't known what her sister felt for the late Duke at the beginning of their marriage, either, beyond satisfaction at having snatched from a host of contenders the biggest matrimonial prize of the last several Seasons, and excitement at becoming a duchess. Had she ever truly loved Fitzhugh?

Claire didn't mean to be disparaging in believing that part of her sister's agreeable nature meant her feelings remained only surface deep. Liliana didn't seem to be profoundly touched by anything, treating even her surviving daughter with a detached sweetness. Unlike Claire, whose emotions could be far too tumultuous for her own comfort.

She'd been better of late, managing to keep them in check. She just needed to continue doing so, concentrating on the welfare of her son, sister and niece, and she would survive this next phase of her life. Wherever it might take them.

Her sister might be well provided for, but as a poor soldier's widow, she definitely was not.

Pushing away the nagging worry acknowledging that fact always produced, she said coaxingly, 'Let Wallace help you into the black silk. You look so ethereally lovely in it the Lieutenant cannot help but grant whatever you ask of him.'

'Now you are flattering me. I've looked old and drained ever since…'

Since she'd miscarried that last child, Claire mentally completed the statement. A loss her husband had railed at her about. Fenniston's unkindness had certainly made that tragic situation worse, and with his death soon after making her sister's failure to produce an heir devastating for her future, it was even more difficult for Claire to try to pull Liliana back from despair. But she would, however long it took.

So she said bracingly, 'Nonsense! That's just depression of the spirits speaking. If you are pale, the colouring suits those golden curls, which not even grief and loss could dim. You are quite as beautiful as you ever were, perhaps even more so with that trace of sadness in your lovely blue eyes. As anyone who gazes upon you knows. As you would, too, if you truly looked at your reflection in the glass.'

That finally brought the hint of a smile. 'You are so good to me. What would I do without you?'

What, indeed? 'You'll not have to do without me—not any time soon, at any rate. Now, let me turn you over to Wallace and go make myself presentable. I'll see you downstairs, then?'

Her sister sighed, then nodded. 'Very well, I'll see you downstairs.'

Relieved, Claire signalled to the waiting maid and walked out. Though she'd assured the Lieutenant that her sister would dine with him, she hadn't been entirely sure she could convince her.

Now to get through dinner. She hoped her sister wouldn't put off enquiring just what the new owner of Steynling Cross had in mind for it—and them. Spending these last months in limbo, a boat with its oars shipped, drifting with the current, had been difficult. She needed to be able to plan, to dip those oars back into the water and guide her little family to a safe harbour. Somewhere that would be best for all of them.

Remaining at Steynling probably wasn't the answer.

* * *

With a frown, Hart regarded himself in the pier glass. MacInnes had ensured he'd wear his best uniform to dinner by the simple means of sending off to the laundry the one he'd travelled in. Before he could protest, his batman told him frostily that if he were not concerned about the impression he made on the household, MacInnes was, and wouldn't have the staff believe him incapable of properly dressing an officer. To say nothing of a duke. But he didn't press his luck far enough to push Hart to put off his uniform and don the new civilian dinner attire he'd acquired in London.

MacInnes seemed to understand without any words exchanged between them just how hard Hart was finding it to relinquish his identity as a soldier and small Scottish landholder and take on the strange and unwanted role of an English duke.

For a little while longer, he thought, brushing an imaginary speck of dust off the gold braid at his collar, he would recognise the reflection he saw in his pier glass. Before losing himself for ever in this strange new destiny.

Not that he believed he wasn't capable of handling all the duties it would require. In any event, Fitzhugh had never seemed concerned about tending to the practical aspects of the job, revelling only in the wealth and status it afforded him.

As a soldier who'd thrived on campaign and survived the worst Boney's Peninsular troops could throw at him, Hart found the potential challenge of running a ducal enterprise hardly daunting. There would be a myriad of details to master, he knew, but at least no one would be trying to put a musket ball through him while he was going about them.

He recalled Mistress Icy Blue Eyes and chuckled. She might not have had a pistol in hand, but if gazes could pierce, the disapproving Mrs Hambleden would have skewered him without uttering a word.

If she continued to be disapproving, it would be partly his own fault for deceiving her with that Scottish brogue.

He admitted, he wasn't looking forward to the inevitable awkwardness of meeting his cousin's widow and having to utter regrets about the death of a man he couldn't mourn with any sincerity. Though he could genuinely regret her loss of husband—and his unhappy assumption of the position the man had unexpectedly vacated.

He also admitted he *was* looking forward to clashing swords with Mistress Icy Blue Eyes again. Pressed into a situation he didn't want and couldn't escape, he simply couldn't summon up the strength of will necessary to stifle the urge to provoke her and make those magnificent eyes flash. Since that looked to be the only pleasure available in this accursed place, he intended to indulge it.

One little change should spark some fireworks, he thought with a smile. After some reflection, he'd decided to abandon the Scottish accent and go back to his usual manner of speaking. He'd only put it on as he'd been piqued by the disdain her tone demonstrated for his mother's heritage—though to be fair, Mrs Hambleden has probably just been echoing attitudes conveyed to her by Fitzhugh—adopting the brogue had been deceiving, and he hated deception.

Would she be more approving once she'd heard him speaking in aristocratically inflected English? Somehow, he didn't think so. After giving his sleeve a final brush, he nodded to his reflection and headed for the door.

A footman scurried to open it before he could emerge. 'Tompkins asked me to lead you to the Green Room, Your

Grace. As you might not remember the way from your previous visits, he said.'

'Kind of him to consider that,' Hart acknowledged. 'As I was just a lad the last time, not old enough to dine with the Duke, I probably couldn't find it without a map.'

Hart smiled as the man suppressed a chuckle before leading him off through a maze of corridors. Fortunately, Steynling had been rebuilt by his great-grandfather, its original Elizabethan parts subsumed into the echoing marble entry section, with massive formal rooms added behind the entry, along with the vast colonnaded wings. Though grand, the building was laid out with geometric precision, which would make finding his way around it easier.

He squelched again his distaste at the idea of having to make his way around, along with a wave of homesickness for Kirkraidy House. One could probably fit five or six of his family home in the space occupied by Steynling Cross.

He would return there, once he initially settled things here, he promised himself. MacInnes would probably abandon him then, he thought regretfully. Hart doubted his batman would choose to stay in England, even if he didn't have some bonnie lass waiting for him back home.

Finding the ideal lady for himself now would be far more difficult. Despite his own distaste for the change, he had no illusions about what his elevation would mean for his bachelor status: every English matron with a marriageable daughter, niece, cousin or young friend would be after him, a huntress gleam in her eye as she attempted to snare such a marital prize for her darling. He'd almost rather stand under the walls of Badajoz again than face the campaigns certain to be launched against him when the inevitable time came to take a wife.

He'd always thought that time wouldn't arrive until he met the lady who instantly captured his heart—as his mother had his father when his Edinburgh teacher and mentor took Papa home on a Christmas visit to his family. One glance, his parents had often told him fondly, and they'd both known they'd met the one person they could love, marry and cherish for a lifetime.

And so they had.

He recalled Moire and smiled. He'd once casually considered offering for his childhood sweetheart, daughter of his mother's good friend and a feisty Scottish lass he'd known most of his life. He'd given her a first taste of whisky; she'd rewarded his first clumsy attempt at a kiss with a roundhouse punch to his jaw.

But knowing he'd be heading off to war with the Royals, he'd refrained from proposing, not wishing to make her a widow before she'd scarcely become a wife. And was later rewarded by a letter from Moire, thanking him for not tempting her with an offer to marry for affection and friendship that would have prevented her from wedding the man she'd later fallen in love with.

'Your parents showed us the best way to wed,' she'd written. 'Not merely for comfort, as my parents did, or for wealth and status, as so many do. To marry someone whom you know within moments of your first meeting to be the other half of your own soul is a joy unmatched by any other. A joy I beg you to wait for and pray you will one day experience.'

Was that still possible when he'd be engulfed by battalions of English maidens intent on capturing a duke? He grimaced—yet another reason to resent the unwanted title that had stolen from him almost all control over his own life.

Selecting a bride was one of the few choices left to him. And when he did, he vowed, patting the letter from Moire he still carried in his pocket, he would follow the path to lifelong happiness she and his parents had blazed, resisting all efforts to push him into marrying for dowry, pedigree or worldly advantage. Despite becoming a duke—and even more because he'd *had* to become a duke—he wanted by his side a woman whose radiant love would inspire and sustain him through the long grim years of carrying the burden of his inheritance.

Fortunately, with so much else to settle, he could put the difficult business of marriage on hold for the foreseeable future.

'The Green Room is just there, Your Grace,' the footman said.

Tompkins, waiting by the indicated door, spotted them and approached. 'Good evening, Your Grace. Let me escort you in for dinner. Normally, the family would gather in the Octagon Salon before dining. But as Her Grace's health is not yet fully restored, she's requested that we proceed directly. She and her sister await you within.'

At the repeated news of the Duchess's ill health, Hart frowned. She'd miscarried a babe the previous spring, he'd been told. Maybe an heir. He thought of asking Tompkins if the child had been a boy, but posing so private a question to a member of the staff would be indelicate. Though Hart was certain so highly placed a family retainer would surely know the answer.

Death of any child was a tragedy. Losing the heir would have been catastrophic.

With two miscarriages followed by the death of her husband, the young Duchess had suffered a number of blows, her formerly secure position rendered uncertain. Regardless of whether or not she'd truly cared for his cousin, Hart must try to be compassionate and understanding.

Hart followed the butler in, a jolt going through him at hearing himself announced as the Duke. After that frisson passed, he looked towards the head of the table to the lady garbed all in black who'd stood as he entered—and involuntarily stopped short.

Awaiting him was not the wilted flower he'd been expecting. The bereaved Duchess was ethereally beautiful, perhaps the most beautiful woman Hart had ever seen. Not as tall as her sister, slender, her hair the purest sun-struck gold, tendrils framing her face before the heavy braided mass was pinned in a shining crown topped by a tiny black cap. A classic oval face, alabaster skin, enormous eyes of deepest blue, and rose petal lips completed the picture. While her sister was lovely, but earthier, the Duchess was a Botticelli Madonna.

Realising he was staring, with his jaw dropped, Hart looked away and closed his mouth. Almost as an afterthought, his gaze slid to Mrs Hambleden, who was standing beside her sister. She wasn't looking at him—not now, at any rate—but staring into distance. There was no hint of scorn in her expression, rather…a deep sadness, almost a stricken look.

She had probably noted him stop short upon entering and witnessed his dazzled expression upon first glimpsing her sister. A memory from long past suddenly surfaced, himself as a young lad standing inside Steynling's grand entry when some neighbours had arrived during his visit. Standing, ignored, while the visitors flattered the Duke and fawned over Fitzhugh. His face must have held just such a look as hers did now—annoyed, hurt, impatient. Sadly resigned.

Had she always been cast into the shadows by the sheer brilliance of her sister's beauty?

Probably.

Then she looked over at him, her expression calm and controlled, become once again Mistress Icy Blue Eyes. Not as beautiful as the Duchess, perhaps—but somehow more alive, more *real*—and much more appealing than a Botticelli angel it would be sacrilege to harass.

Hart suppressed a smile at the thought of the conflict sure to come. But edging that anticipation was a new warmth, a bond created by having shared the similar, if unacknowledged, experience of being overlooked by those who prized appearance and status over all.

By now, his feet had carried him the table, where he bowed to ladies, while Tompkins intoned, 'Duchess, this is His Grace, the Duke of Fenniston.'

Taking a deep breath, senses on the alert for the reaction his next words would provoke, Hart said, 'Honoured to meet you, Duchess, though I am sorry to do so under such sad circumstances. Mrs Hambleden, good evening.'

That lady's eyes widened in surprise, her lips opening on a gasp before, frowning, she curtsied with a curt, 'Your Grace.'

Meanwhile, a crystalline sparkle of tears forming at the corners of her magnificent eyes, the Duchess rose from her own curtsy to give him a nod of acknowledgement. 'Thank you,' came her reply in a half-whisper, her voice as sweet and soft as her appearance.

Hart wondered how many suitors had competed to win her hand. He well understood how she'd captured a duke—especially his cousin. She'd doubtless been the most sought-after prize of her debut Season, and as Fitzhugh always expected the best to be his by right, it was almost inevitable that he had claimed her.

'Please, sit, Your Grace,' the Duchess said, waving a languid hand towards the chair at the head of the table.

As they walked towards their seats, Mrs Hambleden murmured, 'Your speech seems markedly improved since this afternoon.'

'Ah, what miracles can be wrought by several hours in

an English country house,' he replied, unable to suppress a grin.

'Indeed,' she said coldly. 'I shall remember how quickly you can change.'

Despite his delight in teasing her, his conscience tweaked him. 'It was a low scurvy trick, and I do apologise. Can you forgive me? I shouldn't like us to start out on bad terms.'

Looking somewhat mollified, she nodded. 'With so much to be done, nor would I. Apology accepted.'

'Praise be blessed!' he couldn't resist adding before stepping to his place, chuckling at her sharp glance.

By the time he'd taken his seat, she'd recovered her calm. 'I ordered a light repast for dinner tonight, Your Grace. I thought, after your long journey, you would not appreciate a heavy meal.'

'True enough, though after living so long on a soldier's portion, I'm sure whatever you've arranged will be more than sufficient.'

'What treats await you,' the little Duchess said. 'My sister is a marvellous manager. We dine well at every season, whether in company or not.'

'Ducal standards must be maintained,' Hart said smoothly.

Though the Duchess merely nodded, taking the statement at face value, a quick flash of those icy blue eyes told him Mrs Hambleden recognised the comment for the barb it was. Hart waited with anticipation, wondering if she'd fire a volley back.

Instead, she looked to her sister and said, 'Duchess, did you not have some questions of His Grace about his intentions?'

The widow's large blue eyes widened. She opened her lips, then closed them, shaking her head as another large tear rolled down her cheek. 'I...I can't. Now.'

'I have no intentions that need concern you, ma'am,' Hart said quickly, noting the woman's obvious distress.

Mistress Icy Blue Eyes, however, was not so easily deterred. 'Then if I may?'

Raising his eyebrows, Hart said, 'Enquire away.'

She blew out a breath, then forged on, saying, 'If it is agreeable to you, I can continue running the household for the present, Your Grace. Until you've settled in and decided how you want to order things. But arranging mine and the Duchess's…relocation will require a good deal of planning, so I should like to ask outright whether you would have her remove to the Dower House as soon as possible, or whether she might remain in her rooms for the present?'

'Claire!' the Duchess gasped, her expression of dismay deepening.

Mrs Hambleden reached over to press her sister's hand, but her fierce expression undaunted, she continued, 'I know it's upsetting to think about change. But best to know as soon as possible what His Grace expects, so we can begin making the necessary arrangements.'

Hart had spent years assessing the men under his command—especially on the eve of a battle. Under Mrs Hambleden's cool exterior, he sensed uncertainty—and fear.

An unexpected wave of sympathy washed through him. So preoccupied had he been by the huge changes this inheritance meant for his status and position in the world, he'd given little thought to what it meant for theirs. Now, as owner of the estate, he had the authority to cast them both out if he chose.

No wonder the Duchess looked anxious and her sister fearful behind her outward show of calm.

Here was at least one official act as Duke he could perform with heartfelt conviction.

'No, not a bit of that, ladies! This is your home. Your rooms remain your own as long as you wish them to be.'

Releasing a shuddering sigh, the Duchess sat back in her chair. After swallowing hard, Mrs Hambleden said, 'Thank you, Your Grace. That is most kind.' She nodded to the butler, who motioned for the footmen to begin serving the next course.

'You mustn't be thinking me some heartless ogre, ready to cast you into the wilds.' Turning to Mrs Hambleden, he added in a murmur, 'Even if you believe 'tis where I belong.'

Hart was pleased to see that thrust bring a slight flush to her cheeks. But immediately she parried, 'I imagine you make yourself at home wherever you are, Your Grace.'

That exchange had been even, he thought, swallowing a chuckle. While he debated whether to ask the Duchess about her courtship and marriage—wondering whether any such discussion might bring up too many painful memories—Mrs Hambleden said, 'Won't you tell us something of your background, Your Grace? We know your mother's family hails from Scotland and that you grew up there and then joined the army, but almost nothing else.'

'My mother's family owns the Kirkraidy estate, just south of Fife. Flax-growing for linen, linseed oil and cattle feed mostly. My father, younger brother of your husband's father, Duchess, left Steynling to study in Edinburgh, where he met Reverend MacReif, a notable scholar and cleric. As Father was…not on good terms with his own family, the Reverend invited him to spend Christmas holidays at Kirkraidy, where he met his mentor's daughter, my mother Susanna, also a notable scholar.

'I believe they first crossed swords over Shakespeare, she feeling obligated to keep the upstart Sassenach in his place, he upholding the scholarly honour of England. After the initial skirmish brushed the rust off both swords, they decided they had much in common. And almost instantly fell in love.' Hart smiled, remembering the joy on his parents' faces as they gazed at one another. 'They loved as the Good Book said, every day 'til death did them part.'

'They're both gone, then? I'm so sorry,' Mrs Hambleden murmured.

'Father is, as you know, but Mama holds her own, working with the manager at Kirkraidy—the property was in her family and she grew up there, so she knows it intimately.'

'Have you no brother or sisters to help her?' Mrs Hambleden asked.

'None who reside at Kirkraidy. My younger sister, Ainsley, married the owner of a neighbouring estate while I was away in the army. I had a younger brother, but he did not survive childhood.'

Realising that comment could only bring back unhappy memories, he went on quickly, 'And your parents, ladies, are they still living?' Hopefully, he could turn the conversation and learn something of their background—for he knew nothing at all.

After a moment, Mrs Hambleden replied, 'Yes', in a flat tone that didn't reveal much warmth. 'Father is private secretary to Lord Sidmouth, with whom he's worked for many years. Mother resides with him in London, serving as hostess and assistant in his work.'

Which meant cultivating the wives of other politicians, continually engaged in the delicate game of strategy and intelligence-gathering so as to know who had the ear of which man of power and determine with whom to ally oneself to maintain one's position or increase one's influence.

A process Hart understood, as the army operated much the same way. Though at least the army had the crucible of battle to prove the mettle of its participants, so a man was not reliant solely on his wealth and connections.

'Is London home, then?'

'For them, yes. The Duchess and I grew up at Whitley House in Sussex. We didn't spend much time in the city until we went there for our debuts and subsequent marriages.'

It appeared they'd spent most of their childhood separated from their parents, then. Surprised, as he'd never spent much time away from his own before departing with the army, Hart said, 'It must have been hard on them, seeing so little of their daughters.'

'They tolerated the separation well enough,' Mrs Hambleden said drily.

'You mustn't think we were neglected,' the Duchess chimed in. 'They believed the country air healthier. London can be so dirty and smoky.'

'The Duchess was always delicate, subject to ailments of the lungs,' Mrs Hambleden said, looking at her sister fondly, the first expression of warmth Hart had seen from her. 'A fairy sprite who charmed everyone she met. Our parents thought remaining in the country would be better for her, and their physician agreed.'

'Nurse and our governess watched over us ever so carefully,' the Duchess said. 'Mama wrote often to ensure that, as nieces of an earl, we were being prepared to take our proper positions as wives to important men.' She looked over to her sister with a smile. 'Claire took wonderful care of me. We had a very happy childhood, didn't we?'

Mrs Hambleden smiled back. 'We did.'

'We were inseparable until the time came for us to marry. We went to London together, as I couldn't bear to be left behind even though I was not "out" during her first Season. I first met Fenniston—he was still Barkley then as his father's heir—when he called on Claire at the beginning of *my* debut Season. Not until that summer ended were we forced to part, me wedding the future Duke and later that year she marrying Hambleden, the younger son of a long-time political associate of Father's. Though I never quite forgave him for joining the army and bearing her away! Of course, I regret his death, but I could only be happy when she came back to rejoin me at Steynling Cross.'

'Took her away, did he? Did you follow the drum, Mrs Hambleden?' Hart asked, his curiosity now truly piqued.

'I did. Though I spent much of my time overseas in Lisbon.'

'She was so intrepid! Her son, Alex, was born in Lisbon, and she took him on summer campaign as a mere infant!' The Duchess shuddered. 'I can't imagine. Travelling in rough country in all weathers, to say nothing of doing so while *enceinte* or with a tiny child. Managing children is difficult enough in England, with staff to assist.'

'I wasn't that intrepid,' her sister objected. 'But it was… an adventure.'

At the odd inflexion in her voice, Hart covertly studied her face. Her conflicted expression didn't speak of 'excitement' at recalling an 'adventure'. His mind clicked through the facts the Duchess had presented—that she'd first met Fitzhugh when he called on Mrs Hambleden, that the older sister had not married the 'son of her father's friend' until after the younger sister was wed. That Mrs Hambleden had inadvertently called his cousin 'Fitzhugh' when first she mentioned him, not referring to him by title as most would.

Might there have been something between them—on her part, at least? The Duchess was an Incomparable, but only when standing beside such a Beauty would a man gaze past her sister, whose dark good looks and voluptuous figure were sure to have caught his cousin's attention. Hart could easily believe Fitzhugh might lead along a young lady with casual disregard for her feelings, believing himself entitled to dazzle any female he chose. And having no compunction about dropping her when his interest wandered elsewhere.

Had Mrs Hambleden married the family friend and left England seeking adventure—or escape?

'Steynling Cross isn't nearly as adventurous as Portugal, but I'm so glad she returned to me. She's been such a comfort through my...losses,' Duchess said, reaching over to squeeze her sister's hand. 'I hope now we can remain together always.'

Her sister gave her a fond—and Hart thought, somewhat sad—smile. 'I'll be with you as long as you need me...and I'll always protect your interests,' she added, the last said with a faintly challenging look at Hart.

Suddenly the Duchess paled, waving away the course the footman was presenting.

'Are you all right, Sister?' Mrs Hambleden cried.

That lady sat back in her chair, her already pale face going paler still. 'Just feeling...faint, of a sudden.'

Mrs Hambleden jumped up, rushing to her sister and waving a handkerchief at her face. 'You've hardly left your bed these last weeks. I fear you've overtaxed yourself! My fault, insisting you come down to dinner. Should you like to retire?'

'I think I should prefer to return to my rooms,' the Duchess said faintly. Looking over to Hart, she added, 'No insult meant to present company, of course. I apologise for my lack of stamina. As my sister said, I've barely been out of chamber since...'

Another tear formed in the corner of her eyes, one spilling down her cheek. Hart rose too, walking over to offer his arm. 'No need for apologies, Duchess. Let me help.'

When she nodded assent, Hart put a hand under her

arm, lifting while a footman assisted on her other side. Once they had her out of her chair and upright, Hart nodded to the retainer, who relinquished her arm with a bow. 'I'll assist you to your room. Mrs Hambleden, would you summon her maid? Don't worry, Your Grace, she will have you tucked up right and tight in a trice.'

Hart eased along the Duchess's fumbling steps, half carrying her. Though she was hardly a burden, light as child, rather—a fairy sprite indeed. After instructing the butler to summon her sister's maid, Mrs Hambleden came to her other side to take the arm the footman had relinquished. Maintaining a flow of soft encouraging words, she helped Hart guide her sister up the stairs and into her chamber.

That elegant, gilded room was just what he would have expect of the Duchess, its fashionable furnishings rendered in a more delicate, feminine style than the ornate ostentation of the Duke's suite.

Well aware he was out of place in a widow's bedchamber, once he'd helped ease the Duchess into a chair by the hearth, Hart bowed to them both.

'I'll leave you to settle her, ma'am. Goodnight to you both, and better health to Your Grace by morning.'

'You hadn't finished your meal,' Mrs Hambleden said. 'Do you intend to return to the Green Room, or shall I have Tompkins have a fresh plate sent up to your rooms?'

'No need,' Hart said, waving a hand. 'I've had sufficient. Goodnight, ladies.'

The Duchess looked up at him, gratitude and appeal in her striking blue eyes. 'I'm so thankful. Not just for your help bringing me here. For…understanding. For not… pushing me to decide my future before I'm ready.' She offered him one pale hand.

Looking down at that glorious face, Hart could well understand how men enchanted by her beauty and touched by her delicacy would volunteer to move heaven and earth to protect and shelter her. Even he, mostly immune to her appeal, still felt that pull. All those centuries of duty and a warrior's zeal to protect his women, his family, calling in the genes, he supposed.

'You mustn't worry. I'd never disturb your peace,' he assured her.

As he bent to kiss her hand, he saw her sister giving him a look. Did she fear another man falling under her sister's spell, wondering what his possible enchantment would mean for her?

I'll be with you as long as you need me, she'd assured her sister.

Did she worry about what would happen to her if—when—another claimant stepped in to supplant her in meeting those needs?

If someone did, he already knew it wouldn't be him. Much as he appreciated the Duchess's heart-stopping beauty, he preferred a hardy woman who could embrace life with relish, punch him in the jaw or share a snort of whisky, not a fragile doll one must set carefully on a pedestal.

He could at least reassure Mrs Hambleden on that score. Even if it meant delving into what he increasingly suspected had been a complicated relationship between the sisters and his late cousin.

Chapter Three

Early the following morning, Claire rode her mare to the top of the rise behind Steynling Cross. As the fog of the previous night dissipated, she could see the downs unrolling below her, fields upon meadows upon fields. She found the mist-shrouded landscape soothing, as she had the sound of the sea while in Lisbon.

When in Portugal with her husband, she had discovered how calming it was to ride early before any other camp followers were up, just she and her horse alone in a pristine landscape. Relieved for the moment from duties and obligations—if she could never quite outride heartache and regrets. A heartache that today seemed particularly acute.

That ever-present ache sat low in her belly, part disillusionment with Fitzhugh, the man she'd once loved completely, shame that she'd deceived herself about his true nature for so long and regret over losing her life with her husband, Alexander.

Friends from childhood, she and Alexander had become comrades in heartache, both of them entering their marriage of convenience for security and to assuage the loneliness of unrequited love. Over time, they'd grown closer, the fiery physical passion they'd shared a benefit she hadn't anticipated and a pleasure in which they'd both revelled. She'd almost believed he'd grown to love her as she had grown to love him…until the discovery just before his death that turned her affection into bitter ashes of disillusionment.

It was perhaps that pain that had made her so vulnerable to Fitzhugh's seeming kindness and compassion when she returned from the Peninsula, bereft of purpose, uncertain what her role in life might be aside from once again, as she had since childhood, caring for her sister. Longing for the closeness she'd lost, wanting to believe the man she'd never quite got over might care for her as well, she'd almost betrayed herself and her honour, leading to an even more bitter disillusionment.

But there was no use brooding over a past which could not be changed. With the mist vanished, it was time to shake off melancholy remembrances, ride back to consult with the housekeeper, estate manager and then cook so they might present tonight a meal more fitting of a duke.

She thought of the new Duke himself with a mingling of resentment, caution and wary respect. Despite accepting his apology, she'd not quite forgiven the Lieutenant for tricking her into believing him to be the fumbling, unpolished country type Fitzhugh had led her to expect. But she'd have to put that resentment behind her if she was to help him become acquainted with the estate, learn to assume his new duties—and see that he found a proper duchess.

At least she wouldn't need to deal with him until later today. Except…unlike most aristocrats, as a former military man, the Lieutenant probably didn't stay up late drinking and gaming, nor remain in his bed until afternoon. He might even be a habitual early riser.

She felt a sudden stab of alarm, the hope that he wasn't a devotee of early morning rides occurring just as she heard the muffled clatter of approaching hoofbeats.

It might be one of the estate staff. But of course, given her luck, by the time the rider approached near enough for her to recognise the red uniform coat, she realised it was indeed the Duke. Who by now had surely spotted her, so it was too late to slip away.

Trying to suppress her annoyance at having her solitary ride interrupted—the only time in the whole day she ever had truly to herself—she drew up her reins and braced herself for the meeting.

She saw surprise register in his eyes when he drew close enough to recognise her. 'Mrs Hambleden! I didn't expect to see anyone from the house riding this early.'

'I didn't expect to encounter anyone either,' she replied, not sure she'd managed to conceal her irritation.

There was a wisp of smile, quickly suppressed. 'From your tone, I infer the meeting isn't to your liking. Is it because you truly prefer solitude—or is it me in particular you'd rather avoid? In which case, I must assume you have not yet forgiven my little subterfuge.'

'I don't think it's so unusual that I disliked being made a fool of.'

Frowning, Edmenton shook his head. 'Making you feel like a fool was never my intention!' he protested. 'To be completely honest, I didn't *think* about my reaction at all. Since you seemed to expect an uncouth, boorish Scot, I simply fell into the role Fitzhugh had prepared you to anticipate.'

That claim was true enough that her resentment softened a little. By now, she knew enough of Fitzhugh's ability to self-deceive to appreciate his ability to twist facts to suit his opinions. 'I expect you are right,' she acknowledged. 'If I apologise for making a premature, unsupported judgement, can we begin again?'

'If you'll accept my apology for perpetrating the deception—and spoiling your solitary morning ride.'

'Agreed. Since it appears I've spoiled your solitary morning ride as well.'

Not commenting on that, he said, 'With such a vast household to keep running, I expect it's the only time you have to yourself.'

'As it is for you?' she asked before thinking, then felt annoyed with herself when he nodded assent. She didn't want to acknowledge they shared the same preference. Bad enough to have to admit that knowing now that he was not the rough country type he'd appeared had significantly intensified the pulse of attraction between them.

'I used to ride out early to the heights, to reconnoitre the battlefield before an engagement,' he was saying, and then laughed shortly. 'I suppose that's what I was doing this morning.'

Surprised, she said, 'Battlefield? Here?'

'It used to be. When I visited as a child. A battlefield on which I had few if any allies, little artillery and scant ammunition. A battlefield I hoped to escape, which is why I lingered in the army all last summer and even into the autumn retreat from Burgos, hoping there might be news of some…natural issue to supplant me.' He sighed. 'But there was not. A tragedy for the Duchess and for me.'

He wanted to…escape inheriting? Shocked—and disbelieving—she said, 'You mean you didn't wish to become Duke? Why ever not?'

'I've never wished to become anything like Fitzhugh.'

Apparently he'd known of the late Duke's deficiencies of character, deficiencies it had taken her far too long to recognise and even longer to admit. But then, Edmenton wasn't a gullible young maiden to be fascinated. She could well believe Fitzhugh hadn't wasted any of his famous charm on a lowly country cousin.

Not sure what to reply, she said instead, 'If you are so reluctant to assume the title, why did you return at all?'

He grimaced. 'I wouldn't have, were the choice truly mine. But with everyone pressing me about it from the moment I was notified of Fenniston's passing, I managed to delay only until the army reached winter quarters. They all kept emphasising that with the late Duke dying without male issue, were I to be killed, leaving the estate without a male heir of the direct bloodline, the title might go into abeyance or even be reclaimed by the Crown, if no more distant heirs could be found. It would be an abrogation of my responsibility to the land, the tenants and the family not to remove myself from danger and return to England.'

'Your friends were correct, of course. Yours is both the duty and the privilege to carry on the proud tradition of your family name and title. To support and assist your tenants. Maintain and improve your properties. Take your place in Parliament and assist in guiding the nation, as important a protective role as you've played in the army, surely.'

He raised his eyebrows. 'You certainly seem to hold a high opinion of the position.'

'Of course. Aristocrats have ruled this nation for centuries. Only with wise rule can England avoid the upheavals that have occurred on the Continent.'

'Perhaps,' he acknowledged. 'Though from some of the aristocrats I've seen, doing away with them all, as the French have done, might be an improvement.'

'Except they didn't do away with them. After the Revolution chucked them out, Napoleon ushered himself in and has now created a new raft of them. Who's to say his are any better than the old ones?'

Edmenton laughed. 'Maybe so. Maybe not. But I'm no pol-

itician. I understand the business of the army. Parliament—
not so well.'

'You will have secretaries and assistants to help you
track legislation, untangle policy and advise you on what
to recommend and how to vote.'

'As your father does?'

'Yes.' Much as she might have wept as a child at her parents' seeming abandonment, as an adult she recognised the
importance of Parliament's work. 'Assisting the men who
govern the nation is a vital responsibility. It must be carried
out by men of intelligence and education, who possess the
knowledge, understanding and broad experience to make
wise choices. To properly guide the nation.'

'Whether it wants to be guided or not,' he muttered.
'But—' he waved her down before she could protest
'—though I believe your intelligent farmer or well-
educated solicitor or business owner equally competent, I
do concede competence is important.'

'Gracious! Are you to be a Jacobite as Duke?'

He laughed. 'I'll not be nationalising property or calling for a guillotine to relieve my opponents of their heads.
But a bit more widespread representation in Parliament
wouldn't be a bad thing, in my opinion. Or having towns
vote in the delegate they truly want, not the one the nearest powerful landowner wants.'

Despite her desire to maintain a safe distance from him,
Claire found herself increasingly curious. 'You'd truly have
preferred to remain a simple soldier?'

'There's an important duty to be performed in the army
as well, serving England by finally wresting control of the
Continent back from the Corsican usurper. He's a clever
man, a wily general, but ambitious to hold all land from
France to Russia in his thrall. Though saying so may make
me appear a coxcomb, I'm a skilful officer who made sig-

nificant contributions to the fight against him. A fight I intended to carry on until victory, and a career I resent being forced to abandon.'

Claire nodded. Though her late husband had been as eager to quit England as she was for similar reasons, he had also felt this same duty to protect and serve his country. 'But once that battle was won, did you plan to remain a soldier?'

Edmenton—she really must begin thinking of him as 'Fenniston' or 'the Duke'—shook his head. 'Probably not, although I enjoy the army and if England faced another challenge, I would willingly remain in service. Once peace was truly restored, I intended to do some exploring before eventually returning to some of the most beautiful acres in Scotland. Which are now being tended, as I mentioned last night, by my mother and the estate manager.

'Kirkraidy is small by Steynling's standards, but bountiful enough. With Father involved in scholarship, like my mother's father who taught at Edinburgh, we spent part of the year in the city, part in the country. But there's nothing as beautiful as Kirkraidy in the late spring with the bright blue fields of flax blooming.'

She hadn't ever thought he might have a career or a home he missed—one that he resented having Steynling pull him away from. To be sure, she hadn't much thought about him as an individual at all. A man who rode early, a patriot willing to pledge his life on the battlefield—and a near-Jacobin dubious of the rights of hereditary aristocrats?

Her interest engaged despite herself, it wasn't just the powerful physical attraction he exerted that drew her now.

'Does a pretty lass await, too?' she asked, curiosity prompting the question before prudence could forestall it.

'A Scottish lass not suitable to become Duchess, you mean?' he said drily.

That reminder of her earlier dismissal of his heritage chilled the budding entente. 'It depends on her family of course. But such a lady could be totally unsuitable,' she stated flatly.

'And if I suggested that's not any of your concern?'

'My *concern* is to help my sister see that this estate run properly until you are well enough equipped to take it over,' she snapped, her annoyance returning. 'A task which includes steering you towards the selection of a duchess with the proper training to manage such a vast household, who is comfortable mingling in the highest ranks of society, able to maintain the standards expected of a ducal establishment—and provide you an heir.'

'Should I interview suitable candidates? Post a notice in the paper, perhaps?'

'If necessary,' she retorted, truly irritated now. 'Assuming the normal method of meeting eligible ladies in society fails to satisfy. Now, as many duties await, you must excuse me. I'll leave you to continue your ride unmolested.'

Really, the man was so annoying! she thought, turning her mount towards the stables. Fitzhugh might have exaggerated his Scottish boorishness, but he was quite as aggravating as his cousin described. Though why she should be so irritated about his virtually dismissing the importance of properly choosing a bride, she wasn't sure.

Naturally, she didn't want to see her sister supplanted by someone less endowed with the qualities a Duchess should possess: beauty, charm, graciousness, competence, a firm knowledge of the ways of society, someone who would be a glittering ornament to her highly ranked husband. Even if she did allow that the new Duke should have *some* say in that choice.

Maybe it disturbed her because once that final choice was made, the estate ready to turn over to a new mistress, there would be no further duty to fulfil, no more reason to remain. She would have to face the implications of being a widow of slender means and no home, her sole purpose trying to raise her son as best she could.

Putting a hand down to quell the gnawing in the belly that uncertainty always created, she forced her mind to review the myriad domestic details to be decided this day and set her mount to a trot.

Hart watched Mrs Hambleden ride off in a huff. He really shouldn't tweak her, though it was all too easy. He should instead dismiss her as being at heart just another arrogant aristocrat like his late cousin.

But that wasn't entirely true, he acknowledged with a sigh. She seemed unaccountably impressed with title and pedigree, but there was something more there, something that touched him even as her pride irritated. Though her choice of how to go about it might differ from his, she felt the same certainty that Napoleon should be vanquished— having followed the drum with a soldier husband, how could she not? She also expressed the same patriotic conviction that their nation must be governed wisely.

Then, beneath the calm and bravado, he sensed some vulnerability—fear even. Much as she seemed eager to complete her 'duty' acclimating him to his new responsibilities and then being rid of the burden of managing Steynling, there was also a proprietary pride in the place which hinted of a reluctance to move on.

Because she wasn't sure what she would move on to? The widow of a duke would be comfortably provided for. The widow of a soldier might not be. Her late husband had doubtless been a gentleman, but had likely also been a younger son with little inheritance to leave her.

It might not have been just her sister's preference that led her back to Steynling Cross upon her husband's death—if she had no other place to go. And if she were poorly funded, she might have no choice but to hang on her sister's sleeve, unless her parents were willing to take her in.

That sort of uncertainty could make anyone short of temper.

He was too honest to deny the spark that resonated through him at any casual touch. Under that cool veneer, he was certain the heat he felt was mutual. Though the last complication he needed was an attraction to the sister-in-law of his late cousin.

Was he only imagining some jealousy in her enquiry about a Scottish sweetheart? Or was that probing just her need to fulfil her 'duty' by making sure he didn't wed someone 'unsuitable'?

And what, exactly, had been her relationship with his late cousin?

With so many questions about his place here and his future unsettled, if he could distract himself from an unwise attraction and this whole impossible situation by teasing the tantalising Mrs Hambleden, he meant to continue.

Chapter Four

Later that morning, Hart was sitting in the breakfast parlour finishing his beefsteak and ale when Mrs Hambleden walked in.

'Good morning again,' he said, rising. 'Will you join me? I've nearly finished, but a cup of coffee wouldn't come amiss.'

She shook her head. 'Thank you, but no. I broke my fast in the nursery with the children. Tompkins told me I'd find you here.' She took a deep breath. 'I fear I left you rather abruptly during your ride this morning and wanted to apologise…again.'

'I suppose I was a bit abrupt myself,' Hart admitted, recalling his sharp remarks about finding a duchess. 'Shall we offer another mutual apology?'

She gave him a nod. 'I'm willing, if you are.'

''Tis done.' Some imp of mischief induced him to add, ''Naething is ill said if it's no ill taken.''

She looked startled for a moment by the sudden return of the brogue before she shook her head reprovingly, a reluctant smile on her lips. 'I shall try not to take offence, then. Though if you're going to be throwing Scottish phrases at me, I'm not sure I can promise that.'

'Ah, but they have so many apt sayings, the Scots! My dear grannie and my nurse were full of them. "Better a sma' fish than an empty dish." "Haste and anger hinder gude counsel." "Pride and grace ne'er dwell in ae place."'

'Enough, enough!' she said, holding up a hand and laughing in earnest now. 'Lest I insist you apologise again. Those last two border a bit too closely on criticism.'

'The second applies well enough to me,' he admitted. 'Are you sure you'll not tarry for a coffee?'

She looked like springtime this morning, her habit exchanged for a morning gown in a green hue that emphasised the ice-blue of her eyes, her flawless skin and the glossy dark hair. Not only did everything male in him respond to her, after the solitude of his morning ride once she'd left him, he'd been gripped by a sense of isolation and loneliness.

He missed his comrades, the certainty of knowing his job and what he was to do. On the Peninsula now, he'd be seeing to the comfort of his men, dealing with any issues of sickness or discipline. Chatting with his fellow officers before consulting with their commanders on the next military movement, receiving the latest intelligence on the disposition of enemy forces. Checking with his batman about supplies, seeking replacements for worn or damaged kit. Seeing to the care of his horses.

Instead of tending to a myriad of duties amid the bustle of a busy encampment or the city or village where they'd been billeted for winter, he'd ridden through lovely but deserted countryside, its emerging green a stark contrast to the rocky hills and dusty roads of Portugal. The few servants he'd encountered had either silently made their obeisance or quickly scurried out of view.

After returning his mount to the stables and washing up, he'd walked through silent, echoing halls past vast, silent, echoing rooms into this pleasant but only slightly less echoing chamber, the bountiful provisions set out enough to feed his whole squad. And now faced a day in which he wasn't sure what he was supposed to do.

Mrs Hambleden might be more antagonist than companion, but she was intelligent, vital and engaging as well as attractive and the only person with whom he had any connection in all this grand house.

Before he could add any further inducement to his request, she said, 'I'll not have coffee. But I did want to check and see how you were settling in. You may well wish for a few days of quiet and rest before you go about assuming the duties of the estate—'

Hart interrupted her with a wave of the hand. 'Nay, I'm not used to idleness. If you followed the drum, you'll know there may have been months between battles, but every day had its work. My ride this morning was…refreshing, but I'm ready to get on with it. Not anxious to do so, in truth, and still regretting the necessity, but regretting it won't make the duty disappear. So I may as well get on with it. If you are available to assist me?'

'In addition to apologising, I meant to invite you, if you were ready, to begin that process. First, I'd like to introduce you to the staff. Of course, had you notified us that you would be arriving yesterday, I would have had them assembled and ready to greet you.'

'Instead, I slipped in like a thief in the night,' he admitted.

'Or a sheep-taker creeping into a croft, or however you'd phrase it. I imagine there's a saying about that, too—but spare me,' she said, holding up a restraining hand.

While he chuckled, she walked over to ring the bell pull. 'On second thought, I'll have that coffee while Tompkins gathers the staff. Would you…would you like to change out your uniform for civilian attire before the meeting?'

He felt a strong wave of resistance. 'I'm still getting used to that.'

She offered a surprisingly sympathetic smile. 'Even in uniform, everyone will call you "Your Grace." I'm afraid you must get used to that, too.'

He supposed he would adjust—eventually. For now, he wouldn't resist the fierce emotion tightening his chest with the need to cling to his uniform and his previous identity for as long as possible.

A moment later, the butler appeared. Mrs Hambleden gave him instructions while Hart calmed himself by walking to the sideboard to pour her a cup of coffee.

'Who will I be meeting?' he asked after she'd seated herself.

'The Duchess hasn't felt well enough to entertain, so with no need to receive guests, we have a reduced staff. In the office near the stables is Mr Evans, the estate manager. Working inside, in addition to Tompkins, there's Mrs Reynolds, the housekeeper, and Mrs Charis, the cook, who has a baker, two kitchen maids and a scullery maid working for her. Then there's Michelson, the late Duke's valet, and Wallace and Maria, the lady's maids. Six footmen, four housemaids, Mrs Burris, the nurse, and her two assistants complete the inside staff.

'For outside help, we have Greenwood, the gamekeeper, and his assistant, Holmes, the gardener, and his two assistants, and Old Greenwood, the retired gamekeeper who mans the gatehouse. Then there's Parker, the head groom, Stebbins, the coachman, four grooms and two stable boys.'

'And a partridge in a pear tree?'

Giving him another reproving look, she said, 'Are you going to tell me your mother runs the entirety of— Kirkraidy, isn't it?—herself?'

'No, but we've only ten inside servants, plus five in the stables and one gardener.'

'So you didn't exactly grow up in a hovel.'

'No. Although sometimes my mother complained when I returned from the fields that I looked like I did.'

'Hopefully you didn't drag your poor sister through the mud on your travels.'

Hart laughed. 'Ainsley often returned as unkempt as I was, since she insisted on tagging along whenever she could.'

'Wreaking havoc even as a child, I see,' she observed. 'I thought we'd visit the nearer tenant farms this afternoon. It will be several days' ride to inspect all those on the home acres.'

'You will be escorting me?' he asked, surprised.

She flushed a little before replying, 'Soon after I arrived at Steynling, Mr Evans fell seriously ill. Fortunately, he recovered, but only after many months. While he was bedridden, I took over his duties of checking on the tenants. He still is not hardy enough to ride out in all weathers, so I've continued to do the visiting.'

'I see. So just how much acreage will I be inspecting?' Hart asked.

She angled her head at him. 'You truly don't know?'

'I had neither expectation nor desire to inherit,' Hart reminded her.

'True, but you did inherit, almost a year ago now. And have not taken the trouble to learn anything about your holdings or the people they support?'

Hart squirmed uncomfortably at the hint of censure in her voice. She obviously felt he'd been neglecting his duties—and he had to silently admit that she was correct. Once faced with the inevitability of inheriting the dukedom, he should have made it his business to find out all he could about the responsibilities he'd have to shoulder and the people who'd depend upon him.

'Ignorance I will endeavour to eliminate as soon as possible.'

'I should hope so,' she said acerbically. 'But if you were successful commanding troops as an army officer, you should have the experience to handle an estate. Tenants require less management than soldiers, and horses, cows, pigs and crops don't desert, get drunk or turn insubordinate—though pigs can sometimes become quite aggressive.'

Hart smiled. 'I think I shall manage.'

She was silent a minute, then said with deliberate calm, 'Have you given any more thought yet to how you want to proceed—with us? I expect at some point you will want the house to yourself, certainly after you bring home a duchess. I don't mean to be haranguing you about it, but removing my sister to another location, even just to the Dower House, will be a considerable undertaking. One I will have to bring her to by stages.'

'And I expect all the work of any removing will fall on you, with little or no help from your sister?'

She looked away with a sad and troubled expression he couldn't fully read. 'Probably,' she said at last.

'The Duchess, she brak her elbow at the kirk door,' did she?' he asked, unable to resist the urge to tease—or the inexplicable urge to chase the brooding look from her face.

He watched in satisfaction as her expression changed from melancholy to exasperation. 'Recall that you are now in England, please. Whatever did that last bit mean?'

Hart chuckled. 'It's said about a lass who was a busy housewife until she married a wealthy man—as soon as she left the church as a bride, she was suddenly no longer able to do any practical work.'

'Liliana wasn't raised to be a housekeeper, but to grace

a table, charm a guest and please a husband,' Mrs Hambleden retorted, her tone defensive. 'Besides, even were she the industrious housewife you seem to think she should be, she's still physically weak. You saw that for yourself last night. I've been waiting since Fitzhugh's—the late Duke's death to discover where her home and what her status will be going forward. Assisting her back to more robust health will be easier if I know what you envision for her. For us both. If that makes me overanxious and too…importunate, I apologise.'

'No need. I can easily believe uncertainty makes you anxious. I also admit I'd never considered until you first mentioned it last night how precarious you might feel your position is. It will take some time for me to fully learn all the duties I must discharge here, and for that, I'll need the help you've graciously offered. I certainly don't want or intend to take over the management of the house itself. You are both welcome to remain at Steynling as long as you like—permanently, if you wish. When—if—you choose to remove elsewhere, I would then be grateful for your recommendation in finding a competent assistant to take over for you.'

'You are sure you would be comfortable with that arrangement?' she asked, anxiety still clouding her expression, filling those icy blue eyes with a sheen of tears.

With considerable difficulty, Hart resisted pressing her hand—and the even keener desire to take her in his arms. He knew instinctively that the initial urge to give comfort would quickly fire into desire of another sort. A desire that, with his physical attraction to her growing ever stronger, would be difficult to suppress.

He'd indulged in casual carnal relationships over the years, always with knowledgeable matrons interested, as he'd been, only in a temporary liaison. He'd carefully refrained from succumbing to desire for any of the camp followers who hung about the army—or bored army wives looking for a fling. Beginning a liaison with a woman around whom he must live and work would be even more foolish than basing a permanent relationship simply on physical desire.

No matter how tempting he found the frosty but delectable Mrs Hambleden.

Curling his fingers in his fists at his side, he said, 'I'm quite sure. What sort of rogue would that make me?' he added in a jocular tone he hoped would amuse her as it put an end to her anxiety. 'I may be a Scot, I'm not one of Boney's soldiers rampaging across Spain, throwing good people out of their homes, commandeering their livestock and despoiling their daughters.'

She gave him a faint smile. 'No, I suppose the Scots rampaging, commandeering and despoiling of the English ended a few centuries ago. You will tell me in good time if you change your mind, though?' At his nod, she continued, 'Despite your kind offer, I'm sure you will want us to remove once you've chosen a duchess.'

'That's work for another day, and not any time soon.'

She shook her head. 'For all the reasons already discussed, the search shouldn't be put off too long. You might take a month or so to get acclimated at Steynling, but you really should go to London before the end of the Season and begin looking.'

'Won't all the most likely lasses have already been chosen by then?' he asked, trying to put off the discussion and repress his annoyance about being pressed on the matter.

'Not necessarily. In any event, the arrival of a young and handsome duke will have every unclaimed young lady in a flutter—and all the older single females as well, if you don't find an innocent debutante appealing.'

'*She's been raised to grace a table, charm a guest and please a husband,*' he recalled Mrs Hambleden saying of her sister.

Though he'd not previously given much thought to the qualities he'd prize in a wife, he didn't find the idea of a wide-eyed innocent straight from the schoolroom, trained to agree to his every wish and whim, very attractive. He suspected he'd be much more likely to fall in love with an intelligent, competent, forthright lady well able to take care of herself, manage others and not afraid to speak her mind, even if her opinions clashed with his own.

Someone like Moire…or Mrs Hambleden?

Pushing that disconcerting thought aside and wanting to distract her from the conversation, he said, 'So, you think I'm handsome, do you?'

To his relief, whatever argument she'd meant to continue died on her lips as a becoming flush warmed her cheeks. 'You may stop preening,' she retorted. 'The reflection you see every morning in your shaving mirror tells you that.'

As she gazed at him, their glances locked and held. She drew in a sharp breath, and his own pulse stuttered.

He felt it strongly and knew she did, too—that deep, irresistible, potent physical connection, like an underground river surging beneath them, sensed but not acknowledged.

Its strength didn't make the attraction to the sister of his late cousin's wife any less unsuitable. Needing to edge away from dangerous ground, he said, 'I'm glad you've addressed the concern about your future directly, so I might set your and the Duchess's minds at ease. Have you always been so protective of your sister, so vigilant in her defence?'

As if relieved herself to focus on safer topics, she said, 'I suppose so. I began early, if that's any explanation.'

'Caring for your sister as a child? Your parents were often away, you said.'

'Yes. As the nephew of an earl, Father had…ambitions to play a part in political life. Mother, who loved being in London, delighted in assisting him by putting on dinners for his associates and teas for their ladies. Pursuing those wifely aims clashed with her maternal duty to us. Especially to Liliana, whom my parents adored, but whose delicate health required living in the fresh air of the country, far from the ill humours of the city.'

Her tone had been somewhat cool when speaking of her parents, but as she began discussing her sister, her voice became notably warmer. 'Of course, I adored her, too. It was like having a beautiful, pliable doll to dress, tend and play with. Caring for her was no burden, for she is generally as sweet-tempered as she is lovely.

'Watching out for her welfare led me to become more involved in the running of the household, with me eventually writing Papa to request his authority to intervene as I felt necessary. By then, I'd entered my teens, and after turning off several servants whom I discovered had been helping themselves from the household accounts, I took over the direction entirely, hiring a new cook, housekeeper and butler.'

Her face alight now with more enthusiasm than he'd yet seen from her, she went on, 'I'd already taken over the still-room, consulting our own recipe book and the local herb woman on how to prepare remedies for the lung ailments she was prone to. Gradually I became something of an expert in cultivating the most useful plants in our own garden and using them to prepare tinctures, teas and infusions.'

Despite his smiling encouragement, for he truly wanted to learn all he could about the sisters, she stopped abruptly, her bright eyes fading. 'But listen to me, running on like a lonely spinster with a captive guest. You can't really be interested in these ramblings about my childhood.'

'But I am,' he protested. 'I have a responsibility here,

as you've justly pointed out, to the estate and its tenants. I have an equally serious one to my cousin's widow. I did indeed see for myself how far the Duchess is from fully recovering her health and spirits. The more I know about your shared background, the easier it will be to help without inadvertently paining her or proposing activities that are beyond her current strength.'

After he finished, she sat silent for a moment. 'It truly is kind of you to want to…help her,' she said at last, her voice carefully neutral.

Hart's mind flashed back to his bedazzlement upon first encountering the Duchess. 'Don't misinterpret my interest! Though I fully appreciate your sister's astounding beauty, I'm content to simply observe it. There's no danger of my deciding to claim not just my cousin's title, but his widow. I concede that I shall have to choose a wife at some point— when *I* am ready and have met the right woman—but your sister is not a candidate, even if such a choice wouldn't set society on its ear.'

'Are you so sure of that? She can be…enchanting.'

'For a man who appreciates ethereal beauty above all, perhaps. I tend to prefer a more…robust female. Like someone brave and hardy enough to follow the drum. Though I've no ambitions in that direction, either, so you may rest easy.'

There, he'd made his lack of designs on either of them clear enough. Having probably already been too plain, he dare not blunder further still and mention their need to resist the potent physical connection pulsing between them.

Perhaps he was missing an opportunity to engage her help in resisting it, but if he were to admit he considered that attraction unfortunate, she might take it as an insult.

She was wrong, he thought, suppressing a sigh. It *was*

easier to deal with soldiers, with whom one could speak plainly without worrying about arousing untidy emotions.

But he was no callow youth, unable to control his desires. He'd limit his response to Mistress Icy Blue Eyes to teasing and, even without her help, keep physical desire firmly in check.

Was she reassured by his declaration to avoid entanglements? Embarrassed or discomforted at his frankness?

He looked up, trying to read her expression, but she'd turned her face away. 'Well. I expect Tompkins will have the indoor staff assembled by now. Shall we?'

He rose with her, disappointed she'd given him no hint of her reaction to his assurance about maintaining a dutiful cousin's relationship towards the sisters.

'Though we'll host a large gathering later with our staff and all the tenants to celebrate your accession after you return from London,' she said as they walked out of the morning room, 'I should like to introduce you to everyone here as soon as possible. As you might imagine, they are all anxious to meet the new master of Steynling.'

Hart thought of his morning ride, during which the few farmers he passed looked up from their chores at the stranger with only mild curiosity. At envisioning a large gathering where he was the central attraction, like the featured act at Astley's Amphitheatre, dismay rose in him.

He suddenly realised that there'd soon be no more anonymous rides about the countryside—or in London. He didn't question his competence or ability to handle his new responsibilities. He had no difficulty leading men, persuading or commanding obedience, or voicing his opinion with peers or superiors. But the idea that henceforward, when he rode or walked about, he'd be recognised, greeted with deference or outright flattery, always the focus of attention wherever he went on the estate or in the city, made him feel distinctly queasy.

He'd better savour these last few days of relative freedom. Once he'd been invested as Duke, he'd be on public display for the rest of his life.

Resisting the urge to slow his pace and put off a bit longer his first 'ducal debut', Hart set his jaw and paced forward. Fortunately, he could look forward to an extended ride this afternoon in Mrs Hambleden's company.

He'd need a lengthy session of teasing Mistress Icy Blue Eyes to cheer him after taking his first reluctant step into his new role.

Chapter Five

Later that afternoon, Claire waited in the stables for the Duke to join her. After meeting the staff, at his insistence, Edmenton had accompanied the estate agent to his office rather than having Mr Evans bring the books for inspection in the library. No point hefting large ledgers over to the main house, Edmenton replied when Evans said he'd bring over the most recent volume. Besides, he wanted to look at the estate office itself, he'd added, ending the agent's protests.

Claire had an odd sense that he'd been more interested in escaping Steynling Hall than inspecting an office. Though he'd received the congratulations of the staff cordially enough, it had seemed to Claire that she could almost see him…retreating…as he faced the group. Not drawing himself up with haughty reserve, as Fitzhugh often had—it was more like he'd detached himself, his lips making the appropriate comments, his body moving through the proper motions, while the man himself was elsewhere.

Whatever his state of mind, he'd taken himself off with Evans after the introductions were complete, taking with him that energy, charisma and sheer maleness that called to Claire every time she was near him. Leaving behind a void she could almost physically sense.

In just a few minutes she would encounter that force

again—and have to resist it for the entire course of their ride, a prospect that both set her nerves simmering with anticipation and brought a disgruntled scowl to her face.

After reassuring the startled groom who encountered that look that everything was quite all right with the horse he'd just brought her, a shiver passed over her as she sensed, rather than saw, the Duke approach behind her.

Fortunately, the groom engaged him in a short discussion about which mount he would prefer, allowing her to bring her disorderly senses back under control.

You are a mature woman—act like it, she chided herself.

She'd met many commanding, compelling men while following the drum in Portugal. Just because the Duke exerted such a polarising appeal was no excuse for her to become as flustered as a giddy chit in her first Season.

'I suppose I should try all the horses in the stables,' the Duke said as he waited for the groom to bring out the gelding he'd recommended.

'You should, so you can determine which you wish to keep, which you want to sell off.'

'The stables seem full. Did Fitzhugh do much riding?'

'He used to invite friends and go out with the local hunt. In more recent years, he preferred to meet his friends in London.' Answering his unspoken question, she continued, 'The Duchess and I seldom accompanied him. It took her a long time to recover after the birth of their daughter, then again after miscarrying two more babes. The stable boys have kept all the horses exercised, though. You have only to try them and see which ones you like.'

'Did you bring your mount back from Portugal?' he asked.

'No, I sold all our horses, mules and my husband's kit before we returned to England.' She didn't elaborate, but having been with the army, he'd understand from that one terse sentence that she'd had to sell it all to afford passage home for herself and her son. That her husband's death had left her with few resources—on the Peninsula or in England.

Fortunately, he didn't press her for more. 'A fine little mare. Does the Duchess enjoy riding her?'

Claire paused for moment, debating how much to explain and deciding the bare truth would be best. 'Fitzhugh bought the mare for my use after I came here to help my sister. She'd told him how much I enjoy riding. When the Duchess feels well enough to go out, she prefers a carriage. Riding jolts her too much, she says, and she's always afraid the horse may bolt and she might not be strong enough to rein it in.'

Edmenton nodded. 'Some will certainly bolt if they think they can get away with it.'

'Indeed,' she replied, eager to steer the conversation away from any discussion of her relationship with Fitzhugh. 'We owned one like that in Portugal. Great endurance, but he'd nip or try to run away with you, given the slightest inattention.'

He gave her a quirk of a smile. 'I'm sure you managed it. And relish controlling any unruly beast.'

Was he referring to more than horses? But he couldn't know how passionate her relations with Alexander had been. Despite that, she felt her face heat. Ignoring his last comment, she said, 'Despite the horse's uncertain temperament, he was a superior mount in battle, my husband's first choice. Sadly, he was killed by the artillery blast that mortally injured my husband.'

'At Fuentes de Oñoro, you said?'

'Yes. Alexander's comrades told me that a cannon ball struck the horse's flank and came through the other side. My husband lost his leg, the dying horse fell on him, and he lay there some hours before they were able to remove him from the field. By the time they got him to the rear, he was unconscious. He died several days later.'

'I'm so sorry for your loss. My regiment, the Royals, were involved in the battle, too. A desperate fight back and forth through the village and along the riverbanks on both sides. Too many valiant men died that day.'

Claire nodded. 'I brought my son home as soon as we'd completed the burial arrangements and sold off the goods.'

While Edmenton nodded in sympathy, Claire fell silent, the unwanted memories flooding back. Shock, grief at Alexander's death distorted by her desolation over what she'd discovered in their makeshift quarters the night before the battle.

They'd been friends since their youth, but over the course of their months in the Peninsula, sparked by an intense physical passion, their camaraderie had deepened. Warmed by her husband's oft-expressed admiration and his boasts to his comrades about what a lucky man he was to have a wife who could organise a camp, scout out provisions and have a snug billet available when he returned from watch, she'd believed he had come to love her, as she had grown to love him.

Until the night she'd come to tease him into lovemaking, and found him standing in the firelight, melancholy longing on his face as he gazed at a miniature portrait— of her sister.

It wasn't that she hadn't known he'd loved Liliana. Alexander had courted her sister persistently before Fitzhugh discovered her and swept her away. Even if she hadn't been as dazzled by Fitzhugh as he'd been by her—initially, anyway—Alexander had known her family would never allow their beautiful daughter to throw herself away on a nearly penniless younger son once a dukedom's heir came courting.

But Claire had believed that Alexander had, as she had, moved beyond grief at the loss of his first love. Gone beyond a mere marriage of convenience and their long friendship into something *more*.

It made his death all the more bitter to discover she'd been wrong. That once again, as with Fitzhugh after he'd beheld her beautiful sister, Claire was second best.

She looked up to see the Duke studying her. 'Sorry, I was wool-gathering,' she said, glad he was unable to read her thoughts.

'I'm sorry to have brought up unhappy memories,' he said quietly. 'We lost far too many good men in the Peninsula. Instead of the glory of our boyish imaginings, we discovered that war meant pain, suffering, blood and death. Only courage, honour and knowing we were out doing something important for our country made it tolerable. That, and the bonds soldiers develop with those who fight beside them. Ties that last a lifetime.'

Before she could ask him about the men with whom he'd served, the groom returned, leading his mount.

Claire struggled to pull herself back from the disappointment, hurt and disillusion those memories always sparked. It was past time to be over events that had happened years ago, she told herself. She needed to focus on the here and now, on being an effective ambassador between the estate and its new master so he might have the best possible start.

By this time, the groom had helped her to mount and Edmenton had thrown himself into the saddle. 'Who are we off to see first?'

'We'll ride the southern quadrant this afternoon,' Claire said, nodding to the groom who was to ride with them to watch the horses—and serve as chaperon—while Edmenton conferred with his tenants.

'You do like to ride, don't you?' he asked.

'Yes. I'm sure you noted that fact early this morning.'

'Then how about a gallop? I'd like to test the paces of this gelding.'

The anticipation of a race erased the last of her melancholy. 'I'd be delighted. Be warned, Holly, my mare, is very sure-footed and she loves to gallop.'

'Excellent. So do I. We'll see if Charger here lives up to his name. Ready?'

She nodded, then gave the mare her heels. Already dancing at the bridle, the horse sprang forward. Within several moments, the ground was flashing past, the rush of wind pulling at her hat and the curls pinned beneath it. Letting go the worries about her future, the regrets about a past that couldn't be undone, Claire gave herself up to the sheer pleasure of the ride.

They raced neck and neck down the straight farm road, the groom trailing behind. Not until both mounts began to tire did they pull up.

'That was marvellous, thank you!' Claire cried.

'Nothing like good gallop,' he agreed, smiling. 'Blows all one's cares right out of one's head, doesn't it?'

'Indeed,' she replied, more in charity with him than she'd been since his arrival. A little voice whispered it wasn't wise to share any pleasures with him that would make her more susceptible to his appeal, but she hushed it. The pleasures she could allow herself were few enough, this one was unalloyed, and she would enjoy it—even if she did share it with the far too compelling new master of Steynling Cross.

'Shall we walk the horses? You can tell me about the first farm we'll be visiting.'

She nodded agreement, then spent the next several minutes as they ambled down the farm road describing the tenant, his family, his acreage and its likely harvest while the Duke listened attentively.

'You're very knowledgeable,' he commented when she'd finished. 'Do you know all the tenants that well?'

'Most of them.'

At his raised eyebrows, she went on, 'Fitzhugh was often gone, Evans was ill and my sister was too ill to attend to estate matters, so out of necessity I undertook the task. Of course, I'd managed property on a much smaller scale at Whitley, the family manor where we grew up. In addition to attending to estate business, the vicar's wife would often mention when someone was hurt, ailing, or requiring assistance. As I already cultivated herbs for my sister's use, it was easy enough to prepare additional teas and tisanes, while the kitchen could provide broth, bread and foodstuffs for those in need.'

He looked over at her with a dawning respect that warmed her much more than it should have. 'That was kind of you.'

Uncomfortable under his scrutiny, she shrugged. 'Following the drum expanded the expertise I'd acquired tending the household while growing up. As you know, the women who travelled with the army helped each other through illness, childbirth and injury, as well as seeing to provisioning and shelter for their men, caring for their animals and attending the wounded.'

'Your husband must have been proud of so resourceful and accomplished a wife.'

That comment touched so closely on the still-raw wound, she had to suppress a grimace. 'I believe he did appreciate my...competence.'

Even if I never claimed his heart.

Turning away from him, she said, 'Ah, there's the farmer, Mr Johnson.' She pointed towards the man waving at them from the fenced field they were approaching. 'Shall we join him?' Signalling her mount to a trot, she headed off, not waiting to see if Edmenton followed.

She wanted to leave no more opportunity for the Duke to ask questions concerning her relationship with Fitzhugh—or the lingering pain that had been her marriage to Alexander.

After she made the introductions, the Duke asked after Johnson's family members by name, then walked with the farmer to inspect the newly emerged crop, asking questions that showed he'd paid close attention when Claire had described the acreage and its production.

Despite her initial scepticism about the Duke, she was impressed. She'd never accompanied Fitzhugh on a round of his properties and wasn't sure if he'd ever visited all of them. Even if he had, she doubted he could have recalled the tenant's name or those of his family, much less have known any details about his crop.

She was further impressed when the Duke accepted Johnson's invitation to accompany him back to his cottage to meet his wife and share a mug of home brew. Settled on a bench at the rough-hewn table before the hearth, the farmer moved from discussing the spring planting to asking Edmenton about his army service.

While the Duke recounted some anecdotes of army life—choosing, Claire noted, to describe humorous events rather than boasting of battle heroics—Claire chatted with his wife, making sure she had sufficient supplies of herbs to soothe the teething baby and promising to bring her some that would help the four-year-old's cough.

After a cordial leave-taking, Claire walked with the Duke back to where the groom waited with their horses.

'You should take it as a mark of great respect that Mr Johnson invited you to meet his family, Your Grace.'

Though he frowned at her use of the title, he let it pass,

saying only, 'Farmers are much like soldiers, I expect. Hard-working, honest folk grateful for the bounty their efforts produce. It's an honour and a heavy responsibility to oversee the land that guarantees their welfare, just as it was to watch out for the soldiers under my command.'

'Wearing your uniform might have been wise after all,' she admitted. 'The tenants will honour you for what you've been doing to fight Napoleon.'

Edmenton sighed. 'I'd be lying if I said I don't still miss the life. But I'm beginning to understand the importance of the job I've inherited here.'

'I'm pleased to hear that!' Claire said, encouraged. 'Shall we move on? We've time enough to meet several more of the "farmer soldiers" now under your command.'

He nodded and they rode off, Claire cautiously hopeful that the reluctant heir might end up accepting his role and fulfilling its duties after all.

She found her initial resentment of the rough Scottish intruder fading. Of course, he wasn't the country jape he'd fooled her into believing him when he first arrived. Though she had to admit she might have deserved that deception, for when she first received him in the grand drawing room, she probably came across as top-lofty as Fitzhugh. But the Duke was proving to be a good man.

He would doubtless need instruction on how to behave in society, as from what she could gather, he had never played any part in it. But for the most important part of being Duke, caring for the land and its people, he seemed to have good instincts and good intentions. The details of carrying out his duties to them could be learned.

It would relieve her heart of one of its chief concerns to know the estate she had worked so hard to run smoothly these last two years would be handed over into safe hands.

Would *she* like to be in those hands?

A vivid image of the Duke's fingers caressing her burst into her mind with the shock of an exploding rocket, sending a wave of arousal through her before she could snuff it out. She took a shaky breath, trying to calm herself.

So much for managing the sensual awareness always humming between them. She'd have to do a better job of extinguishing such erotic thoughts, or the time she needed to spend with him to familiarise him with the estate and then society would become awkward indeed.

Fortunately, the Duke had ridden on ahead and was chatting with the groom, giving her time to compose herself. At least while Edmenton turned his attention to becoming acquainted with the people of his estate, the disconcerting, shiver-inducing intensity of his gaze would be focused on someone else.

Chapter Six

Hart watched as Mrs Hambleden chatted with the wife at the last farm they were to visit. Over the course of the afternoon, he'd become increasingly impressed with her encyclopaedic knowledge of the farms, the farmers, their wives, children and hired workmen. With an excellent memory for details, she'd called out exact crop yields, recounted any problems encountered during cultivation and detailed such illnesses or accidents as had been suffered by various tenants over the preceding year.

He'd been impressed, too, with the reaction of the estate's people to her. Obviously held in high esteem, she was greeted everywhere with genuine warmth. Though it was easy to understand why, when she knew every individual by name, from the smallest children, for whom sugar treats managed to magically appear out of her pocket, to shy farm hands, to elderly widowers pensioned off in their cottages.

This was no 'lady bountiful' dispensing favours from on high; more like a favoured relation acquainted with the important details of their lives, who understood their problems and stood ready to offer assistance or advice, whether they needed the blacksmith to mend a broken plough, the head groom to help shoe a difficult horse, or nourishment and herbal remedies for the ailing.

* * *

After they headed back to Steynling after that final visit, Hart said, 'You have an admirable talent for dealing with tenants. There are commissary agents who would envy your ability to catalogue and dispense supplies and anticipate the needs of your farmer troopers.'

'As I've said, I've been managing supplies since I was just a girl at Whitley. Travelling with the army in Portugal broadened that expertise in so many ways! It truly was an adventure, as my sister said, even for those of us who were not involved in battle. For one who'd never been beyond the fields of Whitley House or the city of London, what excitement to sail across the sea and explore an austere but beautiful new land!'

'The excitement of cutting branches to create leaky shelters when there were no other billets, and when that wasn't possible, sleeping on the ground in all weathers.'

She laughed. 'Or in a tree, as some of the troopers did! But yes, falling asleep wrapped in a cloak beside the dying fire, to awake dripping with rain or with your blanket frozen around you.'

'Fording rivers up to your shoulders, hoping your horse wouldn't be washed downstream.'

'As least you didn't have to ford them burdened by heavy skirts! How grateful we were, after struggling through rain and mud, when we were offered shelter in a monastery or nunnery. Though my, how cold those stone floors were! Still, we found fine billets in some of the villages, and once spent the winter outside Lisbon in a splendid old stone house.'

He nodded. 'The troopers were often very clever about fashioning chairs, tables, even beds from local timber when we were billeted long enough in one place.'

'The work was hard, but there was merriment, too,' she

continued, her eyes bright with obviously fond memories. 'Regimental dinners and balls when we were billeted in town. Were you ever invited to one of Wellington's? I understand they could be five-course affairs, with wine and dancing.'

'I was not sufficiently important to rate an invitation to one of Old Hookey's affairs. I enjoyed the country amusements, too. Steeplechasing. Hunting. Fishing in the rivers.'

She nodded. 'It's best to remember the good times, not… the hard ones.'

The warmth fading from her face, she fell silent. Hart knew she must be recalling frozen winter journeys and slogs through seas of mud when it seemed they would never reach the promised billets. The days of bloody battles for him; for her, the anxious waiting while artillery shells screamed in the distance, wondering which friend or comrade wouldn't return, who would be brought back wounded—and would her husband be one of them.

A possibility that had become all too tragically a reality for her after Fuentes de Oñoro.

While he struggled to think of what to say, she tossed her head, as if to shake off the grim thoughts. 'I do still miss it, too, despite all. Being constantly on the edge of such danger made one feel so vital and alive! Those of us who followed the troops, assisting with supplies, maintenance and nursing, felt so…*needed*. Performing a service more important than any we could have done in England.

'There was an equality of comradeship, too, despite our different ranks in society. Not that distinctions were forgotten, but the rigidity of the usual rules…softened. It all worked so well, now that one is home, it makes some of the rules and conventions of society one once accepted without question seem unnecessary. Silly, even.'

'I know exactly what you mean. The satisfaction of being

part of something larger than yourself. Something that vitally affects the future, perhaps even the very survival, of your country. Which is why I miss it so,' he added softly to himself.

By now, they'd reached the road that circled the south side of the estate, with the gatehouse in the distance beside the carriage way leading to Steynling Hall. Pulling up, Mrs Hambleden said, 'Let's stop by and see if Old Greenwood is at home. He's the former gamekeeper, you may remember.'

'I may have met him. I often rode into the woods on my visits here as a boy—perhaps the only pleasure available during the purgatory of my stays.'

'If you did encounter him, I'm sure he will remember you.'

Turning back to the groom, she said, 'Everard, you can return to the stables. We've kept you from your work far too long! It's only a short ride back to Steynling—we can manage on our own.'

'As you wish, ma'am,' the groom replied, looking relieved to be excused from what must have been a boring duty.

'Are you sure your reputation can withstand being alone in my company for half a mile?' Hart teased as the groom rode off.

She gave him a darkling look. 'I had the groom accompany us more for *your* reputation than for mine. Showing you are careful about protecting the good name of your female dependents will reassure the staff and win you approval among the tenants and villagers.'

'Demonstrating that I'm not a Scot come to seize, pillage and despoil?'

'Exactly,' she said drily. 'If you care about protecting the widowed sister of the Duchess, a person of little account, they have hope you will be equally respectful of the virtue of housemaids and the daughters of farmers and village tradesmen.'

He gave her a sharp glance, but she didn't appear to be joking. 'You truly believe yourself a "person of little account"?' he asked incredulously. 'You, who from what I've seen thus far, practically run Steynling Cross single-handed?'

She flushed a little. 'I direct much of it, but the staff does most of the actual work. And I have no illusions about my position. I truly am little more than a high-born version of a housekeeper. Not an inch of land or a corner of Steynling Hall belongs to me. I'm only a caretaker for my sister. Or rather, for you, until you make other arrangements. I'll go see if Old Greenwood is at home.'

She slipped from the saddle without assistance, evidence of long practice—which, having ridden with the army, she would have had. Women followed with the baggage at the very end of the marching columns; her husband would have ridden with his unit. Though wives occasionally rode alongside the ranks, she would more often travel with the other women, getting along without her husband's presence or assistance. Fending for herself. As she appeared eminently capable of doing.

Hart found it perplexing that on the one hand, Mrs Hambleden seemed quite confident of her abilities to manage an estate as vast as Steynling, but on the other, seemed to possess such a low opinion of her perceived worth.

Maybe her husband hadn't valued her as Hart suspected she deserved. There was no question that her sister seemed to take her stewardship of what should have been Duchess's duties for granted, with no apparent recognition of the burden her sister willingly carried in her place or how efficiently and effectively she did so.

Hart meant to take note of it. As it appeared Mrs Hambleden would be the one to acquaint him with estate and its needs, he would make sure to express his appreciation for her assistance and his admiration for her expertise whenever possible.

But part of what she'd stated was stark truth. As the Duchess's relation rather than Steynling's mistress, she had no right to manage any of the estate she tended with such capable hands. Everything here belonged to him, as it had to Fitzhugh before him. He could, if he chose and she had evidently feared, relieve her of her duties and turn her out any time he wished.

Even the Dower House, if she removed there with the Duchess, would be not hers but her sister's, despite the fact that it would undoubtedly be her efforts that ensured its smooth running. She could be cast out by her sister, too, should some disagreement arise between them.

Even if they remained together amicably, he would still own it all.

While Hart followed after her, pondering the perils of her position, Mrs Hambleden was greeting the stooped older man who answered the door. 'I've come to present you to the new master of Steynling.'

Old Greenwood bobbed his head. 'Pleased to see you, Yer Grace. Though 'tis more like hello again than a greeting, int' so?'

'Indeed it is, though I wasn't sure you'd remember the knavish brat who rode around your woods disturbing the coverts.'

'Always up to mischief you were, lad. But who wouldn't be, forced to trail after my former master, may he rest in peace? Disturbing coverts be nothing to what that one sometimes got up to.'

From the old man's gruff words, Hart gathered he hadn't

been too fond of Fitzhugh—a fact that immediately raised his opinion of the man.

'Are you expecting a good shooting season?' Mrs Hambleden asked.

'We look to have good hatch out of partridges and we're raising pheasants. Not as many as in years past, as the last Duke weren't fond of shooting. Will ye be reviving the custom of shoots, Yer Grace? Steynling used to be famous for them.'

'Perhaps. I've much to learn about the estate before I can think about leisure.'

The old man nodded. 'Aye, but I recall what a good eye and steady hand ye had. Even if ye didn't bag as many birds as yer cousin.'

'That would have been…impolitic,' Hart said drily.

'Aye, right botheration he'd 'ave raised, should ye have bested him. But I also recollect a time during yer visit when someone shot a hole right through the fancy hat he'd hung on a tree while he and his da were taking tea with their guests.'

'A number of us were shooting that day. As I recall, it was never determined who fired at the hat.'

'So they say. Shot had to been made from a good distance. 'Twere a fine exhibition of marksmanship.'

'Mostly I recall my cousin being highly upset about the ruin of his new hat.'

The old man chuckled. 'He was that bothered, warn't he? So, Army made good use of ye, then?'

'Though as a heavy dragoon, I wielded a sword more often than a firearm, my major did discover I was a fair shot. He sometimes sent me back to assist the rear guard. I had the opportunity to use a Baker rifle when I helped the Ninety-Fifth cover the army's retreat from Burgos last winter. Excellent weapon.'

'Well, both me and yer neighbours hope ye'll be friend to the sport. Some of the best coverts are on Steynling land, and pheasant makes for fine eating.'

'I'll keep that in mind.'

'We'd better be getting back,' Mrs Hambleden said. 'But I did want to stop by briefly, Mr Greenwood. You still have a supply of that liniment I made up for you?'

'Aye, and a right bit of good it does me.' The old man looked at Hart. 'This lady here, she knows summat about physicking. Not that our Duchess ain't a beautiful ornament, but Steynling's lucky to have her sister.'

'Oh, get on with you, flatterer,' Mrs Hambleden said, flushing.

'Only tell truth as I see it,' the old man insisted. 'Well, ye got more important things to do than listen to an old man's tattle. It's pleased I am to see you again, Yer Grace. No longer a promising lad, but a strong man grown. I'm thinking Steynling will be lucky to have ye, too.'

Hart nodded, a bit taken aback by the old man's praise. 'I'll endeavour to justify that confidence, Mr Greenwood.'

As Hart and his companion went to fetch their mounts, he noted Mrs Hambleden carefully avoided his assistance, leading her horse to the mounting block rather than asking for a leg up.

At the rush of heat that coursed through him at the thought of touching her, he decided using the mounting block was a wise precaution. Blowing out a breath, he mounted himself and followed as she guided her mare on to the carriage way leading up to Steynling Hall.

This pesky attraction between them, slowly growing in intensity, was becoming a definite nuisance. One he had no hope of assuaging by indulging it.

Did he?

Hart reminded himself again that any intimate connection between them would be a knave's misuse of the position of power he occupied.

Although he couldn't imagine the fiery Mrs Hambleden meekly submitting to unwanted attentions. She'd more likely abuse his character for attempting such impropriety and send him off with a blistering scold.

Unless…she *wanted* to invite his caresses. After all, she was a mature widow, not an innocent maid. A liaison between two such willing partners, if discreetly conducted, was generally considered quite acceptable. And he was absolutely certain the attraction was both strong and mutual.

But such an interlude would be too dangerous for her, despite the pleasure he felt sure they would both derive from it. They weren't both independent, socially and financially secure enough to pursue their own private interests. Even were she willing, with him head of the household and she a dependent within it, an affair would be inappropriate. No matter how much he regretted that truth.

'Did you really shoot a hole in Fitzhugh's new hat?'

Glad to be pulled from his thoughts, Hart turned to her with a grin. 'It was an ugly hat—however fashionable.'

She chuckled. 'I bet he was furious. Fitzhugh prided himself on being always dressed in the latest kick of fashion.'

'Don't I know it! He never failed to jibe about my backwards Scottish appearance. Tempted me to wear a kilt from the beginning of the visit to its end.' Hart winked at her. 'Maybe I'll save the kilt for that sojourn in London you tell me must be made. To impress all the ladies at my first ball.'

She stared, half-alarmed, half-suspicious. 'I can well imagine you might try to shock society by doing so! Does your mother's family belong to a clan?'

'No, they are all Lowlanders,' Hart acknowledged. 'But I doubt anyone in society would know any better if I donned a Stewart or a Campbell. Unless one of the lairds happened to be attending the same entertainment.'

Shaking her head, she raised a hand. 'No more, or I shall have nightmares envisioning your introduction to society! Let's concentrate for the present on having you master Steynling. There are duties enough to work on here.'

'Aye. But "Feather by feather the goose is plucked".'

'Another Scottish truism?'

'A truth indeed, as I expect you know. I'm guessing you plucked your share of fowl in Portugal.'

She shook her head ruefully. 'I learned a number of new skills while in Portugal.'

'I'm sure I shall learn a number of new skills at Steynling. Shall we ride out again tomorrow?'

She nodded. 'We'll visit the farms to the west. Starting in the afternoon. I've promised my son, Alex, a riding lesson in the morning.'

Softness came over her expression when she mentioned the boy. 'Riding already, is he? How old is he now?'

'He'll be four years old in June. The troopers in my husband's company had him sitting on a horse at age two, our last summer in Portugal. And how he loved having his father lift him up to ride in front of him! Alex already adores horses—and anything outside, really.'

By now, their having reached the path that led from the carriage way to the stables, a groom hurried over to take her bridle and help her down from the saddle.

Hart felt an irrational flare of—it couldn't be *jealousy*. Maybe a wee bit of annoyance that she would not suffer *his* hands on her, but accepted assistance from the groom.

Which was foolish, since he'd already decided that touching her, no matter how the innocent the reason, wouldn't be wise.

Hart walked up with her to Steynling's grand entry. 'I

appreciate the time and care you are taking to acquaint me with the people of the estate.'

'I want you to have the best possible introduction. Their livelihood, yours, the health of the estate—it's all interconnected. The better you know them, and they you, the better all can work together to thrive and prosper.'

Hart closed his lips before he could ask if Fitzhugh had agreed with that adage. From what he'd seen of him, his cousin's only concern about the estate was the income it could provide and the prestige its ownership conveyed on him—both of which he looked upon as his due.

Perhaps Fitzhugh couldn't help being insufferable and entitled. As heir, he'd been doted on by his father, indulged by his mother and given everything he'd wanted all his life. Until he'd apparently believed even a pot-holed, stony road on a dark moonless night wouldn't dare cause a carriage with a drunken driver to overturn if *he* were the driver.

Just what had been Mrs Hambleden's relationship with Fitzhugh? He'd bought her a horse, she'd told him with a hesitation in her voice that suggested there was more to that story. His cousin had apparently paid her a good deal of attention before turning his focus on her sister. Had Fitzhugh dazzled her, as he had so many?

The uncomfortable feeling he didn't want to call jealousy returned. Surely she'd been intelligent enough not to be taken in by Fitzhugh. But he couldn't help feeling… disturbed at the very idea that lovely, competent, engaging Mrs Hambleden might have had a tendre for his cousin.

Chapter Seven

The following morning, Claire took the stairs to the nursery. Her heart lifted at knowing she'd be spending carefree time with her son and her sister's daughter, Arabella, a charming imp a month older than Alex. Having been together since their arrival almost two years ago, the two were more like brother and sister than cousins.

She entered to find her son already dressed in outdoor attire and impatiently walking about the room. 'Mama!' he cried, running over to hug her. 'At last! I thought we would *never* go riding!'

'You make it sound as if you've been waiting for days,' she teased, holding him tight until he pushed away. Already he was growing up, she thought with a pang, brushing off her kisses and allowing only a brief embrace. How she missed his infant days when she'd been able to cuddle him for as long as she liked.

His father had loved holding him, too, she recalled. Alexander delighted in his son and looked forward to having more children. But she'd conceived so quickly, so not wanting to risk her health bearing more children on campaign, they'd both agreed to arrange their lovemaking to avoid another pregnancy until he finished soldiering.

She often wondered if that had been wise. Had they taken no precautions, she might now have another son or a sweet daughter like Bella, who came running over for a hug of her own. As a near-penniless widow with little to offer a potential husband, she expected a child's affection was the only sort of love she would enjoy for the rest of her days. She'd certainly never again let passion rule her, to her anguish and near ruin.

'Can't I go with you, Aunt Claire?' Bella asked. 'I want to learn to ride, too.'

'I'm afraid not, poppet. You're quite small still, and horses are so large, your mama fears what would happen if you should fall. You're her dearest treasure and she doesn't want to risk you. You can start lessons once you grow bigger.'

'If she cares so much, why does she not come see me?' the child muttered. 'You come every day!'

Heart aching, Claire drew the little girl into her arms. 'You know your mama's been very sick. She comes as often as she has the strength to climb the stairs. As she gets better, she'll be able to visit more often,' she added, hoping that would be true.

Her love for her sister couldn't blind her to fact that Liliana paid little attention to her daughter. Perhaps seeing the girl only reminded the Duchess of the sons she'd miscarried, her failure to provide a male heir not just a personal grief but devastating for her position. Much as Claire sympathised with her sister, as a mother herself, she still couldn't forgive her for failing to lavish on her one surviving child all the love and care the girl deserved.

She was trying to decide if she should allow Bella to come to the barn and watch, even if she couldn't promise a lesson, or leave her in the nursery when the door opened. To her considerable surprise, the Duke walked in.

'Good morning, Mrs Hambleden! I hope I'm not intruding.'

'Not at all, Your Grace,' she replied with a curtsy.

After giving her a frown—no doubt for using his title—he said, 'Then won't you introduce me to this lovely lady and this fine young man?'

'Of course. Your Grace, may I present Lady Arabella Edmenton, daughter of the Duchess.'

'Charmed, Lady Arabella,' he said, kissing her hand, which made the little girl giggle.

'And this is my son, Alexander Hambleden. Children, let me present the new Duke of Fenniston.'

Alex made the Duke a very creditable bow while both children chimed, 'Pleased to meet you, Your Grace.'

'Don't saddle me with that title already,' he protested, grimacing. 'We're family, after all. Why don't you call me "Uncle Hart"?'

'They should be brought up to address you properly,' Claire protested.

'And they will do so. If we're in public, and when they are older. I hardly think the nursery demands such formality.'

Bella remained silent, simply looking at him. 'Are you taking my papa's place?' she asked after a moment.

The Duke knelt so he could look directly into her eyes. 'I could never take your papa's place, sweetheart. I'm just taking over running the estate. A job your auntie is helping me learn.'

'Mama's a very good teacher, sir. She's giving me a riding lesson now.'

'Do you think I might accompany you?'

Claire looked over, surprised again. 'Are you sure you wish to?'

'Certainly. I remember how excited I was to learn. My father wasn't much interested in land management, preferring scholarship and his books and content to leave the running of Kirkraidy to my mother. But he loved horses. Sat me on my first pony when I was barely two years old.'

'My papa let me ride when I was two, Mama says,' the boy responded. 'I'm almost four and can nearly ride all by myself.'

'Then you must be making great progress.'

'Please, Aunt Claire, can't I come with you? Even if Mama won't let me ride?'

Claire couldn't resist her niece's pleading look. 'Very well,' she capitulated. 'But put on a cloak and sturdy shoes. And Sally goes with us, in case you get tired and want to come back.'

'I won't! I can walk even longer than Alex.'

'No, you can't!' he protested indignantly.

'Can so,' she shot back.

'If you're going to squabble, neither of you will go,' Claire warned.

'We'll be good, won't we, Bella?' her son said quickly. 'I'd be ever so sad not to see Blaze. That's my pony,' he added, turning to the Duke. 'His face has a big white streak down the middle. Besides, Mama, Blaze will miss me if I don't come groom him and feed him treats.'

'I'm sure he would,' Edmenton said with a smile. 'I'd like to meet him, too.'

Since it seemed the Duke was keen on joining them, Claire capitulated. 'I suppose it's settled, then.'

As the nursemaid helped the children don their coats, Edmenton said quietly, 'Why does the Duchess not allow Lady Arabella to ride?'

'The Duchess does fear she might be injured. Small and delicate like her mother, she doesn't have the strength or co-ordination to manage a pony. Alex is young, too, but he's been sitting astride since he was a toddler, developing his

balance and learning proper technique. Not that I allow him
to ride at more than a walk without a lead line, of course.'

'Lady Arabella is small, but she could still enjoy being
with horses and sitting on a pony's back with grooms walking beside her.'

'You don't need to convince me. Why don't you talk
with the Duchess? Perhaps she will listen to the advice of a
soldier—since she dismisses that of a mere sister.'

The Duke chuckled. 'I doubt you've ever been a "mere"
anything. You mentioned the Duchess has some fear of
horses, so I can understand why she'd not want to conduct
the lessons herself. And having only one chick, she naturally wants to guard her carefully.'

Claire hesitated, then nodded. 'Naturally.' Small chance
of Liliana conducting Bella's riding—or any other—
lesson. But better to agree with the Duke's assumption
than disloyally reveal how little her sister participated in
her daughter's life.

Jacket on, Alex danced around the room. 'We're going
to ride and see Blaze!'

Claire thought the child's boisterousness might give the
Duke second thoughts, but he seemed to take it in stride.
A few moments later, the party trooped downstairs and
headed towards the stables, the two children gambolling
ahead.

'You really don't have to remain for the lesson,' Claire
said to the Duke.

'No, I'd like to. I would like to become better acquainted
with the children.'

'Better acquainted with another of your responsibilities
as head of the family?'

'There is that. But I like children. We always had young
ones hanging about with the army. Being around them re-

minds me of the joy of rousting about with my sister, growing up. Children have such a fresh view on things.'

'And say exactly what they think, bare wood with no gilding, so be warned!'

'I think my self-esteem can handle it,' he said drily.

A few minutes later, they reached the stables. After leaving the nursemaid on a bench inside the barn where she might amuse herself flirting with the grooms, the rest walked to the box stall where Alex's pony and two grooms awaited them.

'Will you be wanting your mare, ma'am?' Parker, the head groom, asked Claire.

'After we do some ground work.' Turning to her son, she said, 'What do we do first?'

'Say "hello" to Blaze and give him his treat. Then go to the tack room to get his saddle and bridle.'

Claire handed some apples slices to her son. 'Go ahead, then.'

'Can I give him a treat, too?' Bella asked.

'Sure,' Alex said, handing her a piece of apple. 'Hold it out flat in your hand. Don't curl your fingers over it, or he might nip them.'

'He can't see directly under his nose,' Edmenton explained as he walked the little girl to the stall rail. 'He has to "feel" the apple with his lips and whiskers to eat it.'

After watching her cousin, Bella held out her own treat, then giggled as the pony scoffed up the apple. 'It tickles! Can I feed him another?'

'Not right now,' Claire said. 'Eating too many could make his belly hurt—like yours does if you have too many sweets.'

'Let's get his tack,' Alex said, loping away from the stall. 'I'm ready to ride!'

Under the indulgent eye of the head groom and his assistant, Alex selected the proper saddle and bridle for his mount, Hart helping him carry them back to the stall.

'You can come, too,' Alex told Bella as the groom held open the stall gate. 'But come on Blaze's left side. And never go behind him. He might get startled and kick you.'

Hart caught Claire's eye and smiled. 'Your son makes a good teacher, too.'

While Bella talked to the horse, the groom helped Alex put on his saddle and bridle. Then the boy led Blaze out of the stall and through the barn to the round pen, Claire and the groom on either side while Hart escorted Arabella.

'Finally I can get in the saddle!' he told his cousin. 'Parker or Mama holds Blaze's head while I take the reins at the top of his neck, then pull out the stirrup and put my foot in. Then, I just swing up. It's easy, see?'

'It doesn't look hard,' Bella said. 'Are you sure I can't try, Aunt Claire?'

'Not today, sweeting. We'll have to talk with your mama first. But you may sit on the rail and watch while Alex practises.'

The little girl sighed, but brightened when Hart said, 'Come, we can watch together.' And giggled again as the Duke lifted her up on to the top rail.

Claire found herself more conscious than she'd like at knowing the Duke's gaze followed her every move. Fortunately, having to concentrate on her son, though it didn't eliminate her acute sensual awareness of him, at least helped distract her from it.

'His form is quite good for one so young,' Hart said as he watched the boy. 'Thumbs up, wrists straight and straight line from bit to elbow. He balances well, too.'

'Yes, he's already proficient at steering the pony at a walk and I'm about ready to allow him off the lead line at a trot. Will you watch Lady Arabella while I claim my horse?'

'Of course. And please ask Parker to have mine tacked up as well. After Master Alex practises in the round pen, I thought you might put him on a lead line and we could ride out to that pretty wood we went through yesterday.'

Claire nodded, touched by his thoughtfulness. 'He would love that. Are you sure you have the time?'

The Duke made a great show of looking about him. 'I don't see anyone else come to claim my attention. Besides, don't you keep telling me I'm the Duke? And therefore should be able to do whatever I want?' Puffing up his chest, he raised his nose in the air and said in an exaggerated, pompous voice, 'I shall ride now, Parker. Summon my horse.'

While Claire chuckled, Bella turned to stare. 'You sounded funny. And you looked so silly!'

'Didn't I just,' he agreed, relaxing into a normal pose. 'That's what happens when one becomes a duke. One turns very strange and silly.'

Shaking her head at him, Claire went to fetch her horse. By the time she returned, Alex had completed his practice at a walk. 'Can I trot now, Mama? I can do it. I know I can!'

Conflicted about whether to allow the more dangerous manoeuvre, Claire found herself giving the Duke a questioning look.

'His balance looks good and he handles the pony well. I think he's ready.'

'Very well, go ahead,' she said, sucking in a nervous breath. Not that she'd needed the Duke's approval, she told herself. She was quite capable of making decisions regarding her son on her own. But the Duke was an excellent rider; it didn't hurt to have another horseman's opinion.

'He's unlikely to hurt himself on the soft ground of the ring, even if he takes a tumble,' Hart murmured in her ear.

Half annoyed, half grateful for his help, she had to bite her lip to keep from returning a sharp reply. It was silly of her to feel...vulnerable. She wasn't going to become dependent on him, just because she might occasionally seek his advice.

Suppressing her conflicted feelings, she concentrated on Alex, who justified their mutual confidence by commanding his pony to a trot and riding with respectable form. After he'd made several successful circuits of the round pen, Claire said, 'That's enough for now.'

'I don't want to stop yet!' her son protested.

'We're not ending the lesson,' she reassured him. 'His Grace—'

'Uncle Hart—' the Duke inserted.

Claire paused, then decided it wasn't worth trying to insist on using his title, which he would probably override anyway.

'Uncle Hart,' she continued, giving him a look that said not to count on such concessions for ever, 'suggested that we ride out to the woods. You must go on a lead line once you leave the round pen, but we'll ride at a trot.'

'Hoorah!' Alex crowed.

'What about me?' Bella asked. 'Must Sally take me back to nursery?'

Claire had intended just that, but as little girl's eyes filled with tears, she hesitated. Before she could decide what to do, the Duke said. 'Back to the house? Oh, no! We couldn't do without the company of the loveliest lady at Steynling. You must ride with me.'

Bella looked up at him, her expression going from dejection to surprise. 'Truly? You will take me?'

Hart made her a sweeping bow. 'If my lady will deign to accept my hand,' he declared, holding it out.

A brilliant smile lit her face. 'Thank you!' she cried, grasping it. 'I would like it ever so much! Even though I'm not the loveliest lady at Steynling. My mama is.'

Wincing, the Duke looked over at Claire apologetically, but she just laughed. 'I told you to expect plain speaking. You may hear more of it when my sister discovers you've taken her daughter riding.'

Hart waved a hand. 'I can send a groom to the house to check but I hardly think she will be concerned. Miss Arabella will be perfectly safe sitting before me, securely held in my arms. We'll not be going faster than a trot, after all.'

Her unruly mind leaping to the image of riding *herself* before Hart, clasped tightly in his arms, Claire hardly heard his comment about the pace.

Bella might be safe riding with him—but she definitely would not be. With her long-deprived senses keenly missing the physical closeness of marriage, were he to sit behind her, pulling her against that broad chest, his arms around her shoulders and brushing against her breasts, his warm breath at her neck…

A shiver went through her. She'd probably lose her grasp on proper behaviour the moment he swung into the saddle behind her.

Enough, she ordered silently, thoroughly annoyed with herself. If she were going to fall into heated reveries every time he mentioned something that made her thoughts rush to the idea of touching him, she would need to severely limit the amount of time they spent together. Which, with all she still needed to do to introduce him to Steynling, to say nothing of assisting with his presentation to society, was not feasible.

She would simply *have* to do a better job of extinguishing these unsuitable thoughts.

By time she'd reordered her distracted mind, a groom had been sent with a message for the Duchess and Parker had brought the Duke's mount. He'd swung into the saddle, and the groom handed Bella up to him.

'I'm so high!' she squealed, clinging to him.

'Don't be afraid,' the Duke reassured her. 'I won't let you fall.'

'I'm not afraid,' Bella said. 'I love it! Let's gallop down the lane!'

'No galloping,' Claire warned quickly. 'My sister would have my head.'

'Very well, no galloping,' Hart agreed with a chuckle.

As they guided their horses out of the ring and on to the lane leading towards the woods, Edmenton said, 'I think Lady Arabella is going to make an intrepid rider, once her mama permits her to begin lessons.'

'I do so want to. Will you ask her for me, Uncle Hart?'

Giving Claire a rueful glance, he said, 'Yes, My Lady. I will ask her.'

'A reminder that no good turn goes unpunished,' Claire observed.

'We shall see. The Duchess might be persuaded after all.'

Claire raised her eyebrows sceptically, but made no further comment.

'You have a very fine horse,' Alex said, his admiring glance taking in the Duke's tall gelding. 'What's his name?'

'Midnight. He *has* been a very fine horse, strong, steady and fearless. He's kept me safe through many a campaign.'

'You were a soldier like my papa, weren't you?' Alex said. 'Did you fight with him?'

'Not beside him, but we were in several of the same battles.'

'He was very brave, Mama says.'

'I'm sure he must have been to have a son who rides as fearlessly as you do.'

'Mama is brave, too. Aunt Liliana says she went everywhere with the army, just like the soldiers. I did, too, but I was little and I don't remember much.' He sighed. 'I wish

I could remember more. You wear a red coat. Mama has a little painting of Papa, but his coat is blue.'

'Different units wore different uniforms,' the Duke explained. 'Some like your papa had blue jackets, some like me wore red. Some hussars—those are soldiers on horseback, too, but they carry different swords—wore light blue uniforms and great hats made out of bear fur.'

'We don't have Papa's uniform, but Mama kept his sword for me.'

At Hart's sharp glance, Claire said, 'I sold everything but that. I wanted Alex to have something of his father's. I only pray he never has to wield it in battle.'

'Please God, this war will be over long before he's of an age to participate.'

'I can show you Papa's sword. Mama keeps it over the fireplace in her room.'

'I should like that.'

Another annoying frisson went through Claire at the idea of the Duke entering her bedchamber. 'Perhaps I could bring the sword to the nursery for him to see.'

'I wish you would leave it there,' Alex said plaintively.

'Maybe when you are older. And only if you promise *never* to try to use it!'

'Can we go faster?' Bella, who'd been remarkably patient, finally broke into the conversation.

'Ready to try a trot?' Hart asked Alex.

At the boy's enthusiastic nod, the Duke said, 'Are you ready, Mrs Hambleden? Then let's go!'

Nervous over her son's first attempt at trotting outside the round pen, Claire was able—temporarily, at least—to put the Duke out of mind as she focused on Alex. Fortunately, he seemed to be having no trouble maintaining his seat or guiding the pony down the straight run of road.

Hearing Bella's squeal of delight, Claire felt a wave of

gratitude to the Duke. It had been kind of him to invite her niece to accompany them. And Bella was clearly relishing having the handsome man's attention.

Reassured that Alex was doing well and Bella was thrilled at her unexpected treat, Claire could finally relax and simply enjoy the excursion.

The Duke was surprisingly good with children—as her husband Alexander had been. The sadness she carried always within her sharpened at thinking how he had been robbed of seeing his son grow up. Alexander would have loved riding with Alex as the Duke was now riding with Bella.

Fitzhugh had been as indifferent to his daughter as her sister was. Because she was not the son and heir he'd craved? Would he have been more engaged with the child if she'd been a boy?

Somehow, with the jaded sense of the man she now possessed, Claire didn't think so. Fitzhugh would likely have accepted the heir as one more thing that was his due, the child's day-to-day upbringing the responsibility of a succession of servants. He might have inspected the boy once or twice a week when his nurse brought him to the drawing room before sending him back to the nursery. And later to boarding school.

The new Duke would be a better father to his offspring, she felt sure. He'd already said he considered Bella—and Alex—his responsibility.

Certainly Bella was his charge to bring up, provide a dowry for and see well married. Would he concern himself with Alex once, as they must at some point, they left Steynling Cross for—wherever they would end up next?

She felt a shock of sadness at the thought of leaving the estate that had been their home the last two years. Where she'd arrived lost and desolate, but eventually felt again almost as needed and useful as she had while following the drum. She would still have her son to care for when they left here—but with what would she replace the duties that now filled her days?

Despite asserting all in the nursery were his 'family', there was no link between them and the new Duke by either blood or marriage. No true connection that would obligate him to look out for Alex.

That truth revived the worry that always hovered just beneath consciousness. A troubling uncertainty about where they would go, what she would do and how she would support her son once the new Duke been had schooled, married and fully taken control at Steynling Cross.

But she'd not spoil this joyful outing with distressing thoughts. As she did whenever that concern pressed upon her, Claire shouldered it aside and told herself to simply be thankful for this day, this place, this moment. She'd drink in the beauty of the countryside, the children's delight and yes, the presence of the man she'd gone from resenting, to suspecting, to liking.

Liking quite a lot, despite the constant struggle to resist how he made her senses sing.

Chapter Eight

The next morning, Hart went earlier than usual to the stables to claim his mount. To his satisfaction, he had only just ridden into the Home Woods when he spied Mrs Hambleden in the distance.

Not until he'd come to Steynling had Hart ever found himself completely without companionship. Even during his boyhood visits, he'd had his father's company for some portion of the day. At home growing up, he'd had his parents and his sister, then his friends at school and finally his compatriots in the army.

After spending these initial days at Steynling, he'd begun to realise how much he enjoyed being always surrounded by such warm camaraderie. Not that he minded his own company, but he'd discovered he preferred his solitude leavened with a good helping of conviviality. With his batman relegated to the servants' quarters and no friend of his own status available, Hart found himself…lonely.

Despite the difficulty of managing his attraction to Mrs Hambleden—and far from familiarity lessening her appeal, that attraction had increased the more time they spent together—she was the only person at Steynling who came close to meeting that need.

She might be acid-tongued at times, hinting of a fiery temper that wasn't always under control, but with her intelligence, keen sense of observation and sharp wit, she made engaging company. Added to that, her impressive knowledge of the estate, the respect she'd won from the tenants and her dedication to her family made her even more intriguing. He wanted to know her better, not least to figure out the reason behind the striking dichotomy between her competence and self-confidence, yet surprising lack of self-esteem.

Was that due to the uncertain position she occupied? As he wasn't a relation, he had no right to interfere in her life, but he would like to discreetly discover what resources she possessed. What she planned or would be able to do if she left Steynling Cross.

Though he'd assured both her and the Duchess that they might remain as long as they wished, at some point they would both have to leave. Much as he resisted being pushed into it, he knew he must marry and hoped he would meet his one perfect lady sooner rather than later. But however sterling the character of his bride, he suspected she would not appreciate housing either her astoundingly beautiful predecessor or the sister her husband found all too engaging.

Still, he found the idea of Mrs Hambleden leaving Steynling inexplicably disturbing. Certainly he needed, and was grateful for, her expertise in acquainting him with the estate. A process he could accomplish on his own but was easier and faster with her to instruct him.

Perhaps her eventual departure unsettled him because he was beginning to see her as a friend whose company he would miss.

Occasionally the observation recurred that she would make a superior duchess. She was competent enough, certainly. He was equally certain that physically they would be well matched. He'd not found her a soulmate at first sight—indeed, he felt she still viewed him as the unworthy Scottish interloper—to say nothing of how extremely awkward and shocking to society it would be to wed the Duchess's sister. A widow of limited means who was both at present his dependent and, in society's eyes, possessed neither the fat dowry nor the social position that qualified her to become a duchess.

Not that he cared overmuch about the opinion of English society. But he wouldn't want to upset the Duchess, nor, for the sake of gaining a passionate bed-mate and a helpful manager, abandon his dream of a soulmate even as he endangered the close bond between the sisters.

A soulmate, his parents' and Moire's examples both proved, offered his best guarantee for a lifetime of happiness, providing him a partner who could help him endure the lifetime of duty he couldn't avoid.

And since he couldn't avoid the duty, he would hold out for that chance of happiness with every bit of determination he possessed. Despite all the obligations of his new position, why should he settle for less?

Besides, he mistrusted a relationship that had begun with a strong physical attraction. He knew too many men who'd wed in the heat of passion only to be disillusioned with their bride when that passion cooled, as it inevitably did.

Fortunately, as he was not yet ready to marry, he didn't need to worry now about his eventual choice. And with nothing more than friendship in mind, he could with good conscience seek out the only congenial company he'd found at Steynling.

Spurring his horse forward, he rode to intercept Mrs Hambleden.

'I'm interrupting your solitude—again,' he acknowledged as, after spying him approach, she pulled up to await him. 'Would you prefer to go on alone, or may I join you?'

Mentally crossing his fingers on the reins, he was relieved when she nodded. 'Join me if you like.'

'You are sure? Not just because I'm the Duke and get everything I want?'

That comment provoked a flash of annoyance in those icy blue eyes, making Hart grin. 'How about a gallop?' she suggested. 'You may *want* to win the race, but you shall not.'

'I'd say "after you", but as a rude Scot not gentlemanly enough to let you win, I won't be coming in after.'

'That remains to be seen. Shall we start?'

As he signalled his mount into motion, Hart's spirits rose at the sheer joy of the gallop and watching the lovely woman racing her horse beside him. As before, the horses thundered down the trail neck-and-neck, Hart pulling up only when both mounts showed signs of tiring.

'You see, I'm not behind you,' he said as he halted at her side.

'But you're not in front, either,' she retorted.

'Would you sulk if I won?'

'Sulk!' she echoed, looking annoyed again. 'I hope I am mature enough not to complain when I don't win at something.'

No, you are used to letting others take precedence, he thought. *Listening while Bella praises her mother's superior beauty. Managing an estate, first your father's, then your brother-in-law's, with a competence that seems to win you little recognition from the family you assist.*

'No,' he agreed soberly, his teasing tone gone. 'I expect you have dealt stoically with whatever setbacks life has offered you.'

Looking mollified, she said, 'I've done my best.'

They'd proceeded only a little way further down the trail when she reined in again. 'As you may remember, the road branches soon,' she said, pointing to the bend in the distance. 'Take the left turning, and after about a mile, it merges into the main farm road. Following it leads back to Steynling's carriage way, so you should be able to find your way without getting lost. I must head back.'

'So soon? But you've barely begun your ride!'

She nodded. 'Alas, too true. I didn't want to miss it altogether, though I knew it would have to be short. I need to harvest herbs before we meet the estate agent this afternoon and then visit the farms on the north quadrant.'

Somehow the prospect of a ride without her company didn't sound as appealing. 'I'll return with you. You can show me the garden.'

She angled her head at him. 'Are you truly interested in herbs?'

Hart didn't want to admit herbs only interested him because their use was for her both a calling and a passion. And he truly *was* interested in learning everything about Mrs Claire Hambleden.

Shrugging, he replied, 'Since all the estate is my responsibility, you might as well show me all of it. While you take me through the garden, you can give me a quick primer on what the herbs are used for. So far, I know you make up ointment for Old Greenwood's back, infusions for teething babes and syrups for a child's cough.'

Her eyes widening, she said, 'You *have* been paying attention during our tenant visits!'

'Mastering details is important for a successful operation—whatever the operation might be. You surely saw that with the army in the Peninsula.'

She smiled wryly. 'Too often because some small detail went awry! If you are going to attend to my words so closely, I shall have to be most careful what I say.'

'When what you say is full of insight and intelligence, it deserves to be attended to closely,' Hart said, seizing the opportunity to express some gratitude to this under-appreciated lady.

Her expression surprised, she looked away, as if she weren't sure what to reply. Which just confirmed to him how unaccustomed she was to praise.

'You mustn't get in the habit of listening too closely to what is said around you,' she said at last. 'You will be presented to society soon, where a great deal of what you will hear doesn't deserve careful attention. Gossip, backbiting, endless discussions of fashion, entertainments and other people, with good dose of pride and arrogance thrown in.'

'Heavens, if that is what awaits me in society, I may feel compelled to avoid it.'

'You might wish to, but you cannot. As the Duke, you have a position to uphold which requires your being in London, for Parliament if for nothing else. Though you might be able to confine most of your social engagements to political dinners or intellectual soirées where matters of importance *are* discussed, courtesy compels you to attend a certain number of balls, routs and such.'

'Where matters of no importance are discussed?'

She sighed. 'All too often, I'm afraid. You must learn to give the appearance of listening courteously, regardless of how inane or trivial you find the discussion, lest you embarrass or offend the speaker.'

'I thought as Duke, I could act as I wished, without regard for who was offended,' he said, teasing her.

Rather than take the remark as a jest, though, she regarded him soberly. 'Some might do so,' she said at last. 'But my impression of you thus far—a man who isn't too proud to share a mug of home brew with a farmer or listen patiently while Mr Evans goes over some minutiae in the estate books—is that you have too much respect for your fellow man to treat anyone shabbily. Even if a lack of wit seems to invite disparagement.'

Surprised and gratified that she'd read him fairly, he said, 'True. I don't hold with carelessly wounding the feelings of others. Even if, as Duke, I would be excused for my arrogance.'

'We shall have to see that you do not develop any. Which may be a harder task than you anticipate, once you are subject to the fawning approval of men wishing to hang on a new duke's sleeve and matrons anxious to win their daughters a duchess's coronet.'

'What, you think my head will be swelled to excessive proportions?'

She rewarded him with another flash of those magnificent eyes. 'I expect it barely fits into your hat at present. Well, I must return. With you, if you still wish to accompany me.'

Chuckling, Hart said, 'Despite your doubts about my ability to resist flattery, I assure you that I can! I'd like to see the place where you obtain the tools to create your magic—easing the aches of old men and the pain of teething babes.'

'No magic, just well-proven herbal recipes. Some from those recorded in the stillroom book at my childhood home, some passed along by other healers, some I developed myself. But you must promise to stop me when you've heard enough. I'm apt to natter on about ingredients, preparations and their effects.'

'Don't worry, I'll cut you off before you've turned me into an apothecary's apprentice. A general acquaintance with healing would be useful knowledge for the "Master of Steynling". Even if I will not be the one dispensing it.'

With the ride shortened, Hart readily agreed to her suggestion that they proceed back at a canter, a pace that precluded further conversation. After arriving at the stables and turning over their horses, Mrs Hambleden escorted him to a walled garden tucked behind the far wing of the house.

He stopped short after she led him through the gate. 'I didn't even know there was a garden here!'

'The plot was cultivated beside the original central part of the house, I'm told, when it rambled on in Elizabethan fashion. When the manor was vastly enlarged, this garden ended up at the outer edge. Including such a central garden would have been thought essential when the first manor was built. After the dissolution of the monasteries, the brothers who'd dispensed healing remedies to their communities were scattered and households had to develop their own source of healing plants. There at the centre is the original knot garden.'

'Very attractive,' Hart noted as they walked towards the pleasing arrangement of silver-leafed plants and small flowers interspersed between an edging of dark green.

'Nothing says what is useful can't also be beautiful.'

'True enough of the healer as well.'

Once again flushing at his compliment, she retorted, 'Remember what Bella said. The true beauty at Steynling is the Duchess.'

Hart studied her as she averted her gaze. She was curiously defensive about having her appearance praised, seeming compelled to remind him that her sister was prettier. Though as he had noted before, only when viewed beside a true Incomparable would Mrs Hambleden not be considered exceedingly lovely. Like seeing herself as 'person of no great importance', had a lifetime in her sister's shadow conditioned her to view herself as being a woman of no particular beauty?

Despite her sensitivity on the subject, Hart couldn't let the comment pass. 'The Duchess is a beauty, true, but she is not the only beauty at Steynling. Since I'm being polite, I'll refrain from pointing out that, unlike her sister, she is *not* very useful,' he added, hoping to tease her out of her discomfort.

He succeeded, for she immediately gave him a sharp glance. 'Beauty is useful in its own right. Merely viewing it soothes and pleases the senses.'

'True,' he allowed. 'And you are a fierce defender of your sister, which is always admirable.'

Waving off that comment, she looked back to the knot garden. 'The dark-leaved plant outlining the knot is box-wood—an ointment made from its leaves is often helpful for joint pain, so I make that up for Old Greenwood. The silvery one is sage, which is brewed into a tea to soothe sore throats, and the one beginning to flower is a daisy, one of the ingredients in the cough syrup I supply to the tenants' children.

'Herbs that grow tall or untidy are planted in beds by the walls,' she continued, pointing to the brick edges of the enclosure, 'while shorter herbs are arranged by their growing preferences. Those in this section like dry soil and full sun, those that need shade and more moisture are over there, where trees on the other side of the wall shelter them.'

She leaned down to run her fingers though the plant edging the sunny bed. 'Most sun-lovers are very aromatic. Like this lavender, which won't bloom until later. The leaves, which are as scented as the flowers, are used in pillow-cases to promote restful sleep, while steeped in oil, it aids in healing wounds. The tiny-leaved thyme growing beside it, combined with ginger root, goes into the rubbing oil Old Greenwood uses on his back. The thyme flavoured with honey also makes a tea that helps to ease breathing—it's my sister's favourite when she has a cough. Oregano, another sun-lover, makes a tea that soothes the lungs.'

'You mentioned your sister often suffered from lung complaints when she was young.'

'Yes, and she's still very susceptible, which is why we grow so many plants for treating that condition. Over the years, at Whitley House and here at Steynling, I've experimented with practically every herb that's ever been used for treating lung problems. Many of them are unruly fellows, so we have them growing near the wall. On the sunny side there's liquorice, mullein and horehound, which are sweetened with honey for cough syrups. On the shady wall are marsh mallow and violets, also for cough medicines. Then comfrey and lady's mantle, both used as a poultice for healing wounds, which along with yarrow, we used a good deal treating injured soldiers.'

'Wound-healing remedies would have been in great demand.'

She nodded. 'Anticipating that, I brought with me as large a supply as I could. Also medications to treat coughs and respiratory ailments. Ginger, mint and fennel to make tea for digestive problems. Calendula flowers, crushed leaves of sweet woodruff and chicory to make an ointment to dress battle wounds. Tansy and willow bark tea to combat fever, and comfrey leaves for compresses that help heal broken bones. The regimental surgeons handled the initial injuries but were always glad of our help tending the wounded as they recovered.'

'I'm sure the doctors appreciated you. I know the soldiers did.' Hart had often witnessed himself the efforts of the women who followed the army and the gratitude of the soldiers they cared for. 'What did you do after your supplies ran out?'

'Some was shipped from back home. Local healers also introduced us to native plants—rock rose to control bleeding, a native type of thyme and fennel, along with curry, that turned out to be excellent for treating wounds. A wild lettuce that produced a sap used as a tranquilliser for the badly injured.'

Her enthusiasm fading, she fell silent, gazing into the distance. 'I used that during my husband's final days, when none of the treatments I'd tried—yarrow, curry, comfrey— nothing helped wounds too grievous to heal. In the end, I had only the wild lettuce and laudanum to soothe his mind and ease his pain.'

'I'm sorry,' Hart said softly, daring this time to press her hand in comfort. The contact brought the familiar, ex- pected zing of attraction, but desire was tempered now by genuine liking and a concern for her that made it easier to hold passion in check. She let her fingers remain in his for few minutes before pulling them away.

'How did you manage afterwards? It couldn't have been easy.'

'Two of Alexander's friends made arrangements for the service and burial. A local stonemason, whose wife I'd helped through childbirth, carved the headstone, and the wife of the town's *patron* planted a rock rose on his grave. The same two friends sold his kit, one escorted me to Lis- bon and made sure I had passage home.'

'Did you return to your parents in London?'

'Yes. I knew I couldn't stay there long, with Father busy and Mother occupied with him, as usual. When I arrived in June of '11, I learned that Liliana was still ailing after miscarrying a son that May. My parents urged me to go to Steynling and help her. She was so grateful, she begged me to stay on. I'd taken care of her for most of her child- hood, and I think it comforted her to have me watching out for her again. Especially after she miscarried another son, after which Fitzhugh was…distraught.'

'Did your husband's family not offer you a home?'

She shrugged. 'They might have offered one, at least for Alex's sake, had I approached them. But Alexander's brother had just become Earl of Lyndenham and was busy with estate duties and courting the lady who would become his countess. Liliana needed me, so remaining at Steynling seemed the best solution for all of us.'

So the new Earl hadn't troubled to invite her, Hart thought, angry on her behalf. Regardless of the other claims upon his time, Lyndenham should have considered it a privilege as well as a duty to look after the widow and son of his younger brother.

'Duties are duties and must be performed—as I concede. But family is the most important thing. It's unfortunate when the head of a family doesn't recognise that truth.'

'I don't like being beholden. If I had gone to Lyme Hill, there would have been nothing for me to do, no way to repay Lyndenham for his hospitality. At least at Steynling, I could offer needed assistance. Not as vital, perhaps, as the healing work I did in the Peninsula, but useful and satisfying. As time went on and I took on more and more, especially after the estate agent's illness and then the Duke's death, I felt I…earned the hospitality I was given.'

She shouldn't have had to 'earn' the support of her family, Hart thought, frowning. He wanted to ask if it had been awkward living under the same roof as Fitzhugh, her one-time suitor, or at least escort—Hart didn't know if his cousin had ever officially paid court to her. But he wasn't sure how to ask. She would probably tell him tartly it was none of his business anyway.

'I shall stop now before I've bored you completely. I must harvest what I need, then check on the children and consult with Cook and the housekeeper before we ride out this afternoon.'

It was a clear dismissal, and not able to think of any excuse to prolong the conversation, Hart nodded. 'I'll come in with you.'

They strolled towards the garden enclosure where she kept her supplies, all the questions teeming in Hart's brain going unvoiced.

The fact that she had not mentioned anything about her brother-in-law's reception or treatment of her—whether he'd been grateful for her help with his ailing wife, resentful of her as a burden on his household, whether he'd flirted with her or ignored her—still tickled his sense that there was more she wasn't revealing.

True, how Fitzhugh had treated Mrs Hambleden wasn't any of his business. If there had been something between them—whatever that something might have been—it ended long ago at his cousin's death. Besides, it should have been even more reprehensible for Fitzhugh to have a liaison with his sister-in-law, both a relation and a dependent in his household, than it would be for Hart to try to seduce her.

But Fitzhugh had always done what he wanted. Had he wanted her?

He'd been married to a compellingly beautiful woman, certainly, though she had been ill. But despite Mrs Hambleden's seeming not to recognise it, she was a very attractive woman herself. An attractive woman whose beauty was enriched by an earthiness and an underlying passion Hart was sure any red-blooded man would sense and appreciate.

If Fitzhugh had wanted her, he would likely have not cared much about sensibilities, hers, his wife's or society's.

He recalled her saying she'd taken a groom on their rides about the estate to demonstrate the new Duke's concern for the reputation of females dependent on him. Had that been a hint that Fitzhugh hadn't felt the same concern?

Hart could well believe it wouldn't have occurred to his

entitled, self-absorbed cousin to spare a thought for such things.

He shouldn't let the question nag at him. Whatever difficulties Mrs Hambleden might or might not have had with his cousin, she had managed to surmount them, her position and reputation at Steynling intact. Anything more personal or private between them had ended without producing negative consequences for her.

But with his attraction to her undiminished and his liking and concern for her growing, he couldn't quite shake a desire to know just how things stood between them. That concern, he regretfully conceded, partly tinged by an ignoble jealousy that Fitzhugh might have enjoyed with her an intimacy Hart could not permit himself—but could not stop desiring.

Chapter Nine

Three days later, Claire strode up to her chamber after returning from riding the estate with the Duke. Shedding gloves and bonnet, she dropped into the chair before the hearth, leaning into its welcome warmth while she stretched out a back that ached after having spent most of the day in the saddle.

They'd been making a methodical circuit of Steynling and had only a few farms still to visit tomorrow. On their way back, they would go through the village so she might introduce the new Duke properly to the shopkeepers, craftsmen and establishments that supplied services and goods to Steynling—some of whom might remember him from his visits as a boy.

She'd need to change into a more formal gown before dinner, as Liliana would be joining them. Delighted that her sister felt well enough to make the effort, Claire suspected it was the prospect of enjoying the company of a handsome man with whom she couldn't dine in her bedchamber as she could her sister, more than any sudden improvement in her sister's health, that was likely the inspiration behind this new show of strength.

Whatever the reason, she could only be pleased. Liliana's improvement was crucial, since Claire would soon complete the essentials of introducing the new Duke to his estate duties, after which he must go to London to enter the Lords and be introduced to society. While it wasn't strictly necessary for her and the Duchess to accompany him, Claire badly wanted to, a trip that would be impossible unless both of them went together.

Claire told herself she wanted to escort the Duke because she knew all too well what it was like to face society as an outsider. As he had no acquaintance with any of the leading families, she could advise him on the subtle interplay of politics and influence among the gentlemen and offer a frank feminine opinion about the merits of the females who would vie to become his Duchess.

She was too honest to deny she was reluctant to see the Duke wed one of the society beauties who would be throwing themselves at him. After an initial disdain, she'd come to like him, to appreciate his competence, to enjoy his cheerful nature, his wit—even when he seemed to delight most in teasing her—and most of all, his fairness and the sense of responsibility he exhibited towards Steynling and all those who lived on its land. Especially since that burden wasn't one he'd sought or been brought up to shoulder.

He showed great promise of becoming an excellent 'Master of Steynling', a name he would call himself to amuse her, puffing out his chest and proclaiming the title in a ridiculously pompous voice that always made her smile. She only hoped he wouldn't grow arrogant under the barrage of adulation he would receive in London.

Then there was that sensual connection that had only deepened as her reservations about his character and competence faded and her liking for him grew. She was frankly jealous of the woman who would end up sharing his bed. A man who possessed the compassion to tell a little farm girl a fairy story to distract her while Claire treated the child's burns, who would patiently listen to the chatter of an elderly widow or a retired old farmer, would probably show equal sensitivity as a lover. Her own senses whispered that he would be a passionate one.

Ah, *passion*. Of all the aspects of marriage, what she missed most was that fiery connection of two bodies becoming one, the bliss of release, the languorous drifting aftermath of lovemaking. She could imagine far too vividly sharing that joy with the Duke.

But she didn't dare. Even if she'd had her own funds and establishment, given how readily she'd conceived, trysting with him would be dangerous. While some men might be unconcerned about illegitimate offspring, Claire was sure the Duke would provide for any child he sired. But such an infant would likely be fostered out, the shame of its illegitimacy hidden by having it adopted by some deserving farm couple who'd been unable to conceive children of their own.

She could never give up a child of her body, especially not one produced with a man she liked and admired.

She needed to guard her heart, too, lest she commit the idiocy of growing to love, once again, a man she could never have.

At least this time, he appeared to be worthy of her regard.

The time she had remaining in the Duke's exclusive company was growing shorter by the minute. She should concentrate on enjoying it here and being the best possible advisor in London. And while doing so, resist the desire that whispered a discreet liaison might be possible.

She must do what duty required her to do for him…and walk away.

To what, she still didn't know.

As always when facing her uncertain future, she pushed away the doubts and dread. Tonight, she'd have not only the Duke's company at dinner but also her sister's. She would simply delight in both.

* * *

Several hours later, the Duke threw down his napkin with a satisfied sigh. 'Mrs Hambleden, please send my compliments to Cook. Dinner was particularly excellent. And you, Duchess, are looking even more beautiful with that healthy glow in your cheeks. I hope that indicates you are feeling more recovered.'

'Thank you, Your Grace, I am,' Liliana said, giving the Duke one of the ethereal smiles that had captured the hearts of so many admirers. Claire felt her teeth clench.

Don't be an idiot, she chided herself. *He assured you he was in no danger of falling for Liliana. And if did, there's nothing for you to say about it anyway.*

'If you ladies are ready to withdraw and can remain for tea, I'll forgo my port and join you immediately.'

Claire looked to her sister. 'Do you feel up to it tonight?'

Liliana smiled—at the Duke, not at her. 'Given such a charming invitation, how can I refuse? Yes, Sister,' she said, turning to Claire, 'I do feel up to it—finally.'

'Excellent,' the Duke said, walking over to offer the Duchess his arm.

As he escorted her sister to the parlour, Claire struggled to subdue a pang of something uncomfortably like jealousy. Until, pausing on threshold, he glanced back to give her a conspiratorial wink.

It was not the look of a man besotted by the company of a beautiful woman.

More like the glance of an adult who'd succeeded in amusing a difficult child. And was sharing his triumph with her.

That shouldn't have made her feel instantly better— but it did.

Shaking her head at herself for being a fool, she followed them into the room.

'Do you enjoy music, Your Grace?' said the Duke.

'Very much. As I was often ill growing up, I didn't manage to practise enough to become truly competent, but my sister is quite proficient. Will you play for us, Claire?'

So Liliana could sit cosily beside the Duke? 'The Duchess doesn't play, but she sings beautifully,' Claire countered. 'Do you think you could manage a few airs, if I played for you?'

'I would very much enjoy listening,' the Duke coaxed.

Liliana tilted her lovely head, as if considering. 'After tea, I might have the strength to perform one or two.'

'It would be a delight to play again for you,' Claire said. 'And you must regain your strength! Soon the Duke must leave Steynling and travel to London. I know he would welcome having us accompany him to introduce him to society.'

'Must it be soon?' Liliana asked, looking alarmed. 'I'm not sure I'm recovered enough to make that journey.'

'I hope you will make every effort to recover,' the Duke said. 'Mrs Hambleden believes it essential that I be introduced to society—'

'And look for a wife,' Claire inserted, needing to remind herself as well as her sister.

Shooting her a quick frown, the Duke continued, 'Before the end of this Season. Of course, I could not possibly begin such a difficult task without your support and advice.'

Looking pleased, Liliana nodded. 'My sister is quite right. You need to take your place in Parliament, and you *should* find a suitable wife without delay. I flatter myself that, as well as we know society, she and I can help with that. It's never too soon to begin the vital business of providing the estate with an heir. I'm still devastated that I...' Her voice faltered.

'You mustn't think of sad past events,' Edmenton said quickly. 'I can't tell you how relieved I shall be to have your steadfast presence beside me when I meet the devouring she-wolves of society.' He gave an elaborate shudder that set her sister laughing.

'We'll not allow them to devour you—will we, Claire? Ah, here is the tea tray.'

As the three settled around it, Claire pouring for the others, she said, 'We'll hope to show you not all society is to be dreaded.'

'I'm sure it held no fears for two such lovely and accomplished ladies. I imagine you dazzled at your debut, Duchess. At a grand ball, filled to overflowing with society's finest?'

Liliana smiled. 'It was grand. Papa, as you know, is much occupied with his duties as Lord Sidmouth's secretary, and Mama in supporting him, so Mama's cousin, Lady Shelford, chaperoned us during my debut Season. She did hold a grand ball at her town house in Grosvenor Square to introduce me.' Her face lit at the memory. 'All of London was there! Such elegant gentlemen and handsome ladies! All so charmingly attentive.'

'How could they not be, to honour the most beautiful girl to debut in a host of Seasons?' Claire said, smiling. She truly had been proud and happy for her sister on that night...even though during her own debut the previous year, she'd been escorted by a baronet's wife whose husband was an associate of her father's. Mama hadn't wanted to ask her influential cousin the favour of sponsoring a daughter until she might introduce the more beautiful younger one. The one most likely to achieve a sterling match.

Of course, Mama was right. Claire had garnered a modest following her first year—including the teasing attentions of Fitzhugh. But Liliana had been besieged not just by the Duke's heir, but by two sons of earls, a viscount and a virtual throng of lesser-titled gentlemen.

There'd been no point resenting her mother's calculated but accurate decision to save her best ammunition for when it might win her the most resounding victory. Or resent the immediate acclaim which had greeted a Beauty like her sister when sponsored by one of society's most powerful ladies.

'I was a bit intimidated at first, truly,' Liliana was saying. 'I was so grateful to Mr Hambleden—a good friend we had both known since childhood—for remaining near me for the first part of my Season, until I'd found my feet. And then continuing to advise me about which suitors to encourage, which to avoid. Of course, he was helpful to Claire as well, as one would expect, since the gentleman had the huge good sense to eventually marry her.'

Her sister looked fondly at her, Claire returning a strained smile. Did Liliana never truly realise that Alexander guarded and watched over her because he'd loved *her*, and had since they were children? Had she never suspected that he proposed to Claire and she accepted him, not out of love, but because neither could bear the idea of remaining in society where they would have to smile and dance and spend time near the one they loved—who was now married to someone else?

Did her sister declare their childhood friend had felt only affection for her and had instead loved Claire to ease her conscience? Or because she truly believed it? Claire had never known for sure.

While she was wool-gathering, the Duke was drawing her sister out about which theatres she preferred, which entertainments she recommended and which purveyors of fashion he ought to visit to acquire the garments essential for a gentleman.

As Liliana blossomed under his questioning, Claire's last niggles of jealousy faded. She'd been trying for months to pull her sister out of the depression and the self-imposed isolation in which she'd languished since the miscarriages of her sons, followed so closely by her husband's death. If the Duke could prompt her to recall happier times and coax her into participating in life again, she could only be thankful.

And he was indeed doing a very good job of it.

Tea concluded, the Duke set down his cup. 'Can I now beg you to finish this outstanding evening with some music?'

'How about "Love Me Little, Love Me Long" and "Cherry Ripe"?' Claire suggested.

Liliana nodded. 'Even though I've not practised in ages, I think I could.'

'Then I need only sit and enjoy,' the Duke said, giving Claire another wink after her sister turned to face the keyboard.

As Liliana truly did have a lovely soprano voice, there was no question the Duke's enthusiastic applause when they finished was genuine. 'Bravo! Dare I ask for an encore?'

Smiling at Liliana, who was beaming at his praise, Claire said, 'What say you, Sister?'

'One more, perhaps. Then I should retire. How about the "Jolly Plowman"?'

It was the first time in over a year her sister had volunteered to do anything. Thrilled, Claire agreed, '"Jolly Plowman" it is.' At her sister's nod, she began playing, blinking back tears.

Whatever else happened, she was supremely grateful

to the Duke for drawing her beloved sister out of her isolation and grief.

They finished to more applause, her sister blushing as she nodded to the Duke.

'Thank you both!' she said. 'I've felt better this evening than I have in months.'

'Wonderful!' Claire said. 'Let me walk you up.'

'No, Wallace can assist me. Stay and pour the Duke the port he deferred to take tea with us.'

After Liliana's maid arrived to escorted her, Claire turned the Duke.

'I cannot thank you enough.'

'For what?'

'Making my sister come alive again. She'd been so mired in grief, I feared I would never be able to rouse her. Now, I hope that by the time you leave for London, she will be recovered enough for us to accompany you.'

He smiled at her with seeming tenderness. 'You are welcome. But I'm not going to London without the two of you, so if the Duchess is not feeling up to it, I'll simply wait until she is.'

'But you must go soon, if only to attend this year's session of Parliament and make yourself known to the peers with whom you will work on England's behalf.'

He shrugged. 'Introducing myself in Parliament could wait.'

'Delay your duty to attend the Lords? We're unlikely to agree on that! But I'm so happy at my sister's improvement, I'll not argue with you tonight.'

'Good. I think you've been instructed to pour me some port. Won't you keep me company while I drink it?'

She shouldn't. Her relief and delight at Liliana's improvement would only cloak temporarily the simmering undercurrent of attraction. But she was too happy to worry about it now. And the little voice in her ear reminded that with London looming, she should savour the time she had in his company before it was no longer hers to enjoy.

Not that the right to enjoy it had ever truly been hers. But soon, it would indisputably belong to the lady he made his Duchess.

Chapter Ten

By late afternoon of the following day, their visits to tenants in the northmost corner of the estate complete, Hart rode with Mrs Hambleden back to Steynling Hall by way of the village.

She appeared lost in thought, giving Hart the opportunity to study her without the danger of being reprimanded for staring—which he certainly would be, if she noticed his scrutiny. Given her response thus far when he complimented her expertise or beauty, she would probably find his close observation unsettling. Which would likely provoke one of her tart remarks, he thought, smiling.

His thoughts then returned to the musical end of the previous evening. Despite the grievous events that had thrown her life into disarray, a lady as young as the Duchess shouldn't shut herself away in a shadowy world of perpetual mourning and regret. Coaxing her to engage once again in society was only right and compassionate.

But watching the serious look that usually graced Mrs Hambleden's face give way to smiles and genuine laughter made doing the right thing especially enjoyable.

He must encourage more duets. Not only to tempt the Duchess into resuming activities she'd once enjoyed, but because for the space of that performance, it seemed to lift from Mrs Hambleden's shoulders some of the heavy burden she carried, making her look younger, happier.

The Duchess had suffered reverses, but so had Mrs Hambleden. She deserved more recognition, more compliments and more evenings when the cares and worries of managing a great estate, trying to restore an ailing sister to health and raise a son and a niece could for a time be forgotten.

Though he didn't want her to lose all the sharpness. He quite enjoyed seeing the flash of those icy blue eyes and waiting, after he'd provoked her, to hear what answering verbal volley she'd lob at him.

'You seem to be more at ease meeting tenants now,' Mrs Hambleden said, rousing him from his reverie. 'Is it becoming more natural?'

'I still have difficulty seeing myself as master of all I survey, but viewing Steynling's people as I do—did—the soldiers under my command makes it easier.'

'Soldiers bearing ploughs and seed drills instead of muskets and sabres.'

He nodded. 'I don't have the worry of finding them nourishment and billets, but providing equipment and supplies is just as important.'

'Fortunately, logistics for that are easier here, too. No long mule trains lumbering at a snail's pace over miles of bad—or no—roads.'

Hart groaned, remembering. 'Thank Heaven! We endured far too many campaigns where we arrived at our next billet hours or days before the supplies, the troopers ready to eat shoe leather from hunger.'

'Did you serve with Wellesley from the very beginning?'

Hart shook his head. 'The Royals weren't in Portugal for his first campaign—or the bitter retreat from Corunna. We didn't arrive until the autumn of '09. Did some skirmishing on the Portuguese border but didn't see real action until we covered the retreat from Busaco to the lines of Torres Vedras before the winter of '10. We were at Fuentes de Oñoro and assisted during the storming of Ciudad Rodrigo and Badajoz. Which is where I met my two best friends.'

She raised her eyebrows. 'They were not from your company, then?'

'Oh, I had friends enough among the Royals. But at Badajoz, while we and several other dragoon units were providing covering fire for the besiegers, French artillery blew up the old stone wall we were sheltering behind. The soldiers not injured in that barrage scrambled to regroup under heavy fire.'

Hart paused, hearing again the crack of rifles and muskets, the scream of flying and boom of exploding artillery, the confused yells between comrades, the cries of the wounded. Tasted again the acrid smoke that obscured one's view and stung lips and eyes.

'Over the next few hours,' he said, 'until the Forlorn Hope succeeded in breaching the walls, our ragtag group dragged rocks, shattered timber, whatever we could find to create a protective screen. Rafe, Charles and I ended up together behind one such shelter. We covered for one another while firing, and when a new blast disintegrated our makeshift wall, dragged each other to safety and helped construct another. By the time the siege ended, we had saved each other's lives several times over.'

'Which created a bond unlike any other, I should think.'

'It did for us. Lieutenant Charles Marsden came from Dunbar's Dragoons. Rafe Tynesley was a lieutenant with the Sixteenth Queen's Light Dragoons. Our units weren't at the same place on any field of battle afterwards, but we had some skirmishing duties together, often met up between engagements and shared a billet during winter quarters.'

Hart smiled. 'In front of the bloody, breached walls at

Badajoz, we pledged that once the war was over and Boney beaten for good and all, we would go adventuring together. My mother had been tending our land since long before Father died, so she didn't need me home. Rafe is a younger son and Charles an orphan, neither needing to return to responsibilities in England. We thought to go out to India or join some colonial army.'

His smile faded. 'Then after Salamanca came the shocking news that I'd inherited a dukedom. My friends were no help. They argued as loudly as the rest that I must leave the army and return home.'

'To be tethered to fields and farms and Parliament, instead of adventuring?'

Hart looked at her sharply, surprised she seemed to realise how he'd seen the inheritance not as a boon, but as a manacle chaining him to a life he didn't want. 'Exactly.'

'I hope, over time, you will come to view Steynling not as just a great inescapable burden, but as a chance to apply the talents you honed in the army for another, equally good cause.'

'Caring for Steynling has been a burden that weighed you down. If I'm grateful for anything about returning, it's relieving you of it.'

'A burden in some ways, yes. A cause of anxiety, certainly. But as I have said before, also an opportunity for me to be useful, to do necessary work well. At least for a time.' She gave him a wry smile. 'Unlike you, I'm just a temporary caretaker at Steynling. I will have to find other fulfilling work once you take over here.'

Hart didn't know what to say to reassure her. She would have to move on from Steynling—as disagreeable as that idea now seemed to him—and he had no more idea than she did where she would go next.

Wherever, he vowed then and there to make sure she

found a comfortable position, either with her sister, if they both preferred, or elsewhere. She might not be his responsibility by blood or by marriage, as her sister was, but she had been the one to keep Steynling running for her sister and for him.

After arriving at Steynling and having the estate agent fall gravely ill, she'd added more work that should have fallen to Fitzhugh. Despite her initial reservations about his suitability, which he hoped he had finally put to rest, she had supported him and given her best efforts to help him settle in and become familiar with the land and its people.

'You will have fulfilling work wherever you are,' he said at last. 'You're not one to lay about, petting your pug dog, eating sweetmeats and tormenting your servants.'

She laughed at the image. 'True enough.' An anxious expression briefly crossed her face before she shook her head and put on a determined smile. 'I will find a way to be useful.'

'Speaking of tormenting, I wrote to Rafe and Charles from London telling them they must join me in England before the summer campaigns begin. If I must endure being Duke, I should at least be able to drag them through some of the activities.'

'If they are able to come to London when you are there this Season, that would be excellent. It's always easier if one has friends to support one when coping with new and unaccustomed circumstances.'

Hart nodded. 'I can shove them before me as covering shields from the sniper fire of marriage-minded maidens. As they are both bachelors, maybe they can deflect one or two of the attackers away from me.'

She chuckled at the image but shook her head. 'Unless they stand to inherit dukedoms as well, they are unlikely to deter any of those maidens who have targeted you.'

'Alas, none of us were *supposed* to inherit titles or position in England. Which was why we had planned to adventure together after the war.'

'I'm afraid they won't be much help in thinning the crowd vying for your favour, then. But dashing single gentlemen with tales about exotic locales will surely draw favourable attention from young maidens, even gentlemen not in line for titles and wealth. So, I might have the pleasure of meeting your friends?'

Hart felt a sudden jolt of uncertainty. His friends would certainly find it a pleasure to meet *her*. An odd proprietary feeling came over him; Mrs Claire Hambleden had become *his* valued friend and companion. He found he was not so happy at the idea of sharing her with his friends, especially Charles, whom ladies usually found irresistible.

'Perhaps. Winter sailing is uncertain, so most officers remain in quarters in Lisbon. Though they'd doubtless find it amusing to view me in my new role.'

'We're arriving in the village now,' she said, pointing ahead. 'Have you visited it since assuming your new role?'

'My batman and I stopped for a glass of home brewed before making our way to Steynling.'

'Did you identify yourself to the innkeeper?' When Hart didn't immediately answer, Mrs Hambleden laughed. 'I thought not. Mr Maitland is going to be dismayed when he discovers he has already served the new Duke with what, I'm sure he will feel, wasn't proper deference.'

Hart waved a hand. 'I'm not Fitzhugh, requiring bowing and scraping.'

She gave him an enigmatic look. 'No, you are not.'

Her reply revived his ever-simmering wonder about just what their relationship had been. How had they interacted when she returned, she the grieving widow, he the husband disappointed by his wife's inability to give him a son?

Since he couldn't figure out an acceptable way to make such an enquiry, it was just as well that by now they were trotting into the village itself.

'Did you stop by any of the other village establishments on your way to Steynling?'

Hart shook his head. 'Just at the Quail and Partridge for a mug of ale.'

'And to put off for a little longer having to ride up to Steynling's gates?'

After a silent moment, he gave her a wry smile. 'Guilty.'

She shook her head at him. 'We'll go to the inn first, get you another pint of ale and rectify your previous omission. Maitland would be embarrassed if others in the village learned of your identity before he did. Shall we proceed?'

A few minutes later, they dismounted before the swinging sign of the two game birds. Seeing Mrs Hambleden walk in, the proprietor smiled at her and nodded to the groom before giving Hart a puzzled look, as if certain he'd seen him before but not sure when or where.

After signalling to the barmaid to serve the groom, the proprietor turned his full attention to them. 'What can I do for you today, ma'am? Returning after visiting the farms, are you? M'wife has a fine stew simmering if you're needing some refreshment before returning to the manor. And for you, Lieutenant?'

'Your Grace, may I introduce the owner of the Quail and Partridge, George Maitland. Mr Maitland, His Grace, the Duke of Fenniston.'

The proprietor bowed. As he rose and glanced again at Hart's uniform, his smile faded to a look of dismay. 'Did you come through the village some time ago, Your Grace, you and your batman?'

'I did. And remember your excellent ale with pleasure.'

'Right sorry I am, Your Grace!' Maitland cried. 'Had you made yourself known, I would have conducted you to a private parlour and attended to your needs personally!'

'You greeted me most courteously and saw me served me with all dispatch. Which is all any honest man need do for one of his fellows, regardless of rank.'

'Gracious of you to say so, Your Grace.'

'What say you, Mrs Hambleden? Shall we try a bowl of Mrs Maitland's superior stew?'

'With pleasure! I know it to be as delicious as Mr Maitland claims.'

'You shall have some at once. May I escort you to our private parlour?'

'No, the taproom is fine,' Hart said. 'Our stop will be brief, as I'm sure Mrs Hambleden is weary after visiting tenants most of the day.'

'Very good, Your Grace. I'll see m'wife brings the stew right away.'

As Maitland hurried off, they seated themselves. 'Would you prefer a private parlour?' Hart asked.

'Since we have only the groom accompanying us, better for propriety's sake that we remain in the common room.'

'So we don't ruin my reputation?' Hart teased, grinning.

'Exactly,' she said drily, refusing, alas, to rise to the bait. 'Do you remember any of the village tradesmen from your visits as a boy?'

'I had no spare coins to spend and Fitzhugh wasn't offering any of his. We rode through once or twice, mostly, I think, so he could show off how deferentially all the merchants and tradesmen greeted him as we passed by.'

Hart hoped that might elicit from her some comment about his cousin, but she merely nodded, leaving his nagging curiosity still unenlightened. 'Then I will briefly introduce you to all of them before we head back. By now, everyone in the village knows the new Duke is in residence, your arrival being the most significant event for the village since the previous Duke's fatal accident. Everyone will watch how you behave to try to glean some insight into your character. Since it will have great impact on their lives.'

Hart nodded, the reflection sobering. He had every confidence in his abilities as a troop commander, but when it came to handling an estate, though he didn't doubt he'd eventually master the task, he was still just feeling his way.

After presenting them each a steaming dish of stew and begging them to let her know if they desired anything else, Mrs Maitland walked away, leaving them to enjoy the meal. Evening had not yet fallen to end the work day, so there were few patrons in the taproom. Still, Hart noted the curious glances sent their way from those nursing tankards of ale or enjoying their own stew.

Mrs Hambleden noticed them, too, nodding towards one staring customer, who quickly looked away. 'You see why it was wiser for us to avoid the private parlour.'

'I imagine even this visit will become the subject of gossip.'

'But the talk will be only curious, not damaging. The villagers all know I've been making the farm visits ever since Mr Evans fell ill two years ago. As I am best acquainted with Steynling's tenants, no one will wonder that I'm the one escorting you to make the introductions. Our being here together may elicit comment, but as we've been everywhere accompanied by a groom, it's unlikely to prompt any salacious rumours.'

'I'm relieved. Such a development would be most unfair—to you, who should certainly not have your stainless character maligned.'

To his surprise, something almost like a...wince? wrinkled her forehead before she smoothed her expression. 'Kind of you,' she murmured.

Kind of him? He'd like to enquire just what that enigmatic reply meant. After a moment's silence trying to find the right words to phrase such a question, he conceded defeat and said instead, 'Who else will I meet in the village?'

'Craftsmen who work at Steynling and merchants who supply the Hall. The blacksmith, the carpenter and the wheelwright, whom we call to the estate as needed. My sister orders her gowns from London, of course, but most of the Hall's residents either make their own clothing from material purchased here or have their garments made up by the village dressmaker or the tailor, their shoes by the cobbler. We'll visit the tailor and cobbler as a courtesy, but naturally as Duke, your furnishings will be ordered from London as well.'

He thought of proclaiming that garments made by a village tailor were quite good enough…but from the look on her face, figured such a protest was futile. 'As they must be, to uphold the reputation of the Duke?' he said drily.

'Your tone suggests such a matter is trivial, but I assure you it is not. The manner in which you dress as much as the way you conduct yourself must uphold the standards required by your position. To do less, appear less, reflects badly not just on you but on Steynling itself.' After a pause, she added gently, 'You shall have to give up the uniform eventually, you know.'

The reminder of that unhappy fact sharpening his tone, he replied, 'Mustn't appear before society like a bumpkin or a pauper, dressed in fustian instead of arrayed by one of London's premier tailors?'

'I'm afraid so.'

Telling himself again that it was useless to fight what couldn't be changed—and knowing she was correct—he tried to smother the resentment. Bypassing the sore subject of his own appearance, he said, 'And your gowns come from London, too, along with your sister's?'

'No, mine certainly aren't. Garments made by a London modiste are far too expensive.'

'Your sister baulks at providing clothing for the woman who is running Steynling?'

'There's no reason for her to bear such an expense. Even if we entertained, which we have hardly done since her illnesses, I would be quite a minor participant, with no need to appear in the latest fashions.'

'Doesn't it also reflect badly on Steynling to have the Duchess's sister appear in anything less?'

Looking uncomfortable, she said, 'The village dressmaker has a very adequate selection of material and I can make up gowns myself, with the help of my maid.' She laughed. 'Believe me, after the time I spent in the Peninsula, having any new gown is a treat!'

She was trying to deflect him, he knew. Sensing that persisting would only make her more uncomfortable, he let the matter drop—for the time being.

After she dragged him to London, though, he would intervene. If he was going to have to leave off his uniform and look the part of a duke, she had better resign herself to looking like the sister of a Duchess.

It would have been a very small matter for the Duchess to see her sister dressed in London finery. Doubtless Mrs Hambleden would never ask for such a favour, but Hart saw the omission as yet one more instance in which she seemed to be taken for granted by everyone at Steynling. She might do the work of a chatelaine, but she wasn't a housekeeper and shouldn't be treated as such.

He would make sure when London finery was bought,

she got her share, and the estate would definitely stand the cost.

Tamping down his anger over this latest slight, Hart finished his ale. 'We should go. It's getting late.'

'Yes, I need to check on the children and consult Cook about dinner.'

They both rose, the innkeeper hastening over to escort them out. Leaving the horses tethered, they walked down the high street, stopping at different shops where Mrs Hambleden introduced him to the baker, grocer, haberdasher, apothecary, cobbler, tailor and dressmaker. On the outskirts of the village, they lingered a bit longer with the wheelwright, carpenter and blacksmith while Mrs Hambleden reviewed the current needs at the Hall and the farms.

As he made his slow progress through town, nodding and chatting, Hart felt an ever-increasing number of eyes fixed on him. By the time they finished with the blacksmith and walked back to collect their mounts, his affability had begun to fray, his dislike for being on display just as intense as he'd anticipated.

Throwing himself into the saddle, he set out at a trot, not slowing his pace until he left all the curious gazes behind. When Mrs Hambleden, who required more time to mount the side-saddle, caught up to him just past the last cottages, he said, 'Shall we have one more gallop?'

She gave him a curious look. 'Maybe a canter. The horses have already ridden far today.'

Realising immediately how imprudent his request was, he blew out a breath. 'You're right, of course. I'm letting irritation blind me to the needs of my mount, a mistake I never made as a soldier. Very well, a canter—for as far as the horses can tolerate.'

The pounding of hooves and rush of wind helped blow away his remaining disgruntlement. Slowing after the horses' flagging pace told him it was time, he turned to Mrs Hambleden. 'I should apologise—to you and to them. Now that we're beyond the view of curious eyes, shall we send the groom back to his duties? Then dismount and let our horses rest before we finish the ride back to Steynling.'

'A prudent plan,' she replied, nodding.

Hart signalled a dismissal to the groom, who rode off with alacrity, doubtless delighted to be released from his day-long chaperonage duty. Sliding from the saddle, Mrs Hambleden gave him a puzzled glance. 'You found the village—irksome? You didn't seem to mind being known as the Duke by the tenants.'

'There was only one of them at a time. I don't like being the focus of everyone's gaze.'

She laughed wryly. 'I'm afraid you will have to get used to it. If you think the curious looks of the villagers intrusive, wait until London, when whole ballrooms of observers will be watching your every move.'

Hart groaned. 'Better not tell me that, lest I flee into the night back to Portugal.' He sighed. 'Which is not such a bad idea. I'll find Rafe and Charles, who harried me to return, and send one of them back to take my place!'

'If only it were that easy. I'm afraid the dukedom is your yoke to bear. It will become easier over time, as you grow more accustomed to the role.'

'Will it?' he asked dubiously. 'But I shouldn't complain about what can't be mended. Especially not to you, who have shouldered so much already. I don't mean to be ungrateful for your assistance, either. You've been an immense help.'

'I want to do what I can.'

He gazed over, unable to help himself. Especially at this moment, when he felt so unsettled and resentful, he thought what *he* wanted most was to fling down the reins, pull her into the shade of the woods and lose himself in kissing her. The passion she awakened would make him forget all about staring eyes, overly deferential servants and townsmen and the gauntlet that faced him in London.

Something of his thoughts must have shown in his face, for she stopped suddenly and drew in a sharp breath. Then leaned imperceptibly closer, her head angled up to his, setting every nerve alight.

Before he could react, she stepped quickly backwards. 'I should find a log to help me remount,' she murmured, not meeting his gaze.

He might well have committed the great idiocy of kissing her if she hadn't suddenly moved away. But fighting arousal, feeling reckless still, he said, 'Let me give you a leg up.'

He expected her to refuse, which would certainly be wiser. Instead, after a long hesitation, she whispered, 'Very well.'

She lifted a booted foot. He took it in one hand, put the other at her waist and lifted her into the side-saddle. He took his time arranging her foot in the stirrup, letting his hand linger at her waist. She sat stiffly upright, looking straight ahead, not at him, but Hart felt her tremble beneath his fingers.

He would never have imagined that clasping his gloved hand about the waist of a lady garbed in a thick riding habit could become erotic. But even that limited contact was sending sparks of desire fizzing from his fingers, speeding his pulse, hardening his groin.

Finally she moved, lowering her hand—to push his away, probably, since he seemed incapable of moving it. Instead, she placed her gloved fingers lightly on top of the hand clasping her waist.

She still didn't look at him or acknowledge the contact

between them in any other way. But he felt that touch of her hand in every part of his body as strongly as if she had laced bare fingers with his.

For a timeless moment they both remained immobile, joined by that glancing bond, a connection so potent, his face heated and his breathing roughened. Then her horse shifted and she pulled her hand up, gently pushing his away.

'You should remount, too,' she said at last, her voice unsteady.

Forcing himself free of the sensual spell, he concentrated on retrieving his mount. Mrs Hambleden began a prosaic recitation of what Cook should be preparing for dinner, as if she needed that inane chatter to distance herself from what had just happened between them.

Hart couldn't decide whether to be relieved or sorry the interlude had ended. Giving in to the temptation to touch her was playing with devil's fire, betting he'd retain enough honour and discipline to draw back from disaster. He beat back the urge to imagine what it might be like to possess her completely, if the mere touch of her hand evoked so intense a response.

By the time she progressed to describing the third course and second remove, his body had settled enough for his brain to resume functioning.

No need to reconsider the prospect of seducing her; he'd already examined that alluring idea from every possible angle before regretfully concluding it was impossible, for a number of excellent reasons.

He needed to do a better job of remembering that, lest he shame his honour and hers. Which would be the worst thing he could do to a lady whom he'd come to respect and value as much as he desired her.

Chapter Eleven

Several weeks later, having made one of their final farm visits, Claire and the Duke walked their mounts back towards Steynling. Having sent their chaperoning groom back to the stables once they reached the estate's boundaries, they rode in companionable silence, letting their horses stop and graze along the verge.

The duke appeared lost in thought, leaving Claire free to study the face that over the last month had become so familiar. She knew the way he frowned when contemplating some difficulty, how the skin beside his laughing eyes creased when he teased her—as he was wont to do far too often. The compassion and gentle courtesy on his face when he dealt with her sister, the firmly set jaw and frosty eyes when he corrected some recalcitrant.

She'd been dawdling during the last homeward section of their rides for several days now, the remorseless clock ticking in her head telling her she couldn't delay much longer that inevitable trip to London.

There was little excuse for remaining at Steynling; Edmenton was now familiar with all the tenants, Evans had inspected the estate books with him in detail and he'd made several visits to the village businesses. Liliana continued to improve, her former lethargy fading as her stamina increased, her enthusiasm to return to the city growing apace.

Yesterday she'd even declared she felt strong enough to enter society, face down the pitying glances and endure the genuine sympathy friends would express at her loss.

But that was only an excuse; in truth, she'd been delaying because of the Duke.

If the Duke's kindness and gentleness when dealing with her sister had soon made him a favourite with Liliana, he had gradually grown to be equally appealing to Claire. How could he not, when he so frequently expressed his admiration for her competence, his appreciation for her diligence in handling the estate duties, her patience and persistence in acquainting him with them?

In addition to giving her unaccustomed praise, in a subtle and often unstated way, he let her know how attractive he found her as woman—even while daily interacting with her much more beautiful sister. Having never before had a man pay her much notice in Liliana's proximity, his continued attentions were balm to a wound deeper than she'd realised.

Over the last month, they'd developed a camaraderie as deep and strong as their potent physical attraction and she was loath to lose it. For once in London, that close bond would end and he would be no longer hers—as much as he'd ever been. He would take his place as Duke and belong ever after to the wider world.

And with him having fully grasped the reins of his role, she would have to finally figure out what do next with her life.

No wonder she was resisting having this halcyon period come to an end.

'You're looking very solemn,' the Duke said, pulling her from her melancholy reflections.

'Just wool-gathering about the future. Have you accepted yours yet?'

The Duke sighed. '"When a ewe's drowned she's dead."'

Claire choked down a laugh. 'I beg your pardon?'

He gave her a wry grin. 'If a lamb drowns in a stream, she'll not be revived. Which means thinking about an enterprise that cannot happen is useless. No, I've not totally banished regret at the loss of my ability to order my life as I wanted. But nothing will change that, so I'm slowly becoming more resigned.'

'I'm glad. In the end, we can only go where life insists on taking us,' she replied, feeling the truth of that more for her than for him.

'Well, I suppose we should ride back now?' he asked, seeming as reluctant as she was to end their private time together.

Then, speaking as the idea struck her, she said, 'Shall we ride to the high bluff east of the Hall first? There's such a lovely vista this time of year, with new wheat and barley already waving in fields interspersed with woods and pasture.'

'Shall we begin with a gallop?' he suggested.

'Absolutely! Let's be off!'

Smiling in anticipation, Claire wheeled her mare and set her immediately to a gallop. For a few sweet minutes, she set aside all the worries and regrets and gave herself up to the simple pleasure of the rushing wind, the breakneck pace and the delight of the Duke's company. Knowing how soon it must end put an even keener edge on the joy of it.

He was smiling as they pulled up. 'You're the best opponent I've had since Charles and Rafe back in Portugal.'

'I remember you enjoyed steeplechasing. Did you race often?'

'Not often. The terrain was punishing for the horses' feet, and a soldier is too dependent on his mount in battle to risk injuring him for a pleasure ride. We were more likely to join an inter-regimental Trigger Club and walk or ride out looking for a good meal—quail, grouse, wild duck, even partridges.'

'We always appreciated having a game bird to roast! Shall we lead the horses as they cool? The trail to the bluff becomes rather steep for riding.'

The Duke nodded and they both dismounted, walking at an easy pace, the horses trailing behind them, until they reached a flat, open space at the summit.

'We can leave them here to graze,' Claire said. 'The best view is to be had from that rock outcropping there—' she said, pointing, '—just below the crest.'

'I'll follow you down.'

After securing the reins, Claire led down the narrow path, a prickling sensation at her back and neck with the Duke following so closely behind her. He answered her quick backwards glance by saying, 'I don't mean to crowd you, but I want to remain near enough to catch you if you trip. Wouldn't want you to go tumbling down the cliff.'

'I'd rather avoid that myself,' she muttered, thinking that his proximity distracted her so completely, she was more likely to trip with him following as he was now than if he left a greater distance between them. She could almost feel the heat of his body and could certainly smell the distinctive scent of his shaving soap.

That acute sensitivity eased a bit when they reached the outcropping, where the vista unfolded beneath them. 'You see? It's one of my favourite spots on the estate.'

'Magnificent! Let me guess. You come here alone when you're in need of calm and quiet to restore you to face your duties?'

Surprised that he'd sensed that, she nodded. 'I do.'

'Is the stream down there the one we crossed on the way back from the village?' The Duke chuckled. 'It reminds me of a crossing we once made. An officer in the next company, wanting to save himself a soaking, ordered one of his men to carry him over the water on his shoulders. The twosome were about halfway across the stream when they were spied by the Light Brigade's General Craufurd. Furious, he barked at the struggling trooper to drop the officer at once—which he did, I'm sure, with much secret glee. Then Craufurd ordered the Captain to wade back to where they'd started and cross the entire stream again, by himself. "All must share alike," the General said.'

'My keenest travelling memory is of one horrid winter march, the ground frozen, hoar frost covering everything with a slick of ice. So frigid was it, the Highlanders were issued trousers. Command said the cold would have killed them had they gone on only in their kilts.'

'Despite all the difficulties, there's much I still miss about campaigning.'

Claire nodded. 'I miss it sometimes, too. As I will miss this place, when we go to London,' she added with a sigh. 'I've grown very fond of Steynling.'

'I should think so, after all the tender care you've given it.' Gazing at her, he raised his eyebrows. 'You say that as if you don't intend to come back.'

'I might well not be. Or at least, not for long, if you bring back a duchess.'

The Duke grimaced. 'Don't spoil the pleasure of our ride by reminding me of that duty. "It's time enough to mak my bed when I'm gaun to lie down."'

She shook her head at him. 'I know you're aggravated when you trot out the Scottish sayings. And I fear you will have to quite literally "lie down" to that duty sooner rather than later. But the duty doesn't necessarily have to be unpleasant. Unlike a female, you won't be forced into marrying any particular person. You will be able to choose, and surely you will find *some* suitable lady who appeals to you.'

'There's a lady who appeals right here.'

A little shock zinged through her nerves. They'd danced around the issue of their mutual attraction, but this was the first time he'd admitted it directly. Telling herself it still made no difference, she said, 'Not a lady who's suitable, however.'

He stopped her with a look. 'She might be. Can you tell me you've never considered it?'

His words filled her with a racing excitement she struggled to subdue. Shaking her head firmly, she said, 'There's no point considering the impossible. And it is impossible, so don't even try to deny it. I am a widow with no dowry, no fortune, no influence. You need a high-born heiress from a prominent family with important connections to maintain your position in society and bear your heirs.'

For a fraught moment, she thought he might deny it, firing her with a ridiculous hope. Which died a moment later when he looked away with a sigh. 'Still, I wouldn't want to have you leave without telling you how I much admire and respect you.'

A bitter, crushing disappointment filled her. 'Oh, yes, I'm *supremely* capable. You needn't waste your breath telling me that.'

'Why shouldn't I praise your competence? You know very well that's not the only quality that draws me.'

If he could be frank, so could she. 'No, there's also a strong attraction between us…which is equally impossible. I cannot say how I much regret that we cannot pursue it. But regret changes nothing. Another task awaits in London, which lingering here does not make any easier. Indeed, it creates a false sense of intimacy that will perhaps make London more difficult.'

She took a deep breath. Coming to this beautiful place, a place of peace and joy for her, had been the impulse of the moment. But perhaps subconsciously she knew she must come here to gather the courage to end her malingering and force herself to do what she must.

'I believe it's time to proceed to London. To…to say goodbye to the companionship we've enjoyed. And I have enjoyed it, so very much,' she added in a whisper.

'Say goodbye?' he echoed. Shaking his head as if in protest, he moved nearer, until he was barely a step away.

He was once again close enough for her to sense his heat, inhale his scent and feel the pull of his nearness. As he gazed down at her, impelled by irresistible impulse, she went up on tiptoe and kissed him.

She'd meant it to be an affectionate goodbye, truly she had, but the moment her lips met his, she stilled. Like a wind-driven campfire spark fallen on the sun-dried grass of Portugal, need so long denied fired from ember to raging blaze in an instant.

The passion she had struggled for weeks to subdue exploded, her brain shut down and all that was left was her senses shouting of need, need, need. Her hands rose up to grip the back of his head, and making a little sound in her throat, she deepened the kiss.

Claire Hambleden was…kissing him?

After an instant of shocked immobility, sensation came roaring back. His brain might be stunned, but Hart's body knew what it wanted, what it had wanted almost from the first moment he met her. Wrapping his arms around her, he pulled her closer and deepened the kiss.

With a little moan she leaned into him, rubbing her body against his torso, her breasts against his chest, her belly against his hardening cock. Then she moved her hand and wound her arms around his back, opening her mouth to him fully, her tongue seeking his with urgency, thrusting, caressing, demanding.

Any idea of control vaporised before his scattered mind could summon it, the kiss and contact he'd craved and denied himself for so long sweeping him into a passion impossible to resist. He welcomed her exploring tongue, the fingers moving up to fist in his hair, her figure pressed against him, contacting his with liquid flame in all his needy places.

He whirled her around and leaned her against the rock wall, instinct urging him to push up her skirts and bare the body he burned to kiss, possess and enter. His fingers caressed her skin as he slid them from the softness of her knees to her thighs, both desperate to reach her hot, wet centre and wanting to linger, savouring every inch of velvety skin.

He was holding her so tightly, it took him a moment to realise that rather than melting into him, she was now trying to push him away. At first he resisted, until the sharp crack of a woodsman's axe chopping away somewhere not too distant finally penetrated his passion-fogged senses. Releasing her, he stepped back, panting.

She looked like a wild creature, panting too, a lock of hair dislodged from her coiffure, her lips reddened from kissing him. She stared up at him, bringing one hand up to touch her mouth, her eyes wide and disbelieving. Then before he could utter a word, she pushed past him and scrambled back up the slope.

Hart followed, but she was too quick for him. By the time he'd reached the summit, she'd seized the mare's reins, levered herself into the saddle and was riding off.

Hart stared after her, not walking towards his own mount until she disappeared in the distance, galloping as if the hounds of hell were pursuing her. Claiming his own reins, rather than remount immediately, he walked his horse, waiting for his breathing to ease, his aroused and frustrated body to settle and his frozen brain to begin working again.

He'd always suspected she felt for him the same deep attraction, but the passion she'd just revealed had gone well beyond anything he could have imagined. Just recalling her reaction sent another blistering wave of arousal through him. He'd imagined they would be well matched physically—and, oh, how true that prediction had been!

But what was he to make of the interlude?

She'd meant it to be a goodbye; she'd made that clear. A goodbye that had also clearly become more passionate than she'd intended.

Had he taken advantage, turning a kiss of respect and affection into something more, something she'd not wanted? But she was first to deepen the kiss, nor had she protested the increasing intimacy of their contact, until the possibility of discovery had driven her away.

He should be glad it had, since he'd lost all semblance of control the minute she'd opened her lips to him. His responsibility, her position as dependent in his household, the possible reaction of her sister—none of that had the slightest effect in restraining his raging desire.

How should he react when he saw her again, as he would at dinner. Apologise? Ignore what had happened?

One thing he couldn't do with any honesty was tell her he regretted it. It would be hard enough to reassure her—and himself—that he would make certain it did not happen again.

Hart might not have been sure how he should act when he met Mrs Hambleden, but she had obviously decided how she meant to treat him. Distant, withdrawn, refusing to meet his gaze, she sat stony-faced and let her sister carry the conversation at dinner, responding with monosyllables when some question forced her to answer. Speaking little and eating less.

Had Hart not already known how self-absorbed the Duchess could be, he would have been astounded that she didn't seem to notice her sister's abnormal reticence.

Even when Mrs Hambleden declined her sister's request that she play for them after dinner, the Duchess merely nodded and said she understood her sister must be tired after her long day.

'Tired, yes,' Mrs Hambleden affirmed. 'And I must be up especially early tomorrow to begin preparations for our removal to London.'

'You've decided it is time to go?' the Duchess asked, her tone surprised.

'Yes. Before the Season becomes any more advanced, we must bring the Duke to London to begin his next tasks— entering Parliament and finding a bride. Fenniston has successfully mastered all he needs to know to begin running the estate. And you are feeling up to the journey, aren't you, Sister?'

'Yes, I think I can support London now,' the Duchess confirmed. 'Perhaps even enjoy it.'

Fenniston.

Hart barely heard the Duchess's reply as her sister's use of his title struck him. She had called him 'Your Grace' on numerous occasions—often to tweak him—but she'd never before called him Fenniston.

'Excellent. As I have much to do, I shall retire now.'

After the shock of her coldness, her sudden announcement and that *name*, Hart couldn't let her just walk away.

'Duchess, will you take tea in the parlour?' he asked quickly.

'Yes, if *you* will play for me.'

'If you wish it. Let me just see Mrs Hambleden out.'

She was already out of the room before he caught up to her and didn't halt until, several steps down the hallway, he grabbed her arm.

She jerked it away, still not looking at him.

Dismayed, Hart floundered for words, finally coming up with, 'Shall we ride tomorrow?'

She shook her head. 'I have many things to attend to if I am to have the household ready to depart for London as soon as possible.'

'Let me apologise then. I'm devastated to think my actions would deprive you of your morning ride.'

To his infinite relief, she finally looked at him with a wry half-smile. 'Not your actions—or at least, not totally. I believe I was mostly responsible for that lamentable loss of self-control today.' She shook her head. 'It's pointless to deny I desired it, that I have for weeks. I thought I was principled enough not to succumb.' She blew out a breath. 'Apparently not. You may now think me a wanton, with good reason.'

'Never that! Only a passionate lady losing sight, for a moment, of propriety. I would have been guilty of even greater blindness, had we...progressed further and the woodsman stumbled upon us.'

She nodded. 'Which is why we must not ride together again. I've shown I can't trust myself. I'll not face the temptation of your company in London, where there will be many others for you to meet, dine with and enjoy entertainments. Of course, I'll be available to advise you, especially on the suitability of potential brides, but there will be no more private interludes to test my lamentable control.'

'You know I wish it were otherwise. That we were both free to pursue...what we desire.'

'Pursuing what one desires is a fool's wish, for a woman at least. There are always repercussions. She can't just walk away afterwards like a man could. Better dreams unrealised than the unpleasant reality of the inevitable consequences.'

She looked up to gaze into his eyes. 'Still, I thank you. For making me feel desirable. Wanted. Appreciated.'

'You are all those things,' he said, thinking how pathetically inadequate the words sounded.

'Then I haven't given you…a disgust of me? I'd be sore afflicted to think I'd lost your good opinion.'

'Of course you haven't! I just hope my irresponsible ardour hasn't given you disgust of *me*. I'd be equally sore afflicted to lose your good opinion.'

Her expression grew tender. 'You have not.'

'Then we can remain…friends.'

She hesitated, then smiled. 'Yes. Friends. Now, go play for my sister. I can only imagine the uproar once we begin packing and she realises we are truly leaving for London. Goodnight… Fenniston.'

Something sharp twisted in his chest. 'I'm no longer "Lieutenant"?'

She shook her head. 'You must accustom yourself to the address and status. As I must. When we go to London, you will arrive as the Duke and will never be simply "Lieutenant" again. Goodnight, Fenniston,' she repeated firmly. Dropping him a deep, deferential curtsy that added a second blow to her use of his title, she turned and walked away.

Hart let her go, paralysed by a tangle of emotions. The simmering aftermath of the kiss his body still craved to repeat. Relief that passion—ungoverned, irresponsible passion—hadn't completely ruined a friendship he had grown to count on. Near-revulsion at her referring to him by title, followed by a searing regret that, all unknowing, with the interlude at the bluff, the last lingering vestige of being just Lieutenant Hartley Edmenton had ended with that kiss.

Now all that awaited him was London, duty and fully putting on the mantle of a job he'd never wanted and couldn't escape.

Were he not saddled with that destiny, would he have pursued her, discovered where passion and friendship might take them?

Unquestionably.

And where would that put his quest to find the lady truly meant for him?

Pushing aside that question, his chest aching, Hart sensed that despite Mrs Hambleden's denial, he had somehow wounded her. Despite her assurance they could remain friends, with her so set upon finding him a bride, was there truly any way to salvage their deeply satisfying companionship?

When he imagined the parade of well-born, well-dowered, predatory females waiting to pounce on him in London, loathing filled him.

Nowhere in that cavalcade, he was almost certain, would he find the lady meant for him.

In the meantime, the thought of losing all contact with the one person who had thus far made this unwanted burden tolerable was…*intolerable*. But at the moment, he couldn't see clearly the way forward for them, both locked into positions neither could escape.

Still, he vowed that though he might not be able to escape being the Duke, he would not be locked into anything else, certainly not his choice of a bride. Unimpressed by pedigree or dowry, he intended to settle for nothing less than a love like his parents had shared.

But after reaffirming that bold resolution, a quiet despair filtered in. With time short and duty pressing, where was he to find the one woman who would send him head over heels in love, as his parents had been with each other?

However unlikely it was for that to occur in London, he would continue to resist settling for less.

And in the meantime, apply all his ingenuity to figuring out how to salvage the healing balm of his friendship with Claire Hambleden.

Chapter Twelve

Ten days later, Claire inspected the public rooms at Fenniston House in London, satisfied that the parlours were tidied, the mirrors polished, the fireplace brass gleaming and all the furniture dusted and out from under holland covers. All was in readiness to receive the flood of guests who would soon be calling on the new Duke of Fenniston.

Fenniston.

Just thinking of him made her sigh. She was relieved their indiscretion on the bluff had not completely ruined their relationship and pleased at how little awkwardness still lingered. Perhaps because that dangerous embrace had been something both of them wanted so badly even though they shouldn't have.

The relative ease between them now allowed her to cherish the memory, instead of having to lock it away. In the privacy of her chamber, she might relive the exciting flush of arousal, the sense of being desired and the embrace that made her come fully alive in a way she hadn't in years. She intended to jealously guard the secret of a time when he had made her feel like the woman he wanted more than any other. When, for those too-brief moments, she'd been *first*.

The recollection was bittersweet, though, as creating that memory had also triggered the necessity of ending any further private rides and turned going to London from eventual necessary to pressing imperative. Imperative to avoid having them be compromised, or worse, falling into an affair that, for her, could only end in disaster.

As painful as the prospect was, after the next few days, once the Duke's presence in London became known and invitations began pouring in, she would turn him over to his destiny. It was essential she do so before she came to place even more value on their relationship. Before she relied too much on his company. Before she found she *needed* him.

For she'd recognised, when she withdrew far enough during their journey to London to look on the relationship objectively, that she'd been skirting dangerously close to falling in love with him, the very catastrophe she'd warned herself to avoid.

Avoiding it would be much easier in London where she would see much less of him. No more long rides or daily consultations. The thought of him marrying someone else still wounded, but she told herself doggedly that over time, the pain would lessen. At least her distress wasn't laced with disappointment; she had known from the beginning he must go on to marry, and soon. She told herself to be grateful to have claimed his friendship for the few weeks they'd had together at Steynling.

Was there any way to salvage that friendship? She deliberately hadn't pondered the question because she feared she would have to conclude there wasn't, and she wasn't sure she could accept that answer just yet. So as usual when contemplating something that promised to be both painful and unavoidable, she pushed the knowledge out of her mind and ploughed her attention back on to work.

As she walked into the entry hall, children's voices from the floor above drew her to mount the stairs. Leaning down to hug Bella and then Alex, who predictably squirmed out of her embrace, she said, 'What are you doing on the stairs, chicks?'

'Sally's taking us to the kitchen,' Alex answered, waving towards the nursemaid trailing behind them. 'Cook is making special iced cakes to welcome us to London. Sally promised to bring some up to the schoolroom this afternoon, but I didn't want to wait.'

'Me neither,' Bella chimed in.

Claire had a brief vision of the tumult in a kitchen with staff still bringing in supplies, chopping food for the evening meal, moving about pans of hot food and assembling dishes and utensils. Probably not the best place for two active youngsters.

'What if I have Sally bring the cakes into the garden? It's stopped raining and it's warm enough to sit out.'

'But we could have some now?'

'If you have them outside.'

The children exchanged glances. 'Then we'll go to the garden,' Alex said.

Swallowing a smile, Claire waved the nursemaid towards the service stairs. 'We'll meet you on the back terrace, Sally.'

They were crossing the hall towards the family parlour where the French doors led on to the terrace when Fenniston emerged from the library. 'I thought I heard voices.'

'We're going to have cake in the garden!' Alex announced. 'Would you like some, too?'

'Cake?' At Alex's enthusiastic nod, he said, 'Then I'd love to join you.'

'You needn't,' Claire murmured as the children trooped ahead.

'I want to,' Fenniston replied, a grim note in his voice. 'Alex and Bella are probably the only people on earth whose attitude towards me will not change over the next few weeks.'

Feeling a little stung, Claire said, 'Mine won't. I value you for the person you are, not your rank.'

'Which is why you call me "Fenniston" now?' he said drily.

Claire felt herself flush. 'I call you that because it's only proper. And reminds me of what *my* proper place is.'

She could see him wanting to dispute that...before concluding he could not. 'I don't have to like it,' he muttered at last.

'No, you don't have to like it,' she agreed. 'You do have to respect the facts.'

They walked out into the small garden tucked behind the town house, a charming arrangement of three allées enclosed by high walls and bordered by plantings. The children were already running down the pathways, eager to explore this new space after being cooped up indoors by rain since their arrival. But as they spied the nursemaid emerging from the kitchen, they ran back whooping.

'I'm so glad you let us come to London, Mama,' Alex said as he reached for a cake.

At Fenniston's raised eyebrows, Claire said, 'I had a mild dispute with my sister, who wanted to leave the children in the country with the nursery staff. I flatly refused.'

She gazed over to her son, now munching cake with a look of rapture on his face, love for him softening her own features. 'If I could give birth to him far from home with a stranger as a midwife, then travel about Portugal with him as an infant, I'm certainly not going to abandon him in the countryside just because we might have a full social schedule in London. In any event, mine won't be as full as my sister's.'

'I don't know about that. You have to introduce me to

all those females *suitable* to become a duchess, don't you?' he asked, a slightly bitter tone in his voice. 'In any event, you must have somewhere to wear all the gowns and furbelows you are about to order.' He held out a hand. 'And before you protest you don't need any, let me tell you that I won't have you embarrass the family by appearing in gowns three years out of fashion.'

He managed an imperious, Duke-like gaze for a few moments, until he couldn't sustain it any more and chuckled.

'Hoist with my own petard,' she muttered.

'Indeed. I'm sure the Duchess is looking forward to acquiring all those gowns and furbelows. I would imagine it's imperative to begin the process immediately so she will have something ready to wear at the events that are upcoming.'

'She is indeed looking forward to new gowns. Thank you, by the way, for assuring her you would escort her to any entertainment she wished to attend. So she would not have to face society with only me beside her.'

'She will be just as much an attraction as I am, don't you think? The "most beautiful girl to debut in host of Seasons",' he quoted, 'returning to society?'

'No one will excite as much attention as an unmarried duke,' Claire said flatly.

'Well, I intend to hold you both to your promise to introduce me and protect me from the ravening female wolves of society. At *every* function I must attend,' he emphasised.

'We'll see,' Claire said non-committally. 'Once you've been launched at one or two balls, you won't require my presence. You can report on which ladies interest you and I can advise you over tea.'

'No, you'll not get out of it that easily! If I must go, you go too. And I won't budge from that position, so don't bother arguing.'

'My, how...*dukely* you sound.'

'Wretch,' he threw back, chuckling.

The children having by now demolished the cakes, Alex turned to him. 'Mama was telling me about all the wonderful places we can visit in London! Seeing fossils and shells and stuffed animals at the British Museum. Jugglers who swallow swords! Riding in the park and best of all, shows with riders and horses at Ashley's Am— Ampa?' He halted, looking at Claire.

'Astley's Amphitheatre,' Claire corrected.

'Mama says they have clowns and performing animals and rope tricks and lots of fancy riding. You'll come with us, won't you?'

Claire frowned, having feared it might come to this. A strong tie had developed between her son and Fenniston, who had often joined their riding lessons at Steynling and occasionally gave Alex a lesson himself.

Shaking her head at her son, Claire said gently, 'It's not like being in the country, Alex. The Duke will be taking his place in Parliament, meeting many new people and have many, many demands on him. He won't have time to go exploring with us.'

'You won't forget us, though, will you, Uncle Hart?' Bella said. He might not be their actual uncle, but it made her smile that they saw him that way.

'Of course I won't. Equestrian feats and sword swallowing? I must see that! Yes, I'd love to join you! If that is acceptable to your mama, of course.'

Claire hesitated. Living in his house on his sufferance, it would hardly be polite to refuse. And with the children along, the outing would be *safe*. She was very much looking forward to witnessing the children's delight at visiting Astley's and the jugglers, but to have his company, too... To enjoy sharing a venue when he was not having to play the Duke, where she did not have to focus on introducing him to prospective brides? She tried to subdue the leap in her spirits at the idea of Fenniston accompanying them.

'Of course you may accompany us if you truly wish to,' she said at last.

'Excellent! I shall look forward to it.'

'And will you ride in the Park with us?' Alex asked. 'Mama said she will continue my lessons.'

'Let's not ask for too much of his time,' Claire warned. 'That wouldn't be fair to all the others who want to meet him.'

'But we met him first,' Alex protested.

Fenniston turned to her with a grin. 'Can't argue with that.'

'Then I shall cease trying to protect your schedule,' Claire retorted. 'You must do what you like.'

Fenniston's face sobered. 'Since I will be doing so much I don't like, you must allow me to salvage *some* pleasures. Especially since I must forgo the one I desire most keenly.'

The smouldering glance he gave her lit her like a flame, making Claire look away. Thank heavens they would be surrounded by children or servants or hordes of people in London. When he looked at her like that, she wasn't sure she would be able to hang on to her resolve to treat him as a kind and favoured friend.

Not while she still yearned for his touch and her lips burned to feel his against hers again.

'Mama, may we play hide and seek down the pathways before we go back in?' Alex asked, jolting her back to the present.

'Of course. But no tag—I don't want either of you falling into the mud.'

'You're it, Bella!' Alex cried, hopping out of his chair and racing off, his cousin setting off behind him.

Smiling as he watched the children speed away, Fenniston said, 'How is the Duchess? I was afraid returning to the London house might bring back unhappy memories. She gave me quite a start after we walked in, turning so pale I feared she would faint dead away.'

'She's much better. Thank you for noticing her distress and immediately fetching her brandy. I'm ashamed to admit I was so busy ordering the servants and inspecting the entryway, I didn't recognise her reaction until almost too late.'

He gave her a grim smile. 'She's not the only one with unhappy memories about Fenniston House.'

Claire looked at him in surprise. 'You have, also? I didn't realise you had ever been here.'

'Not as a boy. But right before I left for the Peninsula, I honoured my mother's wish that I call on the late Duke—Fitzhugh's father. Papa had passed away the year previous and she felt I should inform my father's brother, my nearest paternal relative, that I'd joined the army and would be heading to Portugal. I couldn't refuse Mama, much as I resented doing it. Why should I call on the man who never allowed my mother across the threshold of Steynling Cross?'

'The Duke forbade your mother to visit?' Claire gasped.

'Well...not exactly. But it was made quite apparent that if she came, she would not be welcome. As she didn't wish to go where she was not wanted, she never ventured to England, but insisted my father and I visit on occasion. Blood ties being important, no matter how undeserving the relations might be of affection or loyalty,' he added bitterly.

'At least you only had to deal with the Duke.'

'Oh, no, Fitzhugh was in London then, too. Fortunately, I only encountered him as I was leaving, the morning after my visit with the Duke. After staggering in, drunk, and almost colliding with me with me in the hallway, he paused to ask his equally drunken friends if any of them had seen the monkey who belonged to the circus man in the red coat.'

Claire had eventually discovered how vicious Fitzhugh could be, but this seemed especially unwarranted. 'Did you plant him a facer?'

'I wanted to,' he admitted. 'Then I decided he was not worth bruising my knuckles over and walked out without a word.'

'Probably for the best.'

'You truly don't object to my coming with you and the children to Astley's? I didn't mean to let Alex's enthusiasm force you into it. If you want to maintain the distance you seem to be establishing between us... I can't pretend to like it, but I'll respect your wishes.'

She gave him a melancholy smile. 'We may not be able to explore all we would desire, but I'm not willing to sever all contact between us. It might be safe to continue our friendship here in London, where we will be surrounded by many chaperons...if we both remain vigilant.'

'If I promise not to kiss you again—no matter how much I want to?'

She shook her head and chuckled. 'So much for avoiding the topic. Then I should have to pledge the same.'

'We're agreed, then? Astley's, some rides in the park, the India jugglers and perhaps the menagerie at the Tower?'

'Roaring lions?' Claire chuckled. 'Alex would love that. Very well, Astley's and a few other places—if you can truly spare the time.'

'I'll make sure of it.'

'Don't be too sure,' she warned. 'Once introduced, you'll have the preparation for your entry into Parliament in addition to numerous balls, routs and entertainments, and will likely to be put up for membership at several gentlemen's clubs as well. You may welcome joining those, as they will allow you to escape at any time of day or night when you feel the need to evade feminine pursuit.'

He grunted. 'I'll probably be equally anxious to escape the pursuit of those wanting to toady up to the new Duke. If I am in fact invited to join any. I didn't attend Eton, Winchester, Oxford, or Cambridge with the other toffs. I'm just a Scottish outsider.'

'Growing up, perhaps, but as Duke, you won't remain one. And I know a good bit about being an outsider in society.'

He frowned at her. 'You, an outsider? With your father secretary to a cabinet minister and your mother a well-known political hostess?'

'Just so. My parents were always preoccupied, my father busy with important work and Mama supporting him, so they never had much time for us—for me. Even when I made my debut, Mama delegated the chore of sponsoring me to one of her friends whom I knew only slightly. Most of the other girls were already acquainted with each other, having met in London before their come-outs or at ladies' academies. So yes, I was an outsider. The year would have been quite lonely if Alexander hadn't been in London then. He was as helpful to me when my first Season began as he was to the Duchess during hers.'

'You fell in love then?'

'We were…friends. We had been friends since we were children.'

'And remained friends because you fell in love with… someone else?'

Claire fumbled for an answer. Fenniston had just given her the perfect opportunity to confess her infatuation with Fitzhugh, but knowing his opinion of his cousin, she feared it would lower her in his esteem to admit how blinded she'd been. She felt humiliated herself that it had taken so long for her to see the man for what he was—and ashamed of the sin she'd come so very close to committing.

Before she could decide what, if anything, to reply, the butler walked on to the terrace. 'Your Grace, a visitor has called. The elder brother of one of your fellow officers in the First Dragoons, he said.'

'You'd better receive him,' Claire said, relieved to have the conversation interrupted before she had to explain. Though if not now, she might at some point have to confess.

Or maybe not. Such a conversation wasn't likely to happen while on outings with the children, or when standing in the receiving line at a ball, or while playing cards at a rout. Since she would be taking care not to be alone with Fenniston, she might avoid the humiliation of confessing it entirely.

She smiled grimly. Avoid it and take her dirty little secret to the grave.

'Your society career begins,' Claire continued. 'How nice to launch it by meeting the brother of a comrade.'

'I just hope it isn't the brother of someone I won money from at cards or beat at racing who's urged his London relation to exact revenge,' Fenniston said ruefully. 'Until later, then.'

She nodded, watching him follow the butler inside. Relieved as she was to have this particular conversation interrupted, she was regretful, too. Realising how few opportunities they would have to chat, just the two of them, once the social whirl truly began.

Which was doubtless just as well. Not wise to test again her ability to withstand temptation.

Despite that sensible resolve, she had to place a hand on her stomach to ease the hollow, empty feeling that formed while she watched him walk away.

Ridiculous to feel…bereft at losing his company. She

was going to lose it, probably quite soon. She had best start resigning herself to the fact.

She must suppress the melancholy longing for what could never be. Turn her mind instead to organising the household, preparing her sister to re-enter society and beginning to consider the hard question of what she was to do once all the presentations were over.

Chapter Thirteen

As Hart walked into the formal front parlour, the tall man standing by the hearth turned and bowed. 'Viscount Stannington, Your Grace,' the butler intoned.

'Forgive my impertinence in calling when we've not yet been formally introduced,' the Viscount said. 'But I've been waiting for you to appear. I hastened over as soon as I knew you were in town, wanting to be the first to greet you.'

Hart frowned. 'How exactly did you know I was in town? We only arrived yesterday.'

The visitor waved a hand. 'Oh, you know. Servants notice when the knocker is returned to the door of a residence as prominent as Fenniston House. One tells another who tells another and soon the news is all over town. Especially as your arrival has been anticipated for some weeks, knowing you'd been issued a writ to attend Parliament. But first, let me explain the connection. My younger brother served with you in the Royals—Ensign Laurence Harlburn.'

'Laury?' Hart exclaimed. 'What a good lad! He is well, I trust?'

'Flourishing, when last I heard from him. In any event, he'd written to me about what a stir it caused when you inherited and how it took some time to eventually persuade you to return to England. He knew you'd grown up and attended university in Scotland and had no friends or acquaintances in London. He wrote that such a fine fellow deserved a proper introduction to the city, its clubs and other masculine establishments. If you are willing, I'd be pleased to offer myself as your guide. I don't presume to suggest that I'm a person of any great importance, but I do know most of the *ton*. I can provide introductions and background on those with whom you are likely to deal, both in society and in the Lords.'

Hart was surprised and touched that his company mate had thought of him. 'How considerate of Laury! And gracious of you. I'd be grateful to accept your offer.'

'Excellent! We must make an appointment to dine at the clubs as soon as convenient, so you can meet the members. First, White's,' he continued. 'It's known as a Tory stronghold, while the Whigs favour Brooks's. I don't know your politics—though it's not necessary to agree with the opinions of the majority, as a number of gentlemen, myself included, belong to both.'

'That's fortunate, as I have no politics as yet.'

'Take your time! Now, rumour has it the Divine Duchess returned to London with you?'

Hart looked at him blankly for a moment. 'You mean—the Duchess of Fenniston? Yes, she did accompany me.'

The Viscount laughed. 'Gossip really does fly on gossamer wings! I remember her debut. What an astounding beauty! All of us were green with envy when the late Duke—he was still a courtesy marquess then—made off with her. She will be rejoining society, won't she?'

Hart found himself feeling surprisingly protective. 'She will be, but sparingly. She's not yet fully recovered from mourning. Her sister will also be watching out for her,' he felt compelled to add.

'Has she a sister?' The Viscount shook his head. 'Don't recall a sister.'

'Yes she has a sister, a widow,' Hart said, annoyed that it seemed once again, Mrs Hambleden had been overlooked. 'Her husband was a younger son of the Earl of Lyndenham, a soldier killed at Fuentes de Oñoro. She's been staying at Steynling, caring for the Duchess during her long recovery from illness.'

'I'm so glad she has recovered,' the Viscount replied, obviously dismissing the sister without another thought. 'It will be great news for the clubs.'

'How so?' Hart asked, feeling even more annoyed.

The Viscount grinned. 'Why, because wagers will begin to be laid immediately as soon as it becomes known she's returned—about who will win her this time. She's much too young and beautiful to spend the rest of her life as a widow! Some of the former aspirants to her hand from her debut Season are married now and out of the running, of course, myself included. But it should be an amusing show. Won't this Season's Incomparables be dismayed when they hear the news! I'm willing to bet she will still put them all in the shade.'

'I don't intend to let her be overwhelmed by hordes of potential suitors,' Hart said testily. 'She's still regaining her strength and I am responsible for her well-being. Head of the family, you know.'

The Viscount gave him a speculative glance. 'Any interest there yourself?'

'None,' he said flatly.

'Wouldn't blame you if you had. Such extraordinary beauty doesn't come along very often. Well, I'll take my leave. But I wanted to introduce myself and offer to acquaint you with some of London's most prominent gentlemen before the deluge of females begins. If the Duchess is likely to be besieged, that's nothing compared to the gauntlet you're going to run. Young, handsome, a duke and single?' Stannington shook his head.

'I'd best put you up for membership in the clubs without delay. You're going to need a place where you can retreat from all the young ladies. Fortunately, the dinners there are excellent, the gambling discreet and there's always the reading room if you just want to disappear behind a newspaper for several hours.'

Hart walked him out, bidding him goodbye with a vague promise to dine at his club in the near future. He walked back into the salon with decidedly mixed feelings.

Would he be as on display at the clubs as he would be at balls and routs? Or would it truly be a masculine refuge from the unrelenting glare of attention?

He certainly didn't need another place where he'd have to endure nothing but speculative stares.

He'd go ask the one person who should know that answer, he decided, exiting the salon and trotting up the stairs in pursuit of Mrs Hambleden.

He found her shepherding the children back to the nursery. 'May I have a quick word when they are settled? In the library, but I'll keep you only a moment, so no need to call your maid to chaperon.'

'It doesn't take long for disaster to happen,' she muttered, pulling a grin from him that lightened his mood.

'Too true. But I'll be on my best behaviour.'

'How do you know I can promise the same?'

'I certainly won't promise to save you from yourself,' he warned, warmed by their banter.

'I am forewarned,' she teased back. 'I'll join you shortly.'

Some ten minutes later, he heard her light step at the door and looked up from where he sat behind the massive desk. 'What did you need?' she asked as she walked in.

He gestured towards the desk. 'I've provided you a great barrier to protect you from attack.'

'Or provided yourself one,' she tossed back. 'I shall remain standing, just in case there's a need to flee. So, did you know the gentleman who called?'

'Viscount Stannington? No, but his younger brother Laury is a fine soldier. It was quite thoughtful of him to write and urge his older brother to seek me out. I'm grateful—I suppose—for his offer to present me to his associates and introduce me in the London clubs.'

'Excellent! I'm sure many gentlemen would have volunteered to assist you. But how pleasant that someone with whom you have a prior connection can acquaint you with all the places essential for a gentleman! Something neither I nor the Duchess could help with.'

'Ah, the Duchess. Stannington told me that as soon as the clubs discover your sister has returned to London, members will start laying wagers on who will win her hand.' He grimaced. 'That seems in poor taste to me. I'm not so sure I'm interested in joining a club if all the members are high-born wastrels like Fitzhugh.'

She raised her eyebrows. 'And soldiers don't make wagers about almost anything?'

She had him there.

While he paused, searching for a suitable rebuttal, she continued, 'You should be fair enough not to condemn them all on the basis of your cousin. True, some are wastrels who bet on which of two raindrops will reach the bottom of a window first, but the clubs are also where the leaders of the Lords and the Commons gather. There will be high stakes gaming, but you will also find intelligent, interesting and sometimes vital conversations.'

'Your father is a clubman?'

'Naturally. He belongs to White's, a Tory stronghold, and is a member at Boodle's, too.'

'I will be interested in meeting him.'

'I will invite him and Mama to dine soon, if you like. Though they will have to fit us into their schedule,' she added, asperity in her tone, 'and only accept if no soirée of political importance interferes. But schedule is the reason I intended to seek you out after settling the children.

'We need to begin immediately planning how to proceed with your introduction. If Stannington knew to call, the news that you are in residence is all over London. As early as tomorrow, you can expect to be deluged with invitations. Can we speak about this after dinner? I will bring a diary?'

Speaking with her again...that was something he could look forward to, Hart thought, even if the matter was his accursed presentation. 'Very well, after dinner. Meanwhile, I will bury my misgivings by distracting myself with this very fine library.'

'All of it is yours, Duke. Enjoy.'

'There's something else I'd enjoy more, alas, it is not permitted.'

She shook a finger at him but was smiling as she walked out.

He smiled, too, heartened by the ease that had returned to their relationship now that they had acknowledged their previously unspoken attraction. Bantering about it wasn't as satisfying as acting upon it...but it was a sort of intimacy, the only sort they could permit, and therefore welcome. Especially considering he'd feared after the incident at the bluff, that for the rest of their time together, Claire Hambleden might keep him at the same chilly distance she'd set him at that first night.

Still, the resumption of their camaraderie didn't lessen his distaste for the gauntlet that lay ahead. He'd peruse the shelves and find himself a good book. He suspected that over the next few weeks, he was going to need all the solace he could get.

After dinner, Hart escorted Mrs Hambleden and her sister into the parlour. After serving tea, Claire said to her sister, 'We need to acquaint the Duke with what he can expect during the Season.'

The Duchess nodded. 'Fortunately, I wrote to Lady Downing—one of my dearest friends during my debut Season,' she added to Hart, 'before we left Steynling to let her know when we'd arrive in London. She called this afternoon, so I now have a list of who is in town and which of the most eligible maidens are still on the Marriage Mart.'

Hart grimaced. 'A "mart", is it? My, that makes me feel so much better about the prospect.'

The Duchess gave his hand a slap. 'It's referred to like that only in jest. It's more a meeting of minds than a marketplace.'

'A meeting of purses and pedigrees, more like,' he muttered.

'It could be, but it doesn't need to be,' Mrs Hambleden intervened. 'It's also a gathering of the most lovely, accomplished, well-bred and well-placed young ladies in England. There's every likelihood that you will find one of them can make you not just a suitable, but a cherished wife.'

Hart gave her a dubious look. '"It's ill praising green barley."'

The Duchess's eyes widened in confusion, but her sister laughed. 'His Grace sometimes amuses himself by adopting a brogue and pronouncing a Scottish homily. And this one means…?'

'One shouldn't count on a bountiful harvest when the crop has only just sprouted.'

'Ah, so I shouldn't assume a happy ending to this endeavour hardly yet begun.'

'Exactly,' he said drily.

'Then let me offer a homily back. An endeavour is unlikely to flourish if one does nothing but doubt its success from the very beginning. At least enter upon it with an open mind. If you can find one,' she added acerbically.

Ah, that was the tart rejoinder he'd been missing, he thought with a grin. 'I shall search most diligently.'

'See that you do.'

The Duchess was watching their interchange, still looking bewildered. 'Pay no attention to us, rude as we're being!' Mrs Hambleden said. 'We've grown accustomed to brangling over estate matters. Now, you were to tell us who will likely to be at society gatherings?'

Her sister brightened. 'Yes! Of course, Parliament is in session, so one may encounter any of Lord Liverpool's cabinet members. Lord Eldon—'

'The Lord Chancellor, who will take part in the ceremony when you take your seat in Lords—' her sister interjected.

'Also Lords Harrowby, Westmoreland, Castlereagh and Sidmouth, of course, with whom our father works. Bathurst, Melville, Buckinghamshire and their ladies, along with most of the peers. Norfolk, the Earl Marshall, Somerset, Beaufort and a handful of other dukes are likely to be present.'

'Some of whom may also take part in your ceremony,' Mrs Hambleden added.

'More to point, Lady Downing said three of most eligible young maidens presented this Season have yet to become engaged. A marquess's daughter, Lady Amelia, an earl's daughter, Lady Catherine, and a viscount's daughter, the Honourable Mary. All quite attractive. Lady Amelia is a stunning blonde with superior musical ability who plays and sings delightfully. Lady Catherine, a tall brunette and excellent horsewoman. The Honourable Mary, who is a bit shyer than the others, Lady Downing reported, is a petite brunette who draws and paints in oils and watercolours.

'In addition, there are still quite a few other accomplished young ladies of lesser birth and dowry who are worthy of consideration. Best of all,' she concluded with a touch of excitement, 'Lady Downing will be giving a ball just two days from now, which everyone of distinction in London, including the three young ladies just mentioned, will attend. An excellent venue at which to make your first appearance!'

Hart heard the date fall on him like a noose tightening around his neck. But Mrs Hambleden was correct; he couldn't expect a positive outcome if he went into this dead set against the process. After all, his father had hardly been expecting to fall in love when he accompanied his scholarly mentor to Kirkraidy that Christmas long ago. Maybe the woman to set his heart racing would be present at Lady Downing's ball.

She'd have to be quite something to set his pulses racing more than the lady who now sat opposite him, he thought with a sigh.

'Then there's Almack's,' the Duchess continued. At his puzzled look, she explained, 'It's society's most prestigious social club. A board of Patronesses determines who may be admitted. Lady Castlereagh, whom Mama knows well from her political connections, is one of them, so Claire and I both received vouchers during our debut Seasons. I've already written to her requesting new vouchers, which I'm sure she will send. Only the elite of the elite are granted admission—you can be sure any maiden you meet there will be eminently suitable.'

'If Lady Downing's ball takes place in only two days, we must begin the refurbishing of your wardrobe with all speed,' Mrs Hambleden said to her sister.

'Which will be a delight! I had Wallace obtain a copy of *La Belle Assemblée* today, so we might study the fashions.'

'Why don't you have her bring it up now? The two of you can put your heads together, choose designs and we can begin ordering tomorrow. Is Madame Cecily still your favourite modiste?' At her sister's nod, she said, 'I'm quite sure, for the Duchess of Fenniston's re-entry into society, she will do whatever is necessary to have your first ensemble completed in time.'

'And one for her sister,' Hart inserted. 'I insist.'

'Of course!' the Duchess agreed, unaware of the undercurrents in that conversation. 'Shall you play for the Duke while I peruse the magazine? I'm sure he is not interested in ladies' fashions.'

'I would enjoy listening to you play,' Hart said. 'Or anything that doesn't touch on marriage,' he added to Mrs Hambleden in an undertone. 'And I shall require a very large glass of brandy to recover from this discussion.'

While the Duchess settled on the sofa, awaiting the arrival of the maid with the magazine, Hart escorted Mrs Hambleden to the pianoforte. 'It will be much more enjoyable to sit close beside you…and listen to you play.'

She gave him a reproving look. 'It's fortunate that my sister is here. Her presence will ensure my best behaviour.'

He sighed. 'One could wish you were not on your best behaviour. Are you really looking forward to the endless round of balls and such you've warned me to expect?'

'There are other entertainments available if you want a break from the purely social. Once you join the Lords, you can attend political dinners like those given by my parents. For more learned discourse, the Royal Institution offers lectures on scientific matters, although ladies are not admitted, so I can't speak to their quality. Astley's offers equestrian performances, but you can simply inspect horses at Tattersall's. Which I would love, but that enterprise is another bastion for gentlemen only, the rough talk of grooms and trainers being thought not fit for the delicate sensibilities of a lady.'

She laughed. 'Though after accompanying the army, I hardly have any sensibilities left to be offended. Now that you have Stannington to guide you, he can recommend the best establishments from which to obtain the garments you'll need. A requirement which, like my sister, you should address immediately if we're to attend a ball in just two days.'

'Must I go shopping?' Hart shuddered. 'I do have some formal dress.'

She gave him a severe look. 'If you want to suffer the *least* amount of the intense interest you're going to attract anyway, being properly turned out will help. If you are oddly or slovenly dressed, you will garner even more attention and comment.'

'Very well…' he sighed '…proper garments. You can help me choose.'

'That would be most improper,' she said drily. 'As you very well know.' With a deceptively mild flash of her eyes, 'Perhaps I shall take you to the opera.'

Hart shuddered. Laughing, she assured him, 'People go more to be seen than to view the performance.'

'Since I neither want to be seen nor to listen to screeching sopranos, I must decline. The theatre, perhaps.'

'Very well, no opera. I'll consult the playbills for Covent Garden and Drury Lane, to see what performances you might enjoy. We could hire a box, if any are still available. When do you intend to make your entry into Parliament?'

'I haven't given it much thought.'

She frowned. 'Now that it's known you are in London, you will be expected to go soon. For your first appearance, you must wear a Presentation Robe.' She hesitated, then went on, 'I've spoken with Michelson, Fitzhugh's valet. We still have his robe...which I doubt was worn more than once or twice since his own presentation.'

Hart felt a ripple of revulsion. Giving the Duchess a glance to make sure she was occupied with the maid, who had just arrived with her magazine, he said quietly, 'I'm not normally one to squander blunt and I imagine those robes cost dear. But I refuse to wear anything of Fitzhugh's.'

Letting that statement pass without comment, robbing him of another opportunity to glean some hint about her relationship with Fitzhugh, she merely nodded. 'Then you must visit Ede & Ravenscroft and have measurements taken so they may set about making you one immediately. For a duke, I'm sure they can speed the construction. And if you wish to meet some of the politicians, I'm sure my mother could arrange a dinner with the ministers.'

'I'm not vying for any leadership role now,' he protested. 'I'd prefer for the present to just attend and observe.'

'Very well. It would be useful to have Viscount Stannington present you to the Dukes who will escort you in when you take your seat.'

'I have to be escorted? Can't I just slip in quietly?'

She laughed. 'Certainly not! There's a long-established tradition for taking your seat.'

Hart groaned. 'Something tells me I'm not going to like this. How complicated will it be?'

'Not complicated, just quite formal. While the Lords assemble, you'll go to Robing Room and put on your Presentation Robe, as will the two Dukes who walk in with you and the King of Arms. The Black Rod—the official doorkeeper of the Lords—will then arrive and lead all of you into the chamber, the King of Arms first, carrying his silver gilt sceptre and your patent of creation as Duke, followed by the junior Duke, then you with your writ of summons, then the senior Duke. You will kneel, present your writ to the Lord Chancellor, who will have the Reading Clerk to read it aloud to the members. Then *you* will read aloud the Oath of Allegiance and sign the Test Roll. All three of you Dukes will rise and sit three times, each time doffing your hats to the Cloth of Estate, which is where the sovereign would sit, if he were present. Then you'll rise a final time and shake the Lord Chancellor's hand, after which the three of you return to the Robing Room to remove the Presentation Robes. *Then* you may slip quietly back into the chamber.'

Hart dropped his head to his chest. 'I knew I should have remained at Steynling. Maybe there's still time to flee to Lisbon.'

She chuckled. 'I can imagine the true Scot in you rebels at the idea of bowing thrice to the symbol of the English king.'

'The ghost of William Wallace will haunt me. Enough about that dispiriting possibility, let's talk of something more pleasant. What about being back in London excites *you*? I can't imagine your favourite thing will be gossiping at balls and routs.'

'No, although I do enjoy dancing. And music. I look forward to the concerts at the Hanover Square Rooms. Summer art exhibitions by the Royal Academy and British Institution, with the latest paintings on display. I can never afford to buy any, but I do like to look.

'Then there's riding in the park.' She smiled. 'Childish, I suppose, but I've always loved watching the performances at Astley's. And I will enjoy helping my sister choose new garments. She's always loved fashions and focusing on them will help ease her back into London society. We'll start with just a few entertainments until she finds her stride. I'd not have her overwhelmed.'

'Agreed. We'll ease me in as well.' He paused, thinking she might argue that point, urging him to speed up his own participation, but at length, she nodded.

'I suppose a slower pace will be acceptable for you as well. In any event, we'll have to host a grand ball at some point. But we can wait until you feel more comfortable in society.'

Hart grimaced. 'Ye're nae chicken for a' ye're cheepin'. I doubt I'll ever truly feel the part of an English duke.'

She gave him a reproving glance. 'But as a battle-tested soldier, you're "nae a chicken" either,' she said, trying to mimic his Scottish accent.

Hart laughed. 'Nae, lassie, 'tis a right terrible brogue ye have.'

To his delight, she flushed a little. 'No doubt. But neither do I doubt that you have courage to do what you must. Assume your rightful place in Parliament. And choose a bride to secure the succession.'

Hart waved a hand. 'Ah, that again! If you don't wish to brangle, let's return to music.'

She sighed. 'Very well. Shall we play a duet?'

He nodded. 'One of the few pleasures we *can* indulge in.'

As she took her place beside him on the bench, he felt instantly that shimmering awareness of her body close to his. Looking at that lovely profile as she gazed down to select the music, Hart wished his sojourn in London might be devoted to this. Spending time with her, talking with her, teasing her while she tempted, amused and informed him. Accompanying her and the children to sights rather than being the sight himself, remarked and fawned over and singled out at balls and routs and the theatre.

In two days that gauntlet would begin. She'd asserted he was no coward, but thinking of that gave him chills.

He'd rather volunteer for the Forlorn Hope, he thought grimly as he nodded approval of her choice of music and on her signal, began to play.

He promised himself if he must run this gauntlet, he would reserve time for what he wanted to do—teasing her through the maze at Hampton Court, viewing paintings at the Royal Academy, walking the grounds of the Tower and sitting beside her for concerts at the Hanover Square Rooms.

And during those balls and routs he must attend, if he had to dance with debutantes and husband-seekers, he was going to make sure that for some of those waltzes, he got to hold in his arms the enchanting Mrs Hambleden.

Chapter Fourteen

Two nights later, Claire followed her sister and Fenniston up the stairs towards the receiving line at Lady Downing's ball. She'd had another brangle with the Duke when she insisted her sister must precede her on Fenniston's arm; he'd protested that he had *two* arms and could escort one sister on each. She'd pointed out that to do so would violate the rules of precedence; it was quite proper for a Duke to escort a Duchess, but the widow of Lieutenant Hambleden was not entitled to enter a ball on his arm.

She only won that battle by saying she would refuse to attend if he didn't heed her instructions. She wasn't going to waste her efforts to see him properly presented, she'd told him tartly, if he were going to offend society at his very first appearance by seeming to disregard basic social rules.

She uttered a little sigh as she gazed at him, standing rigidly ahead of her on the stairs. To her relief, he hadn't baulked—too much—at going off with Stannington to bespeak proper garments. When she'd descended the stairs at Fenniston House with Liliana tonight to find him in the entry below, waiting for them, she'd sucked in a breath.

In uniform, he was commanding—but she'd grown used to seeing him in uniform. Viewing him for the first time in all-black evening attire, she'd felt a shock that rocketed from her eyes to her toes.

There'd been no bright colour to distract one's gaze from his arresting countenance, that sweep of dark hair brushing his forehead, those intense grey eyes staring up at her. With his dark coat stretched over broad shoulders outlined against the white of the Corinthian columns framing the doorway behind him, the dark trousers clinging to his muscled legs, he was a portrait of masculine beauty to inspire awe.

Unable to pull her gaze from him, she'd almost stumbled as she finished descending the stairs. Still befuddled, as he bowed over her hand and Liliana's, she'd barely heard his gallant comment on their beauty.

Of course, Liliana did look magnificent. To her relief, her sister appeared excited rather than apprehensive about her first appearance in society since she'd miscarried her two infant sons and then lost her husband. Enlisting Fenniston to assist her, Claire had spent their journey emphasising to her sister how delightful it would be to dance again, see her friends and receive the homage of gentlemen sure to find her just as enchanting as they had during her debut Season.

'I'm not looking for suitors,' she'd protested. 'I'm not even certain I should have put off my blacks.'

'Your wearing colours now is quite appropriate,' Claire reassured, relieved that her sister's friend Lady Downing, who had accompanied them on their trip to the modiste, had reinforced that opinion. The material they'd chosen was a lovely pale lavender that brought out the subtle violet tint in her sister's magnificent blue eyes.

Just then, Liliana looked back at her, 'I'm not so sure I can do this,' she whispered.

Claire reached up to squeeze her gloved hand. 'You'll be fine. Everyone will be thrilled to see you recovered, bravely back in London to support Fenniston despite your own grievous losses. Gentlemen will honour you, not flirt. Unless…' she gave her sister a teasing look '…one happens to catch your eye. In which case, it would be entirely proper for you to encourage him.'

'I wouldn't consider it!' Liliana gasped, looking alarmed.

Claire was not so sure. Not that she doubted her sister meant what she said at this moment, but she suspected the unhappy later years of her marriage had made Liliana forget the heady thrill of being the focus of a man's admiring gaze. She might recoil from any blatant flirtation, but if a gentleman were courteous, concerned and gentle, Claire suspected Liliana might relax, the conviction that she would remain a widow gradually melting away in the warmth of his admiration.

She'd be delighted for her sister if that happened. Even though that would make her own position more uncertain. If Liliana were to marry again, Claire didn't intend to tag along on her honeymoon or instal herself at her new husband's abode.

But no need to worry about that now; this was only their first ball and it would take time for Liliana to find her way again. And settling Fenniston well was Claire's first concern.

The way the Duke looked tonight, had he been only a lowly baron's son rather than the premier catch on Marriage Mart, ladies would be besieging him. As it was…once they entered the ballroom and their hostess swept him away to make introductions to all those wanting to meet him, she would probably not see him again for the rest of the ball.

She forced back a sinking feeling. Her job tonight wasn't to enjoy his company, but to do her best to see that he enjoyed everyone else's. She would watch him, not hoping for him to return to her, but to intervene if necessary. Recalling his flight from the village, she feared that exasperation or distaste with all the attention he would receive might prompt him to try a similar abrupt exit, something she must be vigilant to prevent.

First impressions were lasting, and she wanted society's perception of him to be of a courteous, commanding man confident of his place among them, an assessment he fully deserved. She didn't want him seen as a brusque, irritated outsider plainly unhappy at being thrust in their midst.

As they neared the entry to the ballroom, Fenniston halted so suddenly, Claire almost ran into him. Looking over his shoulder at her, he murmured, 'Why do I feel like the advance guard of the Forlorn Hope?'

That he'd offered that moment of connection just as she'd been mourning his imminent loss, highlighting the shared bond of their background, sent a wave of warmth through her.

She laughed, as he'd expected her to, and resisted the urge to pat his shoulder—a too-familiar gesture that would surely be remarked. 'You may be about to become the focus of all attention, but the firestorm that greets you will hardly come from an enemy and none of it will injure you.'

'I can only hope.'

Then the butler was intoning their names and their hostess turned to greet them. After mutual greetings, Lady Downing invited them to have some refreshments and assured them she would seek them out as soon as she finished greeting her guests. 'So many are anxious to meet you, Your Grace!' she enthused. 'Particularly several charming young ladies.'

Claire held her breath, but obviously on his best behaviour, Fenniston stifled the acid rejoinder she'd feared he might make.

As they walked across the ballroom, Stannington hurried over, bowing to Liliana. 'Your Grace, delighted to see you! If I may say so, you are even more beautiful than I remember.'

Liliana flushed becomingly. 'Lord Stannington, how kind you are to remember an old matron.'

'Nonsense. You will outshine all this year's debutantes. As I'm sure a legion of admirers will soon assure you.'

Seeing her sister's look of alarm at that prospect, Claire said quickly, 'We're on our way to the refreshment room. Can you advise us where it might be a bit more private?'

'My pleasure.'

'Before we go, let me present you to the Duchess's sister, Mrs Hambleden,' Fenniston intervened.

Claire curtsied, thinking sardonically that the Viscount barely took his gaze off Liliana long enough to bow. As she rose, she rolled her eyes at Fenniston, trying to convey the message 'don't bother'.

Gentlemen would not be coming in droves to seek her, any more than ladies would be flocking to them to chat with Stannington.

'There's a snug reception room with a large sofa just off the ballroom where Her Grace might sit and receive her friends,' the Viscount was saying. 'Let me escort you and have a servant bring refreshments.'

After tapping a waiter to supply them, he led them to the salon. Claire appreciated the Viscount's knowledge of house, for the spot to which he brought them was indeed an ideal location. While seated on the sofa—Claire knew her sister wouldn't have the stamina to stand all evening— Liliana had a view into the ballroom, with sufficient space nearby for guests to chat without her sister being overwhelmed by a flood of people.

As they crossed the room, Claire was keenly aware of the many eager, avid glances that followed her sister and Fenniston.

'Thank you, Staninngton, this is perfect,' Fenniston approved as he assisted Liliana to a seat.

Stannington once again showed himself a useful friend, introducing Fenniston to the gentlemen who stopped by and waylaying some of the men eager to approach her sister while allowing past those matrons her sister motioned closer, so that she had a constant stream of visitors while never becoming overwhelmed. Which quite put Claire in charity with the Viscount despite the slighting manner with which he'd treated her.

During the lull while guests formed up for the first dance, Fenniston stepped closer. 'I hadn't been looking forward to dining at Stannington's club yesterday,' he murmured in her ear, 'but now I'm glad I did. It's cut down on the number of introductions I'll have to suffer through tonight.'

'It's not the gentlemen you need to worry about,' she warned.

Practically before the words left her lips, their hostess approached leading two older women, each trailed by a young female who was obviously her daughter. 'And so it begins,' Claire observed.

And what a carousel of beauties circled before him! The Marchioness presented her daughter, Lady Amelia, a blonde as lovely as advertised. The Countess's brunette horsewoman Lady Catherine looked brisk and direct; the Viscountess's Honourable Mary was indeed soft and sweet. Fenniston dutifully requested a dance with each of them as well as with half a dozen other young ladies to whom he was presented.

Meanwhile, Stannington took over watching out for Liliana, as Fenniston was far too overwhelmed by supplicants to be able to perform that office himself. By some prior arrangement? Claire wondered. If so, she could only be grateful to both of them for their foresight. With the number of visitors limited, her initially apprehensive sister had calmed, and now appeared to be happily enjoying chatting with one or two admiring gentlemen at a time while catching up with matrons she hadn't seen in person for years.

Many of them knew Claire, as well, making her the recipient of their attention while they waited to talk with her sister. She turned down several invitations to dance, not wanting to abandon Liliana who, in order to marshal enough strength to remain for the whole evening, had decided she would not dance.

Standing guard on the sidelines also allowed her to keep an eye on Fenniston, who had seldom left the dance floor. Watching him lead out lady after lady, with so many eager aspirants to please, she thought he'd be lucky to escape long enough to gulp a glass of wine.

She felt like a mama must when sending her child off to boarding school: proud to watch him confidently take the next step, sad at having him launched, knowing the two would never again enjoy the same close relationship they'd shared at Steynling.

She tried to fend off the melancholy mood that thought produced. She was here, doing what she'd planned to do and must do; there was no point repining.

About halfway through the evening, she was approached by Lord Telford, an older, wealthy baron who, her hostess confided, had been recently widowed.

After exchanging expressions of sympathy over their mutual losses, Telford asked if her sister was completely recovered. 'Kind of you to ask, and no, not completely. Which is why I'm hovering so closely. I don't want her to become overtired on her first foray into society.'

'I remember her from her debut. Even my late wife remarked on how unspoiled she was for one so beautiful. Her loveliness is only enhanced by the slight air of sadness about her now. I understand she miscarried two sons—that must have been even more devastating than losing her husband.'

'It was. She has a darling daughter, but without an heir...' Her voice trailed off, both of them looking towards the dance floor where Fenniston squired his latest partner.

'It's unfair that life gives so gentle and lovely a creature so little control over her life,' Telford said. 'To have lost her place, her home...it must be nearly intolerable.'

Claire nodded. 'It has been...difficult. Fortunately, the new Duke has been most understanding.'

'I'm relieved to hear it. That doesn't give her back her home and position, however.'

Claire sighed. 'No, it does not. But she will never lack for anything.'

'She should still have everything,' Telford said, an almost angry note in his voice. 'Had not her late husband, that stupid young pup—' He broke off abruptly, and after a moment, continued in more normal tones, 'But I doubt this unhappy situation will last for long. Some astute gentleman is sure to feel compelled to remedy her loss.'

Was he implying he might be interested in assuming that role?

'I don't believe at present she is interested in suitors,' Claire replied carefully. 'But that might change. If a concerned gentleman were kind, gentle and patient.'

'She deserves no less,' Telford said.

Nor does any woman, Claire thought.

'But now I must relieve Stannington,' Telford was saying. 'He enlisted me to help guard her from any admirers who became too overeager or importunate.'

'How kind of you both!' So Stannington *had* been watching over Liliana.

'Fenniston first asked Stannington, and he recruited me.' Telford looked over at her sister and smiled. 'It's certainly no hardship to guard such beauty.'

Ah, perhaps the Baron was not personally interested—just making enquiries to know better how to protect her sister's interests.

And both he and Stannington were watching out for her at Fenniston's request. A subtle but effective precaution she could only approve. He was taking seriously his responsibility as head of family to protect the widow.

He'd been instrumental in coaxing her sister out of isolation at Steynling; now he was making sure her return to society was comfortable and unthreatening. Claire's regard for the Duke, already high, rose even higher.

Curtsying to Telford's bow, she watched him walk over to Liliana and renew their acquaintance while Stannington took his leave. Then she looked to the dance floor to see how her other charge was faring.

Fenniston was nodding at something being said by his current partner. Though his expression couldn't be called enthusiastic, it was at least polite, which Claire supposed was the best she could hope for, given his lack of interest in the whole process of entering society.

Maybe he would meet a lady—tonight or the next night or the next—who would inspire him to dance with delighted eagerness. Someone whose hand he would thrill to hold, whose conversation would inspire him to hang on her every word. Someone who would make him the proper and cherished Duchess he sought.

She truly hoped he would, even as the prospect sent a dismal pang through her.

Which was silly. To see him mingling and her sister

enjoying the small group gathered around her was vastly satisfying, representing the achievement of all her plans.

If she told herself that often enough, she might begin to believe it.

Late that evening, Claire was smiling at an anecdote Lord Telford was recounting to her sister when she felt a tap on her shoulder. With a jolt to her senses, she turned to find Fenniston bowing before her.

'Tonight's duty is done. I've danced with my hostess, all three high-born ladies recommended to me, half a dozen others to whom the hostess presented me, been introduced to more titles than I can remember. I'm ready for my reward. Now *you* must dance with me. And don't think to feed me twaddle about it being "not suitable" or your status being "not worthy" of dancing with a duke, or I shall drag you out on to terrace for a midnight stroll.'

From the look on his face, she suspected he might make good on the threat. 'Very well, a dance. I'll even refrain from reminding you it is *not* suitable.'

'Lord be praised,' he muttered. 'Come, it must be a waltz, I want to be able to talk with you.'

Her whole body tingled at the idea of a waltz—when he might hold her almost as closely as the day they kissed on the bluff. From the dangerous glint in his eye, he was thinking of it, too.

She opened her lips to protest, he angled his head towards the terrace and she closed them.

'While waiting for that waltz, you may converse politely with me,' he ordered.

'My, we are *dukely* tonight!'

He gave her an aggravated look. 'You have no cause to tweak me, I've been doing everything you asked. Although if I must listen to one more lady lisp "Yes, Your Grace" or "No, Your Grace", I won't be responsible for my actions.'

Claire batted her eyelashes at him. 'Yes, Your Grace.'

He blew out of huff of exasperation before laughing. 'I should haul you out on the terrace immediately for that! But must they all say the same thing? They act as if terrified to venture an opinion for fear I might disagree with it. It's all so…contrived and artificial!'

'You are a highly prized matrimonial prospect, as you certainly know. Women don't want to risk alienating such a gentleman. For they must all marry, the most attractive of the few options available to a well-born lady. And since they must marry, you shouldn't fault them for wanting the protection of reaching the highest possible position of rank and wealth.'

'And what of tenderer emotions?'

'Tender emotion is something most females don't have the luxury of indulging,' she said flatly. 'Some lucky few may find it in marriage, but most are thrilled to have kindness, consideration and respect.'

'Kindness, consideration and respect?' he echoed dismissively. 'When I think of the love my parents shared, I find settling for such tepid emotions detestable. They didn't inhabit a dwelling as magnificent as Steynling, but our modest manor filled with affection was a far greater prize.'

'Says the man who has the resources to do whatever he wants,' she scoffed. 'A female can't train for a profession, go off to the army or learn a trade. Faced with penury, taking the most acceptable offer available is her only option.'

'Is that what you did?'

The middle of a ball wasn't the time to explain her tortured romantic past—though Fenniston was obviously interested. 'My late husband and I were…great friends, who offered each other mutual affection and support.'

'Such a feeble endorsement for a woman of your spirit! What of passion, claiming a love to end all loves?'

It was Claire's turn to shake her head. 'Happily-ever-after occurs only in storybooks. Great passionate love more often ends in disaster.'

'Or in a relationship that uplifts and sustains one through all the vicissitudes of life, for all of one's life,' he argued back. 'As it did for my parents and my best childhood friend. Why would one *not* strive for that?'

In the face of his vehemence, her opposition softened. 'I suppose one could. Apparently, your parents and your friend were fortunate enough to find it. I'd be glad for you if you could, too,' she added, truly meaning it despite the hollow ache in her gut.

'Ah, the musicians are tuning up. Our waltz, Mrs Hambleden.'

'It might not be wise,' she said even as her entire body hummed in anticipation.

'I can't compromise you on the dance floor.'

She should offer a more effective protest. But the bald truth was, she didn't want to. She wanted to seize the chance to claim the most intimate contact now possible for them to have, despite his obligations, her duties. Without another word, she let him take her hand.

Her stomach swooped as he took wicked advantage, caressing with his fingers the hand he held as he led her on to floor. She smothered a gasp as he pulled her towards him until their bodies were almost touching. Placing one hand at her waist, he took her trembling hand with his other.

Her mind flashed back to that day at Steynling when he helped her into the saddle…and let his hand rest at her waist. Though he'd not stroked her or increased the pressure at her waist, the light touch of his fingers had sent her heart to her throat and set all her pulses throbbing.

This time his grip was firmer, possessive, the look on his face fierce as he moved her into the position of the dance. Then the music began and he swept her into its rhythm.

She'd intended to converse and discover his impression of the three most promising debutantes, but with the scent of his shaving soap clouding her senses and an intense awareness of his body teasingly, temptingly close, with her mind breathless with anticipation that he might brush against her torso at every whirl of the dance, she couldn't summon a single coherent thought.

After a few moments, she gave up the attempt entirely, concentrating only on movement and sensation, everything female within her delighting at his nearness as she abandoned herself to the pleasure of the dance.

She looked up to see him smiling down at her, tenderness, delight and a hint of mischief in his gaze, and had to smile back. For these few minutes, there was no past or future, no thought of him claiming a bride or the devastation she was beginning to realise would invade her heart when he did.

As he twirled her in dizzying circles, a debilitating realisation swept over her, a recognition she had unconsciously worked hard to suppress over this last week. The dismal reality was it was too late to guard herself against falling in love with him—she already had.

It might not have happened with the blinding *coup de foudre* strike of the love at first sight he claimed to be essential. But despite her resistance, all her precautions, common sense and wariness, somehow she had fallen in love anyway.

How could she bear to see him walk away, as he must when he married, if not before? Marriage or even a passionate affair between them being out of the question.

Well, if she were going to be devastated at the end, she

might as well enjoy whatever scraps of pleasure she could salvage. Like the Canaanite woman who was not one of God's chosen, she would seize the crumbs fallen from the table of the privileged.

Pushing that sobering new knowledge out of mind, she clutched his hand tighter and laughed at the sheer pleasure of the dance while he grinned down at her.

'This,' he murmured. '*This* makes it all worthwhile. You must promise to waltz with me at every entertainment I'm dragged to.'

She should refuse. But why not agree?

Crumbs fallen from table, she told herself.

'Very well. I will.'

'Did I tell you how deliciously beautiful you look tonight, Mrs Hambleden?' he murmured in ear. 'I've have had to wrench my gaze away to stop it following you around room so I might pay attention to these insipid debutantes.'

Much as she discounted flattery, she couldn't help feeling warmed by it. 'Don't be ridiculous. Liliana is far more beautiful, and Lady Amelia, Lady Catherine, and that baron's daughter, Miss Waltham, are all exceedingly handsome.'

'Your sister is still a Botticelli angel—but I told you, I don't favour paragons one must place on pedestals. The misses are all very—maidenly. But you—you are a creature of fire and passion, alive, vital, exciting to behold.'

She flushed. 'You mustn't speak to me like that.'

He caught himself, his fervour cooling. 'You're right. I apologise. It's neither proper nor practical, given our situation. But with you… I don't feel proper, I feel—stimulated. Alive. Invigorated. As if I could go anywhere, do anything.'

'So you can, and will. You don't need me at your side.'

He looked her in the eye. 'You once told me that as a duke, I could have whatever I want.'

Was he asking what she thought he might be? She would never consider that again, even if she loved him. Especially since she loved him. 'Anything but that.'

He blew out a breath. 'What else is worth having?'

The dance ended, he looking as reluctant as she felt to the leave floor. 'Stannington is approaching,' she noted as he walked her off. 'He probably wants to make more introductions or bear you off to the card room. You can certainly repair there if you like. You have fulfilled all your duties tonight, meeting, conversing and dancing with suitable ladies.'

'The best dance of all was with the one you keep telling me is unsuitable. But surely that proves we must salvage our friendship. Somehow.'

'It's not the place or time to discuss it,' she said, trying to squelch the hope those words conjured. Having admitted to herself depth of her own emotion, it was even more important to guard against unrealistic hope.

'Very well, no discussion now. I don't want to spoil the glow left by that waltz. Neither do I intend to get trapped in the card room. The Duchess may tire. I want to be ready to escort you home. And don't tell me that concern is unnecessary and you could find another escort.'

She sighed. 'I won't waste my breath, then.'

'Fenniston, can I tear you away from your lovely partner?' Stannington said, bowing to them. 'Several gentlemen who weren't at the club when we dined yesterday are anxious to meet you.'

'I must check on my sister, Your Grace,' she said. 'Please, do accommodate Lord Stannington.'

'Very well, but I will walk you back to your sister first. And Stannington, I probably won't remain much longer. It's the Duchess's first engagement and we must coax her to leave soon, so she doesn't become overtired.'

'Quite understandable,' the Viscount said. 'I'll bid the Duchess goodnight before I bear you off and promise not to keep you long.'

'Mrs Hambleden?' Fenniston said, holding out his arm.

Giving her little choice but to place her hand on it. Another crumb—and she devoured it eagerly, savouring the connection crackling between them as her walked her back to the small group surrounding Liliana.

'Thank you for the dance, Your Grace,' Claire said as she reluctantly removed her hand from his arm. 'I enjoyed it very much.'

'Not half as much as I,' he murmured before turning to her sister. The group around her parted to allow him to approach as if he were Moses holding his staff over the Red Sea.

'Duchess, are you enjoying the evening?'

'Very much, Your Grace. I'd forgotten how delightful it can be to chat with friends.'

'Your sister tells me she's becoming weary,' he said, ignoring Claire's indignant look. 'I must meet some friends of Lord Stannington's, but would you then be ready to depart?'

'Of course, if you and my sister are. Despite all this charming company, I've grown a bit weary myself.'

'Very well, I'll return directly. Until later, Mrs Hambleden.'

He and Stannington bowed, the latter bidding both she and her sister goodnight.

An anxious inspection of her sister reassured her that though Liliana did appear to be flagging, there was still healthy colour in her cheeks, her smile was genuine, not forced and her conversation spritely. Being back in society did seem to be good for her.

Being back in society—if it meant waltzing with Fenniston—wouldn't be as good for her.

But what was she to do? She couldn't flee back to Steyn-ling Cross and hide away from the feelings she'd been sup-pressing, sensed but ignored. Like a powerful underground river travelled to the sea, they had eventually forced them-selves to the surface, no longer able to be escaped or denied.

Would remaining near, picking up those crumbs when she could, make the eventual parting easier—or harder?

But he'd talked tonight of continuing their friendship—no matter what it took. What could he mean by that?

She hoped he wasn't hinting that he'd decided the physi-cal attraction between them was too powerful to perma-nently deny. That with all the money and resources of a duke, he could persuade her into an affair he would treasure while it lasted and provide for her when he decided to end it.

He'd be generous. But no amount of worldly compensa-tion could repay pain or regret. She knew he was a better man than Fitzhugh; surely he wouldn't ask that.

What did he want, then? She still couldn't see how they could remain close friends, riding together, waltzing to-gether, laughing, arguing, consulting…kissing. Not once he married.

She thought of the praise Fenniston offered sincerely and often for her competence. The admiration he also ex-pressed for her as a woman.

Well, she was now a woman who didn't intend ever again to be second best. To settle for being a mistress rather than a wife. To accept mere respect and affection instead of deep, abiding love. Even if all the love she might have for the rest of her life was between her and her son.

Could they find a way to maintain close and platonic friendship, if that was what he'd meant? Could she bear being just a friend to a man she cared for so deeply?

Even one equipped with a wife?

Her head aching as much as her heart, she fell back on

the strategy she'd adopted to cope with every painful event of life. Her parents' indifference. Her unrequited love for Fitzhugh. The devastation of discovering Alexander did not in fact return the love she'd grown to feel for him.

With no way to change her circumstances, she simply thrust them out of mind. If she could no longer deny her feelings, she'd at least try to rein them in. She had weeks, perhaps months yet, before the Season ended and everything must be resolved one way or another. During that time, she would be seeing Fenniston at the house in Mayfair for breakfasts and dinners, accompanying him to balls, routs and musicales.

Heavens, she'd even agreed to ride in the park, take the children to Astley's and visit the jugglers.

Maybe she should encourage him to spend more time at his clubs. He'd certainly need to attend Lords for his presentation and listen to the debates. She could count on society hostesses deluging him with invitations that might not necessarily include the Duchess, much less her.

Though he had vowed not to attend any social event that did not include them.

She sighed. Trying to puzzle it out just made her headache worse. Abandoning the attempt, she had the dismaying feeling of falling ever deeper into an abyss. How hard was it going to be to claw her way out later, after he was gone and she struggled through a dark future without the light of his luminous presence?

She'd make a plan of some sort. In any event, she had Liliana to safeguard and a future for Alex to assure. Whatever pit her feelings might descend into, she'd concentrate on safeguarding those two most important people, the only ones who truly belonged to her.

Chapter Fifteen

In the late afternoon two weeks later, delighted that for once, he'd be able to escape social activities just as all-encompassing and annoying as he had feared, Hart set down his book with anticipation. Tonight, he'd not have to smile at debutantes—none of whom that he'd met had yet made his body tingle and his heart sing—or maintain enforced conviviality at White's with bunch of rich Englishmen he barely knew or feign enthusiasm at listening to a Parliamentary debate.

By now he'd met most of the available single ladies and time was speeding on. He was beginning to fear he'd not meet the one who would put on his face the rapturous expression he saw on his father's whenever he gazed at Hart's mother. If he didn't…could he delay marrying for another year?

He knew one person in particular would strongly argue against that.

Hart smiled, thinking of Claire Hambleden. This evening, he would spend time in the simple, honest company of her little boy whom he'd grown fond of, a little girl who amused him and a lady whose presence both calmed and energised him.

A lady whose friendship he didn't want to give up, he'd been deciding. Even if she succeeded in finding him a 'suitable' duchess, he didn't want to do without her sharp wit, keen observations and lack of pretension.

Back when he was polishing his sabre on the Peninsula, he could never have imagined he'd be thrilled at the prospect of an evening spent with two children, their nursemaid, a footman and a lady determined to marry him off to an heiress.

At that moment, the lady herself appeared at the library door.

'A successful shopping trip?' he asked.

She nodded. 'I think the Duchess now has enough suitable garments for the rest of the Season. As do I, so don't scold.'

'Good. Have you checked whether the children are ready for this evening?'

She nodded. 'Alex was initially disappointed the destination wasn't Astley's, but I assured him the equestrian acts at Vauxhall would be equally thrilling and the supper much superior.'

After weeks of being constantly spotlighted in society—like the lead actor in a farce, he thought sardonically—when Hart learned Vauxhall Gardens was having one of its occasional early opening evenings, which would include equestrian displays and jugglers as well as concerts, he'd asked to substitute that entertainment for a foray to Astley's. 'I'll try to make sure Alex enjoys it. I know with Astley's diverse audience, I might not be as much the focus of every gaze as I am at a ball, but at Vauxhall, strolling along open walks with people from every walk of London life, I shall feel much less on display.'

'You needn't explain further. Vauxhall isn't the premier attraction for the Quality it once was, so you may well not meet *anyone* who recognises you.'

'A blessing devoutly to be wished! At least for one evening I can be just "Uncle Hart".'

'You know how I feel about that.'

'There will be no one at Vauxhall to gasp in horror at the audacity of children not calling me by my title.'

She sighed, as if knowing arguing over that again was a lost cause. 'If you are ready, I'll fetch the children— *Uncle Hart*.'

Chuckling, he watched her walk out.

Three hours later, Hart strolled with Mrs Hambleden and the excited children down Vauxhall's grand central walk, the groom and nursemaid left for the moment in the pavilion he'd hired while the two of them escorted their charges to watch as the grand lamps were lit, illuminating the path with brilliant colour.

'They're so beautiful!' Bella cried. 'Like flowers, all red and blue and yellow!'

'Bright and pretty,' Alex agreed. 'But I liked the ham and tarts better. The music is nice, but are we going to see the acrobats now?'

'Yes, they are performing in the pavilion we're walking towards,' Mrs Hambleden said.

A few minutes later, they reached the designated pavilion. Urging the children to the front, Hart guided Mrs Hambleden under the shadowy canopy of trees bordering the pathway where their charges were in sight, but it was quiet enough for conversation.

'I apologise if you are missing dancing at the Ravensdales' ball tonight.'

'True, I enjoy dancing. But I enjoy even more spending time with the children doing something *they* enjoy.' She gave him a wry smile. 'And I'm quite certain *you* do not miss going to a ball one bit. How is your…search progressing? We've had little time to chat of late.'

Hart was intensely conscious of how closely she stood beside him, pressed between where he stood guarding her from being jostled by the crowd and the trees behind them. Reach down, and masked by the shadows, he might take her hand…

'Fenniston?' she repeated. 'I asked you a question.'

Jolted back to reality, he said, 'Ah, my dear friend, sometimes I despair of it. I've gone riding with Lady Catherine. She is an excellent horsewoman. I shared my opinion on everything she asked me about, though when she asked about my politics, she twisted her pretty lips in disapproval when I admitted I have none. She's lovely, accomplished, intelligent and about as warm as frost in January.

'I accompanied Lady Amelia to an art exhibit at the Royal Institution, where she expressed her enthusiasm for the colours and composition of the Old Master replicas while seeming to possess no knowledge whatsoever about the Old Masters themselves. And the Honourable Mary— she'd been sweet, gentle and soft as blancmange. Unfortunately, I dislike pudding.'

Shaking her head reprovingly at his assessment, she said, 'They are not the only eligible ladies to whom you've been presented.'

He sighed. 'Where to begin—or end? This one chatters, that one is silent, another's conversation consists solely of the dreaded "Yes, Your Grace" and "No, Your Grace". With that one, I must confess, I finally lost my patience.'

'Oh, dear, that sounds ominous. What did you do?'

'Unexpectedly recovered my brogue and then bombarded her with every Scottish homily I could think of.'

'How bad of you!' she said, trying to suppress a chuckle. 'She probably didn't understand one word in ten.'

'She left my company willingly enough after that,' Hart said, grinning. 'Alas, there were only too many others eager to take her place.'

'Perhaps you should give more consideration to older ladies. Maybe even widows, as long as they are still in their prime and able to give you sons.'

'Ah, the business of getting sons. It was the lack of sons that catapulted me into this position to begin with.'

'It should be pleasure as well as business. Whomever you choose.'

Pleasure.

His body tingled at her tantalising nearness. 'I know only one I've met since this inheritance fell upon me that would make it pleasure as well as business.'

As he stared down at her, her luminous eyes widened, her lips parting. Probably to impart some wise advice he didn't want to hear.

Suddenly exasperated by it all, weary of suppressing his growing fear that he would never find the love he sought and driven by a volatile mix of affection and desire, his tenuous control snapped. Pulling her back behind the tree, out of the lights into near complete darkness, he kissed her.

Once again, his body reacted immediately. The fireworks that were to end the evening were a pistol's crack compared to the artillery barrage of sensation exploding within him. Unable to help himself, he tightened his grip and deepened the kiss.

In the small, rational part of his brain that still functioned, he knew she should push him away and almost hoped she would, ending the madness as he seemed unable to stop.

But she didn't. With a little sigh, she stepped into his embrace, returning his kiss with all the fire and passion he remembered from the bluff at Steynling. Passion he'd dreamed about during long nights in his lonely bed.

He shouldn't be kissing her, his indignant conscience screamed as it fought his reckless senses for control. Finally, mindful of the crowd strolling just a few feet away on the illuminated pathway, the children standing with the crowd applauding the jugglers, he forced himself to release her.

It took a moment for his stampeding pulse and ragged breathing to ease enough for him to speak. 'I'm so sorry. I shouldn't have. After the trust you've put in me, that was a flagrant abuse of our friendship.'

'I'm just as guilty,' she acknowledged. 'I should have slapped your face, gathered the children and stomped off indignantly.'

Hart angled his chin to her. 'There's still time.'

'Would it make you feel better?'

'Not really.'

Sighing, she shook her head. 'It's my fault, but I can't do this. I won't be your mistress. Please, don't destroy the admiration I have for you by asking.'

Horrified, he stepped away. 'I doubly curse my rashness, if my desire for you makes you think I could ask such thing. How *can* you think it?'

'Sorry, I didn't mean to insult you. I know you are not like Fitzhugh.'

'Did my cousin try to make you his mistress?'

She said nothing, which was an answer in itself. Furious, Hart growled, 'That's despicable! How could he treat you with such disrespect? His own wife's sister!'

She looked away, and at first he thought she meant to say nothing more, leaving him desperate to know the full answer to the question that had bedevilled him from the first. Finally, she looked back at him.

'I suppose I should finally confess. It pricks my conscience to have you think me a paragon of virtue when I have fallen so far short. It's not just Fitzhugh who was despicable. You see, I didn't recoil in horror at the prospect when he asked me, as you just did. It shames me to say, but I seriously considered it.'

'You—considered it? How? Why?'

'As you have probably guessed, I fell in love with Fitzhugh in my first Season. Oh, I didn't mean to. I knew his choice was unlikely to fall on the daughter of an earl's younger son with only a modest dowry, not when so many others were vying for his attention and were lovelier and far wealthier.' She laughed. 'I think that's why he noticed me initially. I was probably the only single lady who ignored him. Which, of course, piqued his attention.'

'You've only seen the worst of Fitzhugh,' she continued. 'He could be charming, amusing, wonderful company. The more he tried to beguile me, the more resistant and sharper-tongued I became. I thought it would drive him away before I succumbed to his charm. I didn't realise until later that my opposition just made him more determined to bring me completely under his spell. I tried to never let him see that he'd succeeded, but he must have known. I still didn't dare imagine anything could come of it.

'Once I'd stopped resisting, he continued to see me, but erratically, showering me with attention one week, ignoring me the next. Like you...' she gave him a brief, bitter smile '... I didn't want to settle for wedding someone for whom I felt little more than respect, so I politely fended off any gentlemen who seemed inclined to make me an offer. And went on to a second Season.'

'When Fitzhugh met Liliana,' Hart murmured, guessing what must have happened next.

'When Fitzhugh met Liliana. He called soon after we

arrived back in London for that Season. We were indulging in our usual teasing banter when Liliana walked in.' She huffed out a breath. 'He looked rather like you did the evening you met her at Steynling. Dazzled. Still, nothing might have come of it even then—she had outstanding beauty, but not much more dowry than I—but once she became the Toast of London, the Season's reigning Incomparable...'

'Fitzhugh always had to have the best.'

'Of course, my parents were thrilled. Mama in particular was delighted. She'd called in all the favours she had to persuade Lady Shelford to present Liliana and coax half the Patronesses at Almack's to host balls in her honour. She became the most celebrated debutante of the last several years. Of course, Fitzhugh decided he must have her.'

'So you decide to marry after all?'

She nodded. 'Alexander and I found ourselves in the same situation. He had loved Liliana since we were children, but realised his suit never had a chance once her hand was sought by a future duke. But our families were close, his and mine, after my sister married Fitzhugh, neither of us would be able to escape spending far too much time in their company. Alexander proposed a marriage of convenience. I'd follow him after he joined the army, allowing us both to escape a situation too painful to endure.'

'And after you returned a widow, knowing your affection, Fitzhugh played upon it?'

'I was desolate, the independent life I thought would save me stolen away. Lonely. Liliana was still gravely ill after her last miscarriage. Fitzhugh was so sympathetic, so attentive, so solicitous. First, there were just subtle gestures. His fingers grasped a bit longer than necessary when he handed me into the carriage. Pressure at the small of my back when he seated me at table more intense and lasting than it should have been. Then his gazes grew more long-ing, more…heated.'

'With his wife ill, he would crassly compromise her sis-ter? That's still despicable.'

'Sadly, it's worse even than that. He paid me compli-ments I'd been thirsting to hear from him, even said he'd made a mistake and married the wrong sister. But we could make it right, he said. Liliana could not be a wife to him any longer—her health had become too fragile after the last miscarriage. But he still needed a son. I'd had no trouble conceiving, Liliana had told him. We could have a discreet affair and if I were delivered of a son, they could have the heir they both craved. I'd be saving her from the peril of another childbirth. I'd be saving his inheritance for a son of his own blood.'

Incredulous, Hart stared at her. 'You can't be serious. Fitzhugh—and your *sister* both asked this of you?'

'Just Fitzhugh at first. To my shame, I didn't immedi-ately decline. That annoyed him and frustrated him, which I at first was too confused and conflicted to notice. I'd just been offered the chance I never expected to enjoy intimacy with the man I'd loved for years. In a way that safeguarded the life of the dear sister I'd spent my whole life protecting.'

'The pressure to succumb must have been overwhelm-ing. But…in the end, you didn't succumb.'

'Not, alas, out of noble principle, I'm humiliated to con-fess. But because of Alex. When I thought of how much I loved him, enough to endure the hardships of bringing an infant on campaign, I knew I'd never want to be sep-arated from any child of mine. If I did agree to an affair and conceived a son, I could never tolerate being forbid-den to acknowledge him as my own. Not even for the love I felt for my sister could I give up my child to her. If I had a daughter…she'd be fostered out to some family and I'd never see her again. I couldn't do it. Only after I informed Fitzhugh of my decision did he finally began to reveal his true character.'

Hart took an involuntary step closer. 'Did he threaten you?' he asked roughly, believing his cousin capable of almost anything if his wishes were thwarted. And desire for an heir was as much need as wish.

'Not at first. At first, he was patient, seemingly understanding. He tried again to persuade me, telling me what a gift I'd be giving them both. Then, I should imagine the pleasure he would give *me*. My sister—he noted as you did—was an ethereal beauty, whereas I was a woman of appetites he would willingly satisfy. But by now, firm in my decision, the...tawdriness of it all began to fully dawn on me. The realisation that what he asked was not just immoral but illegal—foisting on the estate an heir who was actually illegitimate. As I became less enamoured of him, more suspicious, Fitzhugh become less cajoling, more impatient and finally furious. And yes, he did threaten to turn me and Alex out of the house. By then, sick and heartsick, I was more than ready to leave.'

'But obviously you didn't.'

'No. My sister came to my room while I was packing. First, she pressed on me the same arguments Fitzhugh had. I was astounded at first that any woman, much less my sister, would willingly solicit someone else to become her husband's mistress. She said she feared another pregnancy would mean her life, but without an heir, her whole future and security was threatened.

'She begged me, but hard as it was, I refused her, too. When I told her Alex and I would be gone by morning, she broke down weeping. How would she cope without me? She begged me to stay, to protect her from Fitzhugh's scorn and abuse. I think she even feared for her life, that if she could not give him a son, he would need another wife who could. So… I stayed.'

'Fitzhugh didn't throw you out in spite of his wife's pleas?'

'I told him if he did, I would expose him. Tell our father what he had asked of me and the deception he was willing to perpetrate. Father dotes on Liliana. He would have taken her away and protected her. He wouldn't have needed to announce Fitzhugh's perfidy to the world, it would have been enough to drop a word into the ears of certain gentlemen, leaders of society with a vested interest in protecting the integrity of the aristocracy. To have them know he'd attempted to act so dishonourably would have ruined his reputation with the only people in his world who mattered.'

'That was an anathema to a man like Fitzhugh. But would your father truly have risked confronting a duke?' Hart asked sceptically.

She laughed. 'Maybe. Fortunately, I never had to find out. Fitzhugh knew Father's privileged position with Lord Sidmouth. He was uncertain enough about whether Father would actually expose him that he abandoned the idea. After that, he ignored both me and Liliana while his behaviour grew ever more reckless. He spent most of his time in London, which suited everyone. Then came the wager, the carriage race…well, you know the rest.'

'I might want you as much as he wanted you. But I give you my solemn word of honour, I would never disrespect you by trying to make you my mistress.'

She looked away, the crystal tear on her cheek illumined by the lamplight. 'Now you know me as not just a wanton, but immoral, too.'

'"He's lifeless that's faultless", my old nurse would say. It's not immoral to be tempted. Only to succumb. Something I understand better than you may know. You may have heard rumours that after Badajoz, battle-crazed soldiers subjected the town to such a reign of pillage and debauchery, Wellington finally sent in officers with orders to shoot any soldier who didn't desist from theft, rape and destruction. I could easily have been one of them.'

'You?' she gasped.

He nodded grimly. 'I've told you how we were pinned down. How we watched the French mow down our comrades, shoot them off ladders, jeer at them as they threw lighted barrels of gunpowder down on their heads. How Charles, Rafe and I escaped death several times over. Not just the troopers entered the town in a haze of fury when the walls were finally breeched.

'We went in after the first wave, Rafe and Charles and I. I told you we made a pledge to adventure together after the war. What I didn't tell you was we made it after we'd almost shot down some townspeople who ran towards us in the street. That near-murder shocked us all back to sanity. Extreme conditions try the soul. In the end, we resisted. In the end, you did the right thing, too. After all, if everyone who was tempted was to be condemned, no mortal soul would pass the test.'

She brushed away the sparkle of tears. 'Thank you.'

'Thank you—for trusting me with your story. I can only guess how painful it was to relate, and I'm so very sorry for what my cousin put you through. Never would I want to cause you such pain. Your experience with him inspires me to set an unbreachable guard on my own passion. I want to offer you only the most profound respect and affection.'

'Respect and affection,' she repeated in a whisper. 'Well, I see the jugglers are completing their performance. We should probably get the children home. If we linger much longer, it will be time for the fireworks to begin. We'd never pry them away from that.'

After her shocking revelations, he sensed she was feeling drained and vulnerable. He wanted to continue to reassure and protect her—and he didn't want this special evening, the only one he was likely to pry out of his overfull social schedule, to end. 'Why not stay and let them enjoy it? The Duchess is out with friends and won't return until the wee hours. She'll never know.'

She angled her head, considering. 'We may have to bribe Nurse, the nursemaid and the footman to not say anything.'

Hart waved a hand. 'I'm a duke. They'll listen to me.'

He watched her as she debated with herself while he considered all she had confessed. That she'd loved Fitzhugh came as no surprise—he had suspected as much from the beginning. But that his cousin had been despicable enough to use her love for him and her sister to try to force her into an illicit affair to conceive an illegitimate son to pass off as the rightful heir?

Only a man who believed himself entitled to anything and everything he desired would consider such a plan acceptable.

'Very well,' she said. 'I suppose we can ask them, just this once.'

He nodded agreement, still marvelling at the pressure she'd sustained and resisted. And knowing if his cousin were not already beyond the pale, he would have been hard pressed to keep from seeking him out and pummelling him within an inch of his life.

They made their way forward through the watching crowd to the children who stood at the front of the group, enthusiastically applauding the bowing jugglers with the nursemaid.

'Can we stay a little longer, Uncle Hart?' Bella begged as they walked away.

'Your aunt has agreed to let you have a rare treat.' Bending down, he whispered. 'But it must remain our secret.'

'Ooh, I love secrets,' Bella said, clapping her hands.

'I hadn't said anything, because I thought we must leave right after the juggler's performance,' Mrs Hambleden said. 'But it's such a special evening, we can stay for the fireworks.'

'Fireworks?' Alex cried.

'They are said to be splendid,' Hart said.

'You're the best Mama in whole world!'

As if involuntarily, she glanced up at Hart, pain in her eyes. Was she recalling how being Alex's mama had saved her from committing a sin that would probably have destroyed her? Or still castigating herself for having been tempted in the first place?

He hoped relating his own experience would help her forgive herself, but he knew such forgiveness didn't come easily. He'd been shocked by his capacity for violence at Badajoz, by how close he'd come to taking a life not out of duty or necessity but out of blind rage. It had taken him a very long time to make peace with that.

'She is the best mama in the whole world,' Hart agreed. 'A lady of principle and courage, able to persevere even when placed in almost impossible situations.'

'Can we have more cakes while we wait for the fireworks?' Alex asked.

'Of course. We'll have Tom the footman fetch some when we return to our box.'

After the cake, they watched a second equestrian performance that proved even more exciting than the first, the horses racing in circles while riders stood, sat, or performed leaps on their backs. The fireworks that ended the evening were spectacular, even if Bella had to hold her ears against the noise.

* * *

After they'd returned the children to the nursery—and Hart dropping a coin into the palms of the nursemaid and footman for their efforts—Hart walked Mrs Hambleden back down the stairs. 'Take a glass of wine with me in the library?'

Having had her share such a traumatic episode made him feel even closer to her, an intimacy as powerful as their physical connection, making him loath even now to end their evening together. Knowing that society, expectations and eager marriage-minded maidens awaited on every evening to come.

She shook her head. 'Tired as I am, I might not be equal to the struggle to resist kissing you. Which absolutely cannot happen again.'

'The attraction between us is…inconvenient,' Hart admitted. 'Though I can't quite make myself regret it. But I hope our mutual respect and affection is equally strong. If we are both diligent, can't we have both friendship and honour?'

'Friendship and honour,' she repeated. 'I would like that. But to ensure it, I'd better bid you goodnight now.'

It would be wiser, he knew. Even if he didn't like it. Even if he would still be fighting against desire for as long as he knew her.

As she walked away, Hart blew out a breath. And said a little prayer that he'd meet that one special woman soon, before friendship and honour was not enough. Before desire betrayed him into betraying a woman who had already borne too much abuse from a Duke of Fenniston.

Chapter Sixteen

In the early evening a week later, Claire followed the housekeeper to check that Fenniston House was ready for guests. The Duke had received word that his two friends had indeed taken leave and would be arriving today. In honour of their visit and with Fenniston's reluctant agreement, she would be arranging a grand ball to honour them as friends of the Duke and heroes of the Peninsular War.

Having soldiers about would help distract her from her continual turmoil over Fenniston. They'd attended several balls in the week following their visit to Vauxhall, interspersed with a few evenings where Fenniston repaired to his club to escape the relentless feminine pursuit. He'd even attended a meeting of political gentlemen organised by her father, who told her later that he quite approved of the new Duke and hoped to steer him into Liverpool's coalition.

During those balls, she'd seen no sign yet that the Duke had met the woman who would inspire him to fall headlong in love in the manner he craved. She still thought it a hope unlikely to be realised.

After that night at Vauxhall, it was painfully obvious *she* was not that woman. He wanted to protect her and honour the 'respect and affection' between them. Given the confession she'd made to him, she should count herself fortunate that he was still offering respect and affection.

She'd dreaded making that revelation and had hoped she might finish their time together without doing so. She'd not intended to reveal it that night until, blundering on to the subject when anxiety made her blurt out her reluctance to become his mistress, she more or less cornered herself into revealing it.

But being Hart—she now secretly thought of him as the name he called himself, 'Fenniston' carrying too many overtones of Fitzhugh—he'd not just understood, he'd urged her to forgive herself. She wasn't sure she'd ever completely manage that...but having revealed her worst secret to him she felt...lighter. No longer carrying such a tawdry, humiliating burden alone.

And his kiss in the dark shadows of the magical, lamp and moonlit Vauxhall Gardens, was one more crumb from the table to treasure.

It was unlikely she'd have many more.

Respect and affection.

Oh, Hart! She felt that for him, but so much more. Unlike the love he was waiting to experience, hers for him hadn't developed all at once with the sudden force of a thunderclap. She'd gone only gradually from resentment and suspicion, to at first grudging respect, to genuine admiration, to love...all the while struggling to resist the passionate attraction that *had* been present from the first.

She shook her mind free of that useless observation to wonder instead what would happen if Hart did not find his special lady before the end of the Season.

She wasn't sure she could endure standing by watching him through another Season—though by then he would no longer need her help. He was steadily building a circle of friends to advise him on ways of society and a small coterie of influential hostesses who could counsel him about the character and accomplishments of potential brides, steering him towards someone suitable.

She wasn't sure either that she could endure returning to Steynling with him unwed, where it would be all too easy to fall back into their former camaraderie, a bittersweet closeness and a dangerous attraction. To walk the difficult line between continuing friendship while avoiding the ever-present temptation to take the ultimate of crumbs available and become his mistress.

She told herself she was wiser now and had too much self-respect to settle for being merely his *chère amie*. She hoped.

Which brought her back to same conundrum: if she did leave, where would she go?

Nowhere yet, she told herself, nodding to the housekeeper who'd just finished showing her the newly made-up guest rooms.

'Excellent work, Mrs Reynolds. I'm sure His Grace will be pleased with the accommodations for friends. Is everything progressing for dinner?'

'All is in hand, Mrs Hambleden. Cook is delighted to prepare a meal for the heroes who are ridding us of Boney's menace!'

'Please convey my thanks to the staff for their hard work.'

As the housekeeper hurried off, Claire hesitated. It was too early yet to dress for dinner. She could visit the schoolroom and read the children a story, which always cheered her. And would distract her from the ever-present temptation to seek out Hart in the library where he often retreated from the bustle of the household.

Sometimes she could be with him and shut out all but the delight of his company. Forget the sorrow that he didn't feel for her the depth of emotion she felt for him. Forget the sense of gathering doom, that even their limited friendship could only last a bit longer.

Today was not one of those occasions. Instead, she seemed to be especially aware of the creep of time and tide carrying him inexorably away from her. Why seek him out, when gazing on him, talking with him at this moment was almost as much pain as pleasure?

Before she could decide what to do, a footman trotted up the stairs.

'Mr Tompkins sent me to tell you the guests have arrived. The Duke took them into the Grand Saloon.'

Glad to have her indecision ended, she followed the footman downstairs. She was looking forward to meeting Hart's friends, dragoons like her husband who'd likely participated in many of the same battles and shared the experience of campaigning. Talking with them would reconnect her to a time when she had been content, fulfilled, with almost every day bringing a new adventure…

A time when she'd believed she'd finally found love as well as satisfaction.

Pushing away that disappointment, Claire entered the Grand Salon after a brief knock. The three men within rose, bowing to her curtsy.

'Welcome to London, gentlemen! I hope we will make your visit very pleasant.'

'With your arrival, ma'am, it already is,' the tall blond soldier in a scarlet coat said.

'Mrs Hambleden, may I introduce my friends? The shameless flatterer in the red coat is Charles Marsden of Dunbar's Dragoons, the one in the blue is Rafe Tynesley of the Sixteenth Queen's. Gentlemen, your hostess, Mrs Claire Hambleden.'

Hart came over to escort her to a place on the sofa. Not even curiosity about her guests muted the instantaneous response his touch evoked, she noted with resignation. Determinedly turning away from him, she smiled at the soldiers.

'Officially, your hostess is my sister, the Duchess. As she's only recently recovered from a…lengthy illness, she is at present resting, but will join us for dinner.'

'Mrs Hambleden followed the drum in Portugal,' Hart told them. 'Her husband was a lieutenant in the Fourteenth Light Dragoons.'

'He…fell at Fuentes de Oñoro,' Claire said, a catch in her throat.

The two soldiers' smiles faded. 'Very sorry for your loss, ma'am,' the blue-coated Tynesley said quietly.

Claire nodded and took a deep breath. 'Did either of you happen to know him?'

'The Sixteenth was at Fuentes,' Tynesley said. 'A hard-fought engagement. But we didn't work with the Fourteenth. Whereas Edmenton—'

'Remember, Rafe, it's Fenniston now,' Marsden interrupted. 'Or Your *Grace*.' He emphasised the word with a flourishing bow.

'Stuff it, Charles,' Hart said. 'Considering the two of you were primarily responsible for harrying me back here to assume the wretched title, I'll take no grief from you over it.'

'How are conditions on the Peninsula?' Claire asked, smiling at banter so achingly familiar from her time with the army. 'Are you in winter quarters in Lisbon again? Any word on what Wellington intends for the spring?'

The soldiers' response was delayed by the arrival with Tompkins and the tea tray, Claire serving all of them.

'Ah, to enjoy tea poured by graceful feminine hands. Won't have need of sugar,' Marsden said.

Claire laughed. 'Lieutenant, with your charm, you certainly had tea poured in Portugal by hands just as dainty— and probably more alluring.'

'She has you there,' Hart said.

'No mention of Marsden's Portuguese ladies,' Tynesley warned. 'Gentlemen never tell.'

'You were going to describe the upcoming campaign?' Claire interposed.

'I'll pass on as much information as lowly lieutenants are privy to,' Tynesley said. 'We expect the French to attack through central Spain. But rumour says Old Hookey intends to send his main force north across the Douro and hit the French from behind their lines. We expect orders to move one way or another some time in May.'

'If he can bypass central Spain, outflank Joseph's French army and head north towards the Pyrenees and the French border, he could shift supply lines to the northern coast of Spain and be primed to move against France itself,' Hart observed.

'That's what we're thinking,' Marsden agreed. 'But enough talk of war! With a lovely lady in our midst, surely there are more agreeable topics of conversation.'

'When must you take passage back?' Claire asked. 'We were hoping to fête you at a dinner and a grand ball, the first hosted by the Duke since assuming his title, if you can remain for a week.'

'I think we can manage a week's stay, although we'd need to leave immediately after the ball,' Marsden said. 'Can't miss troop movements, once Old Hookey decides he's ready to march. But I'm quite ready to be fêted! It can make up for the many miserable rainy marches when there were hardly any provisions to be found after we arrived, much less a grand dinner.'

'I'm looking forward to sleeping in a bedchamber not constructed out of canvas or tree limbs,' Tynesley said.

Claire laughed. 'I fondly remember those huts! Thick posts supporting a roof of pine, broom or straw, a thatch of branches for walls with the space between stuffed with moss or grass? Snug and fragrant! And much warmer than a blanket tossed on to a stone convent floor.'

'My, you were an intrepid campaigner, Mrs Hambleden,' Marsden exclaimed.

'I can assure you your accommodations here will be much more comfortable. Saying that, shall I send you upstairs to rest before dinner?'

'I hope to continue our reminiscences then,' Marsden said.

'The Duchess will be joining us. We mustn't bore her with too many soldiering stories,' Hart warned.

'I'm sure the Lieutenant can easily switch to conversation that will charm my sister,' Claire said, looking up at Marsden with a smile.

'I ever aim to please,' he said, winking back.

'You can count on it,' Hart said acerbically. 'Charles never met a lady he didn't feel obligated to charm.'

The Duke seemed a bit put out by his friend's flirtatious ways. Amused, Claire said, 'If only all gentlemen were so accommodating. Again, welcome to Fenniston House, gentlemen,' she said, standing.

'I'll escort you up,' Hart said to his friends as she walked out.

Claire returned to her room to dress for dinner, bemused and thoughtful. She would enjoy reminiscing with Hart's fellow soldiers, a reminder of a time when her most pressing problems were establishing a comfortable billet, finding food and concocting medicines to treat the sick and injured.

It reminded her how different London society was—how foreign Hart must have initially found it, where what was meant was more often implied than stated plainly, where every remark could contain innuendo, where subtle interconnections between families, political allies and adversaries shifted and realigned like sea grasses swaying with the tide.

No wonder Hart longed for the days of plain talk and straightforward action. She hoped his amusing friends could remain long enough to immerse him in a satisfying dose of that lost world.

An hour later in the drawing room, Claire introduced Hart's friends to her sister, looking forward with amusement to how the flirtatious Lieutenant Marsden would react. She wasn't disappointed.

Both men were initially awestruck, though Tynesley was more subtle about it. Marsden gave an audible gasp, swept Liliana a bow more suited to acknowledging royalty and exclaimed, 'Most honoured to meet you, Duchess.'

'And you, sir,' her sister returned, colouring prettily.

Marsden turned to the Duke. 'Fenniston, you wretch! You didn't warn us you'd been blessed to live with goddesses. First we met Athena, and now Aphrodite!'

'Would that I did possess all wisdom,' Claire said drily, exchanging an amused glance with Hart, who rolled his eyes at his friend's extravagant praise.

'Behave yourself, or she will have to smite you like Aphrodite did Psyche,' Hart said.

'Oh, I would never smite anyone!' Liliana protested.

'Indeed not, for I will take care only to please you,' Marsden assured her.

At that moment, the butler bowed himself in to announce dinner ready.

To encourage a more convivial evening, the two visitors had been seated on either side of her sister with Claire across from them and Hart taking the place of honour at one end of the table. As the courses were brought and removed, Marsden kept her sister engaged with a constant stream of light chatter.

Claire herself sat silently for the first part of the meal, enjoying her sister's enjoyment and the banter between Hart and Tynesley, in which their soldier's bond and genuine affection was evident.

But after some time, Tynesley said, 'You must allow me to apologise. We've been droning on about regimental matters and people you don't know, most rudely ignoring you.'

'Not at all. I've enjoyed listening to your experiences.'

'How much time did you spend in the Peninsula?' Tynesley asked.

'My husband and I married in late summer of '08, just after he joined the Fourteenth Light Dragoons. We left for Lisbon in time for him to participate in the Battle of Porto in May and Talavera in July of '09. I had remained in Lisbon that spring, being delivered of my son in June, just before the battle.

'Our little family reunited that autumn in Lisbon and the following spring, my son and I followed the army, my husband being involved in the battles at Barquilla and Coa River in July of '10. We retreated with them after Busaco behind the lines of Torres Vedras, going out again the following spring when he…he was wounded at Fuentes de Oñora. He succumbed to his wounds in June, after which my son and I returned to England.'

'Again, my sympathies for your loss. You did quite a bit of campaigning, then.'

Appreciating his attempt to direct her thoughts away from her loss to happier times, she smiled. 'Yes. One felt very useful. My sister often suffered from ailments of the lung as child, so I'd become something of a healer. In addition to making a home for my husband, I was able to assist with the sick and wounded, which was very satisfying.'

'I know we soldiers appreciated a lovely smile and soothing hand on the brow when ill or ailing,' Hart said.

'Along with the Portuguese maid who also served as nursemaid, I became very adept at laundry and cooking.'

Tynesley laughed. 'I was so relieved when there were ladies about who one could hire for those services! My batman's idea of washing my shirt was to take it by the collar, give it a few shakes in a river and hang it out to dry. Were you billeted in any of the tent cities?'

'Twice. Amazing to consider how, after the tent mules delivered the canvas and the bugle to "stand by tents" sounded, in a mere few minutes a hundred tents stood where a moment earlier there had been only bare ground.'

'Aye, the lads grew proficient—as they should have!' Hart said. 'Considering some of the places one had to sleep, having a dry, cosy tent was a blessing.'

'I must say, I'm in awe of you, going on the march with an infant,' Tynesley said. 'That cannot have been easy.'

'Oh, but the troops were always ready to assist. While I rode one of the mules, my maid Benedita carried Alex, well wrapped up against the dust or rain, my husband's batman assisting her and the baggage mule trailing behind them. Once in camp, with their help, we arranged whatever billet was available and generally had dinner ready when my husband returned from picket duty, several of his friends joining us for a meal and some cards afterwards. Or some alfresco songs.'

'Sounds as if you enjoyed campaigning,' Tynesley said.

Claire smiled, the memories bittersweet. 'I did, on the whole. After time, I suppose, one puts out of mind the difficult bits—the marches in pouring rain or freezing sleet, slogging through mud that sucked the boots off your feet. The burning summer heat. The battles. One just remembers the adventure, the camaraderie, the sense of doing something important. I hope it will be so for you when your sol-diering days are over.'

'A blessing devoutly to be wished,' Tynesley said.

'Dinner was excellent,' Marsden said as the staff cleared the table. 'Have you plans for us for tomorrow?'

'I thought you would enjoy dinner at my club,' Hart said.

Tynesley shook his head. 'I'd rather dine with these lovely ladies and then attend whatever entertainment was planned, if you are permitted to bring guests.'

Liliana looked up, a bit shamefaced. 'I nearly forgot, Sis-ter. Of course, I'd be pleased to dine with everyone. But at the last minute, Lady Downing asked if I might accompany her to the Sullivans' musicale and perform with her. The friend who planned to sing developed a ticklish sore throat and had to cancel. We were to attend the Brixtons' rout to-morrow night, were we not? You go and make my excuses.'

'Of course, accompany Lady Downing if you wish it,' Claire replied. She felt both a little let down that her sis-ter preferred a friend's company to her own, but also en-couraged. It would be the first time Liliana had ventured out without Claire's support since she returned from Por-tugal. She had to view that as a positive step in her sister's recovery.

'Speaking of music, shall we have some?' Hart asked. 'After months in the wilds of Portugal, I believe my friends would rather have tea, conversation and music with you la-dies than sit at the table drinking port with me.'

'We can always do that after the ladies retire,' Marsden said. 'I'm sure your voices are as lovely as your appearance.'

'Is he always such a flatterer?' Claire murmured to Hart as they walked to the salon.

'He does tend to empty the butter boat over the ladies,' he murmured back. 'Are you charmed?'

'Amused. But pleased that my sister does appear entertained.'

They enjoyed tea, after which she and Liliana favoured the company with several songs before they drew partners for cards. Tynesley, who was left as odd man out, seemed content to sit silently, sipping his wine and watching the play.

After the initial shock Liliana's appearance produced in every gentleman encountering her astounding beauty for the first time, he hadn't seemed as enchanted by her sister as Marsden. She hadn't thought he'd particularly noticed her, either, other than with his polite efforts at dinner to include her in the conversation.

But as she and her sister bid the gentlemen goodnight, leaving the men to their delayed port and conversation, he followed her out.

'Thank you again for your kindness in chatting with a rough old soldier. I've seldom enjoyed an evening more.'

Unlike voluble Marsden, she knew by now Tynesley spoke little, observed more and only said what he meant. 'That's very kind of you. Any lady would be pleased to entertain a soldier sacrificing so much to defend his country.'

Tynesley chuckled. 'She might be, but it was the company of *this* particular lady that made the evening so remarkable. I hope to enjoy as much of it as I can before I must return to soldiering.'

Then he bowed and walked back to rejoin his friends.

Nonplussed, Claire wasn't sure what to make of his attention. She was flattered, of course, but somewhat puzzled. As a soldier soon to return to Portugal, he didn't have time for more than gallantry. But unlike his friend, Tynesley didn't seem the type for idle flirtation.

She did note, though, amusement supplanting her curiosity, that Hart was glowering at his friend as he walked back to the group. She'd been aware of the Duke watching her closely throughout the evening, hopefully pleased that his friends were obviously enjoying their hospitality. Surely he couldn't be...jealous of Tynesley's attentions?

When pigs fly.

Dismissing that ludicrous thought, she hurried to catch up with her sister.

Chapter Seventeen

In the afternoon a week later, Hart was reading in the library when Rafe rapped on the door. 'I'd like a chat, if you're not busy.'

Hart motioned him in. 'Some wine? I thought you were with Charles, doing a last-minute check in with Horse Guards and replacing some kit before you leave tomorrow.'

Nodding to Hart's offer, Rafe said, 'We finished at Horse Guards and I didn't need to visit the shops. I've enjoyed all the entertainments you've laid on for us, but we've not had much chance to talk seriously. How are you adjusting to your role? I know you dreaded returning to assume it.'

Sighing, Hart handed him a glass of wine. 'It has been... difficult. Mostly I put out of mind all the plans we'd discussed for after the army. I am finding some aspects are similar to soldiering—having troops, in this case tenants, to watch over, planning large movements, like spring planting, rather than disposition of army units.'

'I understand another crucial element is finding a wife to provide the estate and title with an heir. I didn't notice at the entertainment last night that you had your eye on any lady in particular, though you were certainly besieged by a number of lovelies.'

'I haven't found that special lady...yet. I just hope, despite the imperative to produce an heir, I can resist the pressure to take a bride until I do.'

Rafe seemed to take an inordinate amount of time to pick a speck of lint from his sleeve. 'I should think you had a superior candidate right under your nose. And I don't mean the Duchess, exquisite as she is.'

'Mrs Hambleden,' Hart confirmed with a nod. 'A superior female in every way. I'm very fond of her.' He wasn't about to confess his attraction to her, hoping the usually perceptive Rafe wouldn't notice it; certainly he'd been trying his best to keep his desire under tight control.

'You know my background, we talked about it often enough around a campfire. The special relationship my parents had, the all-encompassing love they felt from their first moments together, a love that never dimmed. A marriage different from most of the unions we've witnessed, especially with the army. Troopers wedding solely for comfort some woman following the army. The women themselves who might acquire a succession of husbands, one after another as the predecessor was killed.'

'You can't fault the ladies too much, Hart. The women are resourceful, but they depend on their husband's connection to the army for billeting, food and transport. Widowed without that connection, a woman would be completely on her own, and most had few resources. So you are still holding out to experience that *coup de foudre*?'

Hart nodded. 'I am. I was forced to assume the title, but no one can force me into wedding someone who's merely "suitable"—' he spat out the word '—no matter how much I'm pressured about providing for the succession.'

'Then…you have no designs on Mrs Hambleden.'

'Designs?' he echoed, afraid for a moment his friend sensed his barely leashed longing. 'No! Not if you mean marriage.'

'Then you wouldn't mind if I…got to know her better?'

Unpleasant shock rocketed through him. 'You? Why would you do that?'

Rafe laughed. 'The usual reason. I find her both attractive and fascinating.'

Everything within him rose up in protest. 'You can't mean you'd want to…court her? That would be entirely unfair! She's already lost one soldier husband. It's beyond cruel even to suggest enticing her to take another. She sacrificed her bit for the nation, caring for him and other soldiers, waiting for him, agonising through every battle he fought in. Ultimately getting the devastating news that he'd been seriously injured. Staying behind as the army moved on, faithfully nursing him until his death. No, she's done enough! She deserves to remain safe, secure and protected in England, she and her son.'

Unmoved by this diatribe, Rafe said mildly, 'I'm not proposing to abduct her and carry her off to Portugal. But I'm not waiting for some magical bolt from the sky to inspire me with starry-eyed love.' Rafe held up a hand. 'Not that I'm denying such love happens. I hope it happens for you. But I've experienced a touch of ecstatic love before and I'd just as soon not do so again. I prefer a quieter, more rational path.

'Mrs Hambleden is lovely, intelligent, witty and to have followed the drum as she did, both courageous and resourceful. I like her very much and could easily see that attraction deepening into a satisfying, life-long affection. All I intend for the moment is to ask if she would write to me and let me call on her when I'm next in England.' He shook his head. 'I wish I had time to court her properly now, but I don't. Not on this visit.'

While Hart sat, too shocked to speak, Rafe continued, 'Though I admit, carrying her off to Portugal has immense appeal. The idea of returning from picket duty or battle on a day of pouring rain or a night of freezing cold to have a hot meal served by those sweet hands. And having that loveliness to embrace through the—'

'Enough!' Hart barked, cutting him off. 'Obviously, I can't forbid you see her. If she wishes to write to you, that's her own business. Just be careful. It's my responsibility as head of the family to watch out for her—and letting her hare off to face all the dangers of life on campaign again... well, I would be failing in my duty if I were enthusiastic about that.'

Rafe studied him a minute. 'She's just the sister of your late cousin's wife, isn't she? Not really a part of your "family". Not really *your* responsibility. Unless you've chosen to make her one.'

Hart didn't want to get into the complexities of how she'd cared for the estate and the widow, how she'd helped ease him into his role, supporting him every step of way, even when at the beginning she'd neither liked nor trusted him.

'A relative by connection is just as valid as one by blood,' he said stiffly.

'If you say so. Even so, the protection you offer still leaves her dependent on your charity and good will. Not to mention that of your wife when you do wed. Which isn't as secure as having a husband of her own to support her and provide for her son. I won't inherit a title, but I do have some money of my own, which would go to my wife if anything happened to me. Something apparently her late husband didn't offer her.'

Hart tried to find some objection to that argument. And couldn't.

'Well, I'll get off to see what mischief Charles is up to. See you at the ball tonight.'

'Very well,' Hart said, disgruntled and upset.

'And Hart—I think you are navigating troubled waters as well as any man could. I hope you find that special lady you're looking for.'

Hart nodded, an unsettling mix of conflicting emotions roiling in his chest. He loved his friend. He wanted only the best for Claire Hambleden. But he'd been thinking 'the best' would be for her to remain where he could continue as her friend, watching out for her well-being and that of her son.

If Rafe wanted to eventually beguile Claire Hambleden into wedlock, Hart didn't think he could wish him well.

Still disgruntled early that evening, as Hart left the library to return to his rooms to prepare for dinner, he spied the lady in question standing in the upstairs hallway, talking with the housekeeper.

While they chatted, Hart focused on Claire Hambleden. He hadn't needed Rafe's praise to appreciate how lovely she was…that wordless sensual connection hummed between them as fiercely as ever. Likewise, he appreciated her efficiency and competence—he'd seen evidence of that from his first day at Steynling Cross. Was he being unfair, selfishly wanting to keep her close?

But he hadn't stood in the way of her forming an attachment to someone else, he defended himself. Someone from society, someone *suitable*. A soldier about to return to war, even a man of character as excellent as Rafe, was not the best candidate to offer her lifelong support and protection.

Not of the kind he could offer.

Was he wrong to wait for the blinding strike of rapture he'd believed since childhood to be the only true measure of lasting love?

Rafe had shaken his certainty.

If he did come to doubt it, Rafe was correct. Standing

above him was a woman eminently capable of being a duchess. One who already enlivened his discussions, brightened his table and could fulfil every erotic daydream in his bed.

That conclusion left him feeling even more uncertain and unsettled.

But there was no confusion about the warmth that filled him when Claire Hambleden smiled at him as she dismissed the housekeeper and descended the stairs. Or about the intensity of desire her nearness evoked when she halted beside him.

'I see you are venturing out of Fortress Library,' she said. 'Sorry the house has been in such an uproar these last two days, but no such large-scale entertainment been done here, Mrs Reynolds informed me, since Fitzhugh's mother died. There was much to clean, dust, polish, unearth and rearrange. I want everything to be perfect for you tonight—and for the guests, of course.'

Looking away, she said, 'Wouldn't it be romantic if the lady you've been searching for were to appear tonight, at your very own ball? So you might fall in love during a dance, like Cinderella and her Prince?'

That sort of love was a fairy tale, she'd once claimed. Was she right? Except he knew it happened. He'd grown up basking in the reflected glow of it.

'As long as I don't afterwards have to go about town trying glass slippers on the feet of the ugly stepsisters.'

Chuckling, she said, 'I'm going up to fetch my own slippers—and gown—now. You're going up to dress as well?'

But as she looked at him, their gazes locked and her merry expression died.

Was she thinking—as he was, as he couldn't help it—of the two of them in a bedchamber, stripping down the outer layers of afternoon dress in preparation for donning evening wear?

She'd be in a fine, nearly transparent linen chemise that revealed the voluptuous contours of her body, her breasts barely covered. He, standing shirtless as he kicked off the pantaloons that concealed his desire for her. And there would be no dressing for dinner until after a passionate interlude fulfilled them both...

Maybe she *was* thinking of that, for a rosy hue lit her face as she jerked her gaze away. 'I...I assume your batman has your dinner dress prepared?' she asked, drawing them both back from fraught moment. 'You won't try to sneak down in uniform?'

'I thought appearing in it would make a fine farewell tribute to my friends, as they will be in dress uniform. Or there is another alternative.'

'Not the kilt again! You've been threatening me with that ever since I induced you to agree to hosting the ball.'

'Well, it is my ball and I *am* Scottish and I *am* the Duke. So can do whatever I want...can't I?'

'I already mentioned there are some limits on your powers,' she said drily. 'Besides, you're only *half*-Scottish and you told me family doesn't have a tartan.'

'Mama does have a distant connection to the Campbells. Close enough. I almost think you'll be disappointed if I don't wear it.'

'I know it will take an act of forbearance to refrain from thumbing your nose at all those who've been fawning over you.'

'Since if this half-Scot weren't a duke, most wouldn't give me the time of day, much less clamour for me to attend their parties and parade their marriable daughters in front of me. You told me you'd been an outsider, too. Don't you ever want to thumb your nose at all of them—so obnoxiously self-assured, as if they own the universe by right, as if all its workings should adjust themselves to their satisfaction?'

'As Fitzhugh thought it should,' she murmured.

'Exactly.'

'Growing up, I used to think so, too.'

'But you don't any longer?'

'Now I don't think so. I saw in the army how men from merchant families and tenant farms could exhibit the same courage, tenacity and persistence I always ascribed to high-born leaders. And then, there was the disillusionment of Fitzhugh.'

'Again, I'm so sorry for what he subjected you to. It was inexcusable.'

Her face twisted with remembered pain. Wanting to distract her from it, he said, 'I appreciate all you've done for my friends.'

'I've enjoyed having them here—and recalling memories of happier times.'

'I hope I've given you some memories of happier times here and at Steynling.'

'You have. And some regrets—which you know and understand only too well—but most of the memories will be happy.'

An odd pain pinged in his chest when she spoke like that, as if she were leaving. 'You must waltz with me tonight. Yes, yes, I will honour all the influential matrons you invited and all the silly debutantes. But I really only want to dance with you.'

He felt the truth of that deep within. Had he always felt it—or was it only Rafe, pointing out her perfections, offering her as alternative to his hazy dream of a wife, that sharpened his own perception of her?

'Well, I'd best go up.' With a smile, she was gone, a haze of rose perfume and gracefulness lightly tripping up the stairs.

Hart watched her go. Yes, he'd wear the formal dress

she insisted on. Yes, he'd dance and converse with all their guests. But as he told her, what he'd really be waiting for all evening was that waltz, when he could hold her in his arms even in the full glare of a ballroom.

Could he fend off having Rafe do the same?

A number of guests joined them for dinner, including Mrs Hambleden's parents, to whom Hart had been introduced when they called the day after his arrival in London. They'd not yet met for dinner, as they'd been unable as yet—Mrs Hambleden said drily—to co-ordinate their calendars.

The Duchess sat at the opposite end of the state dining table from him—observing proper protocol, her sister insisted again—with her parents and sister nearby, while his friends were placed near him, along with the most distinguished guests. Dispersed between were other leading lights of society, the Duchess's friend Lady Downing and Lord Telford near her, Viscount Stannington and several other members from White's at his end.

Much as he enjoyed his friends' engaging banter, he was really waiting for dinner to be over so he might chat with Mrs Hambleden. From the way Rafe's gaze often wandered down the table towards her, his friend was waiting for that, too.

Hart cursed the fact that at his own ball, he'd be forced as host to chat and dance with most of the guests. Whereas Rafe, attending only as a guest, would be free to monopolise Claire Hambleden. Would he?

His friend was an excellent soldier, a master tactician. Given the interest in the lady he'd expressed in the library, Hart bet he'd be laying the groundwork to lure her into committing to a correspondence that might continue and strengthen their relationship. Would she be amenable?

None of his business, Rafe would say. But Hart couldn't wait to talk with her and claim the waltz she'd promised. As the Duchess led the ladies away and the butler brought in the gentlemen's port, he ground his teeth and tried to summon patience.

Too many hours later, with dinner over and the ball in full swing, Hart felt he'd sufficiently fulfilled his obligations as host and could finally seek out the lady he'd been waiting for all evening.

Rafe had spent a good deal of time with her. Of course. He'd have been foolish not to, given his interest and the fact that he must leave on the morrow. Hart couldn't help resenting it, though. After sidestepping a matron eager to claim a dance for her daughter, pretending not to hear several voices summoning him, he paced towards where Claire Hambleden stood in the small salon adjacent to the ballroom, conversing with—of course, Rafe.

Was she smiling at him with particular interest? Hart wondered, inspecting her closely. No matter, as at a signal from him, the musicians began to tune up for a waltz. He walked over to them and bowed.

'Mrs Hambleden, I'm holding you to your promise. Sorry Rafe, but I'm going to carry her off.'

His friend gave an ironic lift of his brows. 'You're not sorry at all. But as Mrs Hambleden has been gracious enough to spend a good part of the evening with me, I can't be churlish enough to monopolise her completely.'

Hart held out an imperious arm. She looked down at it and back at his face—heaven knew what she read in his clenched-jaw expression—and placed her hand on it. 'I very much enjoyed chatting with you, Lieutenant.'

'The dance is beginning,' Hart reminded, with a none-too-gentle pull on her arm.

'My, so...*dukely*!' she said, looking up at him as he led her from the salon towards ballroom. 'Has someone been impugning the honour of Scotland? Did some maladroit young lady step on your toes? You seem uncommonly out of sorts. Or is it only that being host places you even more squarely at the centre of everyone's attention?'

'A little of all that. But mostly, because I've become spoilt being able to chat with you at dinner most days, able to solicit your opinion and compare notes on the company with you while riding to entertainments. Now it's practically midnight and this is my first opportunity to talk or dance with you. If I had to endure any more innocuous drivel spouted by another of the most "eligible" debutantes tonight, I swear I would have stormed out of the ballroom and returned in my kilt with a brogue to match.'

She laughed. 'I almost wish you had.'

'There's still time, so don't tempt me. Tynesley monopolised you enough, it's my turn. What do you think of him, by the way?'

'Lieutenant Tynesley? I see why you like him. Lieutenant Marsden is outrageously amusing, but one senses he never takes anything seriously. Tynesley is quieter, more observant, so...steady. A man one could count on no matter how difficult circumstances become. Not as immediately approachable, perhaps, but once he offers friendship and support, I expect he would be fiercely loyal and unwavering.'

Hart nodded. He wasn't surprised she'd formed such a good opinion of his friend. Rafe deserved it. Still, unable to help himself, he said, 'You find him...attractive?'

She angled a glance at him. 'Why do you ask?'

'Just curious. As you say, ladies tend to gravitate to Marsden, but you seemed to prefer Tynesley.'

'Well, Marsden is devoting himself mostly to amusing

my sister. So I must approve of any gentleman who pays attention to me when in my sister's vicinity.'

She hadn't really answered the question, but he didn't feel he could press the point without her wanting to know why. If Rafe hadn't yet made his serious interest known, Hart wasn't going to advance his agenda.

They reached the ballroom just in time to join the other couples stepping into the rhythm of the waltz.

Hart pulled her as close as he dared, delighting in the scent of her rose perfume, the warmth of her waist beneath his hand, the fingers clasped in his own. Yes, this was what he'd been waiting for, he thought exultantly as he twirled her at dizzying speed around the room. This closeness, the giddy pace that made the people around them, the room itself, blur into a haze, so that for these few moments it felt as if nothing existed but the two of them, wrapped in music.

Like breathing a deep lungful clean air again after surviving a battle, leaving behind the smoke, cinder and wreckage.

No need now for conversation and she attempted none. She seemed, like he did, to find simply moving so closely together through the hypnotic circles of the waltz too great a pleasure to spoil with words.

How could he let her go? To Rafe or anyone else. Was he being foolish, wishing for something that might never happen, overlooking the jewel right before him?

He wanted with keen urgency to slip with her out on to balcony and kiss her again. But at his own ball, he was under too much scrutiny to quietly disappear. Besides, if he did sneak away with her, tongues would wag. Some might already believe his attentions towards her exceeded what one would expect towards the woman who was merely a sister of the Duchess.

Unless he decided to take Rafe's advice, stop tilting at

windmills of romantic fantasy and begin courting her in earnest, he mustn't dishonour her by having society whisper he was offering only the same tawdry arrangement Fitzhugh tried to press on her.

But for now, he would push aside worries about finding a wife and how he was going to salvage his friendship with a woman who'd come to mean so much to him. Submerge these new doubts about whether he'd even been seeking the right sort of match.

He'd simply enjoy this moment, holding her in his arms.

He wished the music might go on timelessly, since he couldn't claim another waltz without inciting gossip. But if he couldn't dance with her again, he decided in the moment, he would keep her near him the rest of the evening, to converse, play cards with, and enjoy.

Those watching his every move could make what they liked of it.

Late that night, Claire drifted back into her room and over to the window, gazing out at the moonlit night. Though the beginning of the ball had been pleasant, Lieutenant Tynesley distracting her from the painful process of watching Hart sought after, flattered and danced with by the many females clamouring for his attention, the end of it had been…glorious, from the moment he swept her into that waltz.

Of the crumbs of attention she was allowed to devour, save only the forbidden pleasure of kissing him, waltzing was the most delicious. To be held so tantalisingly close, his gaze focused on her, his body brushing against hers, striking sparks at every sweeping turn…

Just as well they were watched by attentive, curious or jealous eyes throughout, which helped her hold in check the always simmering desire to lean up and kiss him again.

Then to her surprise, after the dance, he'd tucked her hand in his arm and kept her near him.

Walking her with him to chat with guests. Asking her to accompany him to visit with the political figures present, letting her direct the conversation so, he murmured, he might listen and learn. Taking her in to the second supper after midnight.

He'd seemed to have eyes for and interest only in her. Had his friend Tynesley's attentions made him jealous, prompting him to devote himself to her?

Were it Fitzhugh, she would think he had done so to draw her away from another gentleman and refocus her attention on him. But Hart wasn't an egotist like the late Duke.

Might the shock of his friend's particular regard have made him examine more closely his own feelings for her? Might he have suddenly recognised that what he felt for her, if not the sudden strike of love at first sight, was love none the less?

She pushed away the speculation as soon as it occurred. She didn't dare imagine he had come to love her as she did him; the disappointment if—when—that hope turned out to be fantasy would be too crushing.

She'd told him she hoped he would find his Cinderella, and perhaps that's who she had been tonight. Princess for one evening before her ball gown turned back into a servant's garb. There might never be a glass slipper for her to slip on her foot, but she'd have the memory of when, for a few golden hours, nothing in the world was real save only she and Hart. Just one glorious dream to sustain her.

Once she returned to her inevitable place among the ashes before the chill hearth of reality.

Chapter Eighteen

Claire was daydreaming in the hazy afterglow of the ball early the next morning when there was a rap on her door, followed, to her great surprise, by the entry of the Duchess.

Her sister was never out of bed this early. Springing up from her chair in alarm, Claire cried, 'Liliana! What is it? Has something happened? The children?'

'No, no everything is fine,' her sister assured her. 'Well, more than fine. Wonderful, in fact. I hope you don't mind I've invaded your room so early, but I just couldn't wait a moment longer!'

Whatever the news was, it must be good, she thought with relief. Her sister was beaming.

'I asked Wallace to have chocolate sent up. We can enjoy it while I tell you my news.'

'I'm much too anxious to wait on chocolate. Tell me at once!'

She took Claire's hands and drew her down on the sofa. 'Dearest Sister, no one could be more kind and loving. I'll never forget or repay the love and support you've given me these last two years! Were it not for you, I'd still be languishing on my bed back at Steynling.'

'It makes me so happy to see you moving on with life. Give credit to Fenniston, too, for encouraging you.'

'Yes, he was a tremendous help in boosting my confidence. Without the two of you, I would never have had the courage to come to London. Now, I'm so glad I did!'

Wallace knocked, Claire biting her tongue with impatience while the servant brought in the tray and curtsied herself back out. 'Out with it! I can't stand the suspense another minute.'

'You always assured me I was not meant to be a widow the rest of my life. I didn't believe you. But you were right. Oh, Claire, I'm going to be married!'

Of all the things Liliana might have said, that was the one Claire was least expecting—this soon in their London sojourn, anyway. 'M-married? To whom? When did you decide? Are you sure?'

Liliana laughed. 'Quite sure. To the dearest, kindest, most wonderful man! Lord Telford proposed at the ball last night, and I accepted!'

Telford?' Claire was shocked by the suddenness of it, but not at the sort of gentleman her sister had chosen.

'He's been so considerate and courteous from the very beginning. So supportive and protective! At first, I thought he was only being kind, but over the last few weeks, he's become ever more attentive. Then, when I feared he might have serious intentions, I tried to draw away. Because... well, you know I couldn't risk childbirth again. But when he offered, and I initially turned him down—tearfully, I fear, for until that moment I hadn't realised how much I wanted to accept—telling him I couldn't give him a child, he assured me it wouldn't matter! That he already has several children and an heir in robust good health.

'He said it would be his honour and privilege to cherish me the rest of his life. That he never again wanted me to live on charity in another's man's house, but be mistress of my own, for ever. Of course, he's only a baron, but quite wealthy, he assured me, so I will never lack for anything.

Oh, Claire, it was so…romantic! Never have I felt so special and valued, not even when Fitzhugh first came courting! Wedding a duke's heir was a *grand* match, but my union with Telford will be something even better—a marriage of tender love and genuine respect!'

Claire sat, frozen, nodding as her sister enthused about her fiancé for several more paragraphs. Finally, when Liliana stopped for breath, she asked the question screaming in her head since the minute she'd heard the news. 'When do you intend to wed?'

'As soon as possible! We could call the banns, but I really don't want to wait the month that would require. Telford said he rather not delay being able to call me his very own! He's off this morning to fetch a special licence. I must talk with Mama later today, but I hope to have a small private ceremony at their town house within the week. It would be more suitable to have it there rather than here, don't you think?'

A week. She would have to sort out her own future, hers and Alex's, in just a week?

'Will you remain in London after the ceremony?' Claire asked, still trying to wrap her mind around all the implications her sister's news had for her life.

'No, Telford wants to whisk me away to the country to tour his estates—his is quite an old barony, you know, and he owns properties in several counties. He said we could honeymoon in the Highlands, or on the South Downs, or in the Lakes. I just need to decide. Perhaps you can help me later—all sound lovely.'

'Maybe that's something to decide with your fiancé,' Claire said drily.

Liliana giggled. 'Yes, you're probably right. Oh, I shall need a few new gowns, but little else! He said the house-keepers at the various properties are all very efficient, so

I wouldn't have to concern myself with domestic matters. I need only grace his table, sing for him and charm his guests.' Her sister sighed. 'After the last few years at Steynling—oh, it all sounds like heaven! Well, I must away. I shall dress and go see Mama immediately, so we may put our heads together about the wedding.'

She hopped up, gave Claire a hug and danced out.

Leaving her sitting with her cup of now-cold chocolate that tasted like ashes.

Cinderella's ashes indeed.

She tried to order the thoughts flying around in her head. The first, most important, was that once her sister married, she could not remain at Fenniston House. Or return to Steynling Cross.

An ironic smile curved her lips. She had thought it would be Hart's marriage that forced her to decide what to do about her future. She hadn't expected to be blindsided by her sister's.

Her once again wholly self-absorbed sister, who apparently had yet to give a thought to how her plans would affect Claire's position.

She'd expected to have weeks, maybe months, before she lost the magic of Hart's company. Now she had days.

Unless…unless he truly had deeper feelings for her.

She thrust the thought out of her mind. Nothing about her unsuitability to become his Duchess—her lack of dowry, high rank or important family connections—had changed. She needed to make other, surer plans.

She needed to pay a call on Mama.

Predictably, when she called late that morning, she could hardly fit in a word in as her mother enthused over their tea at the prospect of Liliana's upcoming wedding.

'I *knew* she was too young to remain a widow! Of course,

she won't have the same precedence she had as Duchess, but the Telford barony is one of the oldest in England and he's extremely wealthy. All in all, it's a good match.'

Only then did it occur to her mother to enquire about Claire's future. 'Will you stay with her once they return from the honeymoon? She's always counted on your help, and it's not as if you have any duties elsewhere.'

'Stay with her? I hardly think her now husband would be pleased to see his sister-in-law sitting on his doorstep when he returns from his wedding trip.'

'Oh, nonsense. Another capable of pair of hands is always welcome. Liliana isn't accustomed to dealing with household affairs, as you know.'

'Telford has been widowed for some time, and assured Liliana that his several properties are all managed by competent housekeepers. She's not anticipating having to deal with domestic matters.'

'Then what do you intend to do? You can't remain at Fenniston House…and much as we love you, you know we can't house you here with the child. There's no nursery or staff who could attend to him.'

Claire took a deep breath. 'I had hoped to take him with me back to Whitley House. You and Father seldom go there, so we wouldn't be in the way, and as you know it's quite large enough to accommodate all of us whenever you choose to visit.'

Looking uncharacteristically uncomfortable, her mother said, 'Well, ordinarily that would be acceptable but…but I'm afraid you can't return to Whitley. I'd been quite bursting to tell you the news, but wanted to wait until everything was finalised, which it just was this week. Your father is to stand for Parliament, which you know has long been his dream! Lord Sidmouth knows of a pocket borough where he will propose him as the candidate, so he'll almost certainly be elected. But such things as campaigns and sitting in Parliament are…expensive and we've long since used up my dowry funds maintaining this London residence. The short of it is, your father has leased out Whitley House. The new tenants intend to take up residence immediately.'

Claire swallowed hard, her first, best plan just disintegrating before her eyes.

'Do you know what you'll do?' her mother said, an atypical expression of maternal anxiety on her face.

Which didn't last long; before Claire could decide what to reply, her mother patted her hand. 'Well, you'll figure out something. You always do.'

'Yes, Mama, I always do,' she echoed, unable to mask the bitterness in her tone. 'Thank you for the tea.'

'Of course, darling. You will be helping Liliana with the wedding plans, won't you? I would offer to assist, but with your father getting ready to campaign, I—'

'Don't worry, Mama. I'll take care of her.'

Equilibrium restored, her capable daughter stepping in to allow her to focus as always on her husband, her mother smiled. 'Well, I shall see you at the wedding, then, shan't I?'

Dread beginning to seep in, Claire didn't remember what she replied or even how she made it out the door and back on to the street. But as she stood, trembling, to summon a hackney, she knew there was only one other place she could go.

One she'd managed to avoid ever since Alexander's death. But with no other alternative, for Alex's sake, she would have to call on the Earl of Lyndenham, her late husband's older brother.

Half an hour later, Claire paced the grand parlour of the Earl's town house on Brook Street. She'd called without notice or an appointment, so having to wait to be escorted into the Earl's august presence wasn't surprising. Though she couldn't help wondering if part of the delay was deliberate.

Alexander's family hadn't been pleased when he, a younger son with no land, money or title, had married a girl with only a modest dowry. Their chilly politeness at her wedding had made her eager to speed away from England and never see them again.

Since that day, she'd seen the Earl only once, when she called on him after returning to England to inform him of Alexander's place of rest in the little cemetery outside Fuentes de Oñoro. His signet ring, along with his sword, were the only objects of value she'd kept, the proceeds from selling the rest thankfully enough to pay their passage home. The Earl had been frosty then, too—perhaps suspecting she intended to beg him to take in his deceased brother's little family. She'd been fiercely glad that, thanks to Liliana's invitation to Steynling Cross, she hadn't had to ask.

Now she would have to.

After pacing for another fifteen minutes, the butler finally returned to usher her into the Earl's library, where he sat behind his massive desk, his expression as she walked in as stony as the sculpted lion paperweight securing the documents on its corner.

Girding herself, she curtsied. He didn't rise in response.

So that was how this would go. After an exchange of meaningless pleasantries, he said, 'So why have you come to see me?'

In a few brief sentences, Claire related that her sister's intention to remarry, which would mean she must leave Steynling and that due to her father's campaign, her childhood home was unavailable, nor did her parents have space to house her in London.

'I suppose you have come here to ask for my charity?'

He shook his head. 'I tried to warn Alexander what an imprudent match he was set on! But there's no reasoning with impetuous youth. I suppose we can take the boy in. My brother's son, after all.'

Claire swallowed hard. 'And what of me?'

'Are you not going to remain with your sister? I understand you've been taking care of her since she failed to produce an heir several times.'

'As I just informed you, she is to remarry. I can't remain with her. I could go elsewhere, but I should like to stay near my son.'

For a long, silent moment while she seethed with suppressed anger and humiliation, Lydenham stared at her. 'I expect we could find a place for you. My wife's elderly aunt has been complaining about her companion of late. Another poor relation. If you tend her, you'd be at Coldwater Manor, which is not far from Lyme Hill, where the boy could join my own sons until he's old enough for Eton.'

Though the words were like hot coals burning her tongue, she said, 'I would be most appreciative.'

'It's settled, then. Consult with my housekeeper about arrangements to transport the boy to Lyme Hill. I'll have my wife write to her aunt. She'll let you know how to proceed.' Staring at her, he shook his head again. 'Younger sons.'

'My lord,' Claire said, rising to curtsy and then walked out, back rigid.

Once on the street outside, Claire paused to take a deep breath, trying to contain her anguish and burning, impotent fury. Were it not for Alex, she would have hired herself out as a housekeeper before subjecting herself to that humiliation.

But a housekeeper could do nothing for her son. The Earl could guarantee that he would be well housed, well fed, well educated and eventually established in the aristocratic world into which he'd been born.

Maybe she'd take that housekeeper job later, once he was grown and didn't need her any longer.

For now, she had packing to do and a wedding to prepare for.

And she had to break the news to Hart.

Chapter Nineteen

'She's to marry? That's sudden, isn't it?' Hart asked after a subdued Claire Hambleden tracked him down in his library.

He'd felt a lift of his depressed spirits as she walked in. Parting from his friends this morning as they left to return to Portugal had been solemn affair. He'd enjoyed immensely the revival of their comradeship here in London, which made the unspoken knowledge that this morning might be the last time he saw one or both cut even deeper.

He found it hard to face returning alone to a world he didn't want while the friends he cherished returned to the one he did want, without him. But shock at her unexpected news had distracted him from those melancholy reflections.

'I suspected Lord Telford might be interested in her. Stannington had no trouble recruiting him to watch over her at her first ball. When I think back on it now, he was always a guest at the entertainments we attended and at Lady Downing's more select small parties. Their attachment happened more quickly than I'd anticipated, but I always thought she'd marry again. An older gentleman, someone who already has an heir, is ideal. She might not survive another pregnancy.'

Hart lifted his brows. 'Her husband might not be pleased about a *marriage blanche*.'

'There are ways to enjoy intimacy and still avoid conception.'

His brows lifted higher. 'Indeed? You are acquainted with these ways?'

Feeling her face colour, she stumbled, 'Well, y-yes. Because I conceived so easily, we didn't want to risk another pregnancy while campaigning. There are ways of giving pleasure while…adjusting the final act —' Noticing him grinning at her, she stopped abruptly. 'You are enjoying this!'

He chuckled. 'You do look adorable when you're angry.' Then his smile faded as the implications of her sister's marriage suddenly dawned on him. 'When is she to be wed?'

'In a week.'

Shock went through him. 'So soon? What will you do afterwards?'

'I can't remain at Fenniston House, of course.'

He wished that weren't true, but he knew it was. 'Will you move to your parents' town house?'

She shook her head. 'They have no facilities there for Alex, and I'd not go without him.'

'You'll take him and Bella to one of the Duchess's new husband's properties and watch over them there?'

'I don't believe that's advisable. Move in with newlyweds?'

'Then you'll return to Whitley?' he asked, trying to make sense of her options. 'You once said you might go back there if your sister no longer had need of you.'

She looked away. 'That won't be possible either. My father has let Whitley House and the new tenants arrive shortly.'

He shook his head, appalled. 'I don't expect your late husband left you enough to set up your own establishment?' he said, compelled to ask, though he was certain he already knew the answer.

'He did not. However, I have spoken with the Earl of Lyndenham, his elder brother. He's agreed to take Alex into his household with his own sons.'

It took him a minute to comprehend what she *hadn't* said. 'And what of you?'

'I've been offered a position as companion to his wife's elderly aunt.'

'A *companion*?' he burst out, but she held up a hand to halt him before he could launch into the tirade she must have sensed was coming.

'I don't expect Lyndenham to support me. They never offered to after Alexander's death. But being raised alongside the sons of an earl, Alex will have every advantage. Be sent with his cousins to school. Be found a position like my father's when he's finished with university. It's a good opportunity for him.'

'What of you? Buried away in the country at the beck and call of some old biddy?'

She attempted a smile. 'I expect my herbal expertise will be useful. It's not…ideal, I admit. But I can't expect to hang on Liliana's sleeve for ever.'

'Has she even asked you to?' Her silence after that query was enough answer. 'After all you've done for her, she will just…cast you adrift?'

'She's always been fairly self-absorbed—not her loveliest trait. In any event, I'd rather earn my crust as a companion than remain with Liliana as a poor relation. This is better for Alex. Living with the Earl's family, he has a much brighter future. That's all that matters. Now, if you'll excuse me, I'd better get started with the planning.'

She walked out, leaving him staring after her, furious on her behalf at her self-centred sister, her oblivious parents, her indifferent in-laws. How could they not recognise her worth?

It would be impossible for her to remain with him once her sister married; even he, much as he disparaged society's rules, understood that. So in a breathtakingly short time, he was going to lose his guide to London, his tutor about the estate and the one person who'd understood how difficult he'd found it to accept his role as Duke. The person who'd eased and assisted him whenever possible. Who'd amused him with her wit, impressed him with her intelligence and competence, constantly tantalised his senses with her smouldering passion.

He got up to pace around his desk. What was he to do without her? Coming on the heels of having his best friends leave for Portugal, the idea of losing her too yawned ahead like a bottomless pit of loneliness and isolation from which he knew not how to emerge.

With what was he to replace her friendship and support? Stannington was a good enough fellow, but they were hardly close. He could barely tolerate conversing with most of the ladies he'd had to talk to or dance with. He was nowhere close to discovering the lady he could fall in love with.

Then he remembered Rafe's advice, and everything fell into place.

If none of the 'suitable' debutantes appealed, why not marry Claire? With the Duchess wed again, society might find his marrying her sister a bit less shocking, and his choice certainly wouldn't hurt her sister. Though he felt some dismay over abandoning his cherished dream of falling in love, in every other way, wedding her made perfect sense.

He would be able to keep her permanently by his side. A woman who'd already impressed, inspired, challenged and delighted him. Ah, ecstasy unleashed, he'd finally be able to indulge the passion that had sparked and fizzed between them since their first meeting. Just imagining claiming her completely made his pulse pound and his head dizzy.

Most importantly, a beautiful, valiant, admirable woman would finally be given a place worthy of her. He'd see that she was cherished and cared for, her son given every advantage she could want. And if…when…they had children of their own, he'd have an heir of whom he could be proud and she another son to delight her.

He ran the arguments through his head again, just to make sure in his enthusiasm—brilliant images of taking her to the bedchamber did somewhat impair rational thought—he wasn't overlooking some impediment.

But after reviewing all the circumstances several more times, he reached the jubilant conclusion that wedding Claire Hambleden would solve all their problems, his and hers.

Now he needed to find her and propose before she got too far into her planning.

It was possible that at first, as she could occasionally be argumentative and stubborn, she might turn him down. But she was too intelligent and practical to resist for long recognising all the advantages.

And he wouldn't mind a bit having to kiss her into agreement.

He discovered her directing a footman to bring trunks down from the attic. Once the man had deposited his burden outside her door, leaving them alone, he turned to face her. 'You must have a thousand things to do, but there's something urgent we must discuss. Now. If you'd walk in the garden with me?'

Where they were unlikely to be either seen or overheard.

Where, if the interview went as he hoped, he'd be able for the first time to kiss and caress her thoroughly without any trace of guilt.

She'd avoided looking at him directly, but at this, she glanced at his face. Apparently reading aright that he wouldn't be put off, she nodded. 'Very well. But I can only spare a few moments.'

'I won't keep you long.' Not a promise he intended to keep if everything went well. Little eddies of desire coursed through him at the possibilities.

But after she'd gathered her shawl and walked into the garden with him, halting by the first bench out of view from the house, Hart found himself suddenly at a loss for words.

After a few minutes of silence, she prompted, 'You had something urgent to discuss?'

'Y-yes. I was…quite disturbed by your news earlier. Oh, happy for the Duchess, of course. But concerned about what you tell me is planned for your own future. So concerned, I cannot help but intercede to try to change it.'

This was sounding awkward even to his own ears, but then he'd not awakened this morning with the expectation of making someone an offer of marriage. Thinking it would be better to just get it over with, he dropped to one knee. 'Claire Hambleden, would you do me the honour of becoming my wife?'

She stared at him for a long moment, going pink, then white, then pink again. After opening and closing her lips several times, she said at last, 'I believe in such circumstances, I'm supposed to first thank you for the compliment of your proposal. But I cannot accept it. Now, if you'll excuse me, I have…' Her voice trailing off, she turned to head back to the house.

'Wait!' Hart cried, catching her elbow. 'Why? Why won't you marry me?'

She pressed her lips together, as if she were harbouring under strong emotion. 'I understand why you've offered, and I'm…very touched by your concern. I know you want the best for me and for Alex. Granted, a duke might have a slight advantage over an earl in what he could offer my son, but not a significant one. As for me, I know you respect me, that you would always treat me with kindness and consideration. For almost any other single female in London, that would be enough. But it's not for me.'

'You'd truly prefer to be companion to some old woman than be mine?' Hart cried, stung.

'Had things turned out differently—had Liliana not become attached so quickly—I would happily have remained here as your companion for the rest of the Season, perhaps even beyond. Remained your friend and advisor until you met the lady you've been searching for, the one with whom you could fall in love completely. I still hope for you to find her. And when you do, I don't want to be your competent, convenient wife, running your house and breeding your sons while you mourn the love you can never wed. Can you vow you feel that sort of love for me?'

While he fumbled for words, she shook her head sadly. 'I didn't think so. Which means there's nothing else to be said. I appreciate your kindness. But I cannot marry you.'

With that, she left him staring after her and walked back to the house.

For the next several days, they avoided each other, she not appearing at breakfast, Hart dining at his club while he tried to decide what to do next. Despite telling himself it was a possibility, he hadn't really expected she would turn him down—the advantages of marrying him for her son alone would be enough to convince her.

An earl's sponsorship would probably be sufficient,

though. He was still insulted she'd think fetching and carrying for a querulous old woman preferable to remaining at his side.

Not to mention the blazing physical connection she was forfeiting. She'd not even given him a chance to try to kiss her into submission.

But her question—did he love her the way he'd anticipated loving a wife?—always stopped any further indignant reflection. He hadn't fallen in love with her at first sight and couldn't pretend to either of them that he had.

So what should he do now? Let her move forward into the future she seemed to prefer? Press her again to accept him, even though he couldn't return the right answer to that question?

He didn't really want her just as an amusing, competent companion and a passionate bed-mate...did he?

The third evening after his failed proposal, Hart found himself dragged to a ball he hadn't been able to avoid by an annoyingly cheerful Stannington, who promised to introduce him to the stunning daughter of a diplomat, a viscount who'd just returned from being posted abroad. The girl had looks, a fat dowry and having lived in foreign parts, should possess a sophistication Stannington thought would appeal to his finicky friend, who had already dismissed from consideration most of the desirable females in the Marriage Mart.

With the ladies of Fenniston House occupied with planning the wedding, both had sent their regrets to upcoming various social events. Lord Telford showed up at the house every day to confer with his bride, and Claire Hambleden seemed to spend most of her time at her father's town house or packing, preparing for her sister's nuptials and their removal from Fenniston House.

As Hart accompanied Stannington through the receiving line at the ball, he realised how much he missed having the sisters with him. The Duchess, to watch over and protect. Claire, to enjoy her company and to tease until those icy blue eyes flashed.

After mechanically greeting his hostess, he was smiling slightly at the memory of those eyes when Stannington walked up, a stunning brunette on his arm. 'Miss Beauford, may I introduce the Duke of Fenniston?'

'Your Grace,' the girl said, curtsying deeply.

'Why don't you take a turn about the room with him?' Stannington suggested, flashing Hart a smile. Mentally damning his overly helpful friend, Hart could do nothing but say, 'It would be my great pleasure.'

Miss Beauford was lovely, witty, intelligent, well read and well travelled. A skilled conversationalist, she elicited Hart's opinion about Lisbon, the Portuguese, the progress of the war and how he suspected Wellington meant to win it. In short, she was everything Claire Hambleden told him he needed in a duchess.

And gazing into her large green eyes, scanning the impressive figure well displayed in her low-cut gown, he felt... nothing.

Nothing but a yearning for a sharp-tongued, argumentative female who was entirely undeferential to his opinions. He realised that in all his London soirées, he'd not met anyone who appealed to him like Claire, who fired his blood like Claire, who could make him laugh or warm his heart like Claire.

The idea that she would soon be gone and he would never see her again filled him with desolation.

His circuit of the room with the eminently 'suitable' Miss Beauford complete, Hart bowed himself away. With neither the card room nor the dance floor appealing, he ignored the greetings and invitations offered him as he stalked across the floor, headed down the hallway in the opposite direction of the brightly lit entertainment rooms and found the library, which he'd remembered from a previous visit had doors that led on to a balcony.

His memory being accurate, he soon strode out into the cool evening air. Music and conversation floated towards him from the terrace outside the ballroom, where a number of couples were strolling and chatting. He smiled, remembering the time he'd coerced Claire into waltzing with him with the threat of hauling her out to such a terrace and kissing her.

How he wished she was at his side this moment so he might draw her close, even if he wasn't allowed to kiss her. His confusion, anger and annoyance faded to a deep loneliness.

And as he gazed at the distant couples on the ballroom terrace, he suddenly realised that while he'd been waiting for the dramatic strike of a *coup de foudre*, a quiet but ever-deepening, no less profound love for Claire had been silently building, until it now completely filled his heart.

He didn't need to *fall* in love; he was already in love. And he knew with a deep, sure confidence that he loved the woman who'd become indispensable to him as much as he would ever have loved the mythical lady with whom he'd hoped to fall in love with at first sight.

He'd been devastated as well as angry after Claire refused him, feeling certain that letting her go was wrong. Now excitement filled him to seek her out, confess that he'd been a stupid fool who hadn't recognised the truth in his own heart, and that he was ready to offer her all the love she deserved. With no worry that he might some day fall for someone else.

Which also made him recognise that in his shambles

of a declaration, he'd made no mention of his feelings at all—not even *affection*.

What a nodcock! No wonder she'd turned him down. She'd probably had more passionate invitations to dance.

But now that he realised he did in fact love her... He was certain she cared for him. Coax her to wed him, and he would build on that base—aided by ardent seduction and all the tempestuous lovemaking she'd allow, to make sure she grew to love him as well and never regretted accepting his offer of companionship over that of Lyndenham's old aunt.

After all, he already knew she was quite susceptible to the amorous invitations he'd offer her.

Hurrying off the balcony, stopping only long enough to bid his hostess farewell, Hart made his way back to Fenniston House.

Chapter Twenty

It was nearing midnight when Claire returned from her parents' town house. An evening that had been solitary; Liliana had accompanied her fiancé to a private dinner with his friends, her parents had been out attending a political affair, and Hart, she knew, was at a ball.

He wouldn't return for several more hours, so now she was back at Fenniston House, she could refresh herself with a glass of wine in the library, her body tired from packing boxes and unpacking the champagne glasses to be used for her sister's reception.

Though the real reason, her mind informed her sharply, for choosing the library was so she might breathe in the subtle scent of Hart's shaving soap that lingered in the space he used most often. Wrap herself in the sense of his presence that filled the room in which he'd spent much time reading. Where they'd often conferred.

Before Liliana got engaged and her world fell apart.

She'd been carefully avoiding Hart, knowing how hard it would be to resist the temptation to accept him if he persisted in his suit. But she would not, *would not*, once again become someone's convenient second choice. She'd done that—twice. And it hurt too much.

More than never seeing him again? her heart whispered.

Not sure she could keep answering that enquiry in the

affirmative, her only option was to empty her mind of all thought, deaden her heart to all feelings, and leave as quickly as she could. The very day of her sister's wedding, she'd take Alex off to her brother-in-law's estate and remain there until the position with his wife's aunt was arranged.

Her melancholy gaze focused on the fire, she only belatedly heard the footsteps in the hallway. Before she could spring up, Hart himself came striding in.

'Just the lady I wanted to see.'

She ought to nod and smile politely and walk out. But she seemed to be frozen in place.

He crossed the room and took her limp hand in his. She couldn't find the words to object.

'First let me apologise.'

'Apologise?' she echoed, finally finding her voice.

'For making you such a hash of a declaration. Oh, I was angry—and hurt—when you refused me. But I've come to understand why you had to.'

Trying to armour herself against any new argument, she said, 'Nothing else you say will make any difference.'

'Oh, but it should. "A full heart lied never", and mine is full—with love for you. I do love you. I burn for you. I don't want to live without you. Please put me out of my misery, and say you'll marry me.'

Anguished, she pulled her fingers away. 'Ah, so you figured out you'd omitted any mention of affection in your first proposal, did you? Don't try to distract me with another Scottish saying! And you don't need to remind me of the passion you can elicit. But affection isn't love. And passion…doesn't mean love either.'

'How can you believe that? When our mere touch—'

'From experience!' she burst out. 'My late husband gave every evidence of loving me while we revelled in the ecstasy of completion. But I never claimed his heart. The evening before his death, I spied him gazing at a miniature of my sister...hopeless longing in his eyes.'

She gave a self-deprecating laugh. 'We'd begun with a marriage of convenience, but I'd come to believe he loved me, you see. As I'd come to love him. But I was wrong. And then there was Fitzhugh—again. Seeming so kind, so compassionate. But in the end, wanting to use me as a brood mare for his own ends. I know that's not what you want, but I'm done with being *convenient*, a capable woman who performs all a wife's duties, warms a man's bed and provides him an heir. I deserve more. I won't settle for less.'

'You do deserve more. Can't you see—that's what I'm pledging to give you!'

'Only because you know I won't agree to wed you unless you do.'

He stared at her, studying her distraught face. 'You don't believe me.'

She shook her head, willing the tears not to fall.

'If you don't believe my words and won't allow me to kiss you, how can I convince you?'

'You can't.' Unable to take any more, she jumped up and ran from the room.

Safe in her chamber, heart pounding and spirit shredded, she threw herself on the bed. She didn't believe him. She didn't dare believe him. Being wrong—again—would destroy her. She couldn't take that risk.

She would simply need to survive the week until Liliana's wedding and she would be gone. And have the rest of her life to figure out how to exist without him.

Once again Hart was left to gaze after Claire, the memory of her grieving, pain-filled eyes haunting him.

After so many betrayals—her husband's, Fitzhugh's, her

sister's—small wonder his sudden conversion hadn't convinced her. No matter how genuine it was.

So how might he convince her?

For having realised he truly loved her, he wanted no other woman to fill his life and his bed. And he wasn't about to give up.

She did deserve more than his easy words and easier kisses. She needed action, some tangible sign that would convince her of the sincerity of both.

What was nearest to her heart, her greatest concern? Her son's welfare, undoubtedly. What else did she want more than anything?

I never belonged... I was always an outsider.

After all her years tending her parents' manor, improvising on campaign, overseeing Steynling, she craved a place of her own where she belonged and that belonged to her and her son. Where all the effort and care she devoted to it would benefit them, not some indifferent owner.

Hart sprang up, pacing the library, thinking. A frontal assault hadn't worked. Maybe stealth would serve better. He'd outflank her and hope that for her happiness and his own, the tactic would succeed.

The afternoon before her sister's wedding, Claire made one last inspection of her bedchamber. Her trunk and the children's were packed; she'd agreed to take Alex and Bella to Lord Telford's Lake District estate and watch them until the newlyweds returned from their wedding trip. Then she'd take Alex to Lyme Hill before proceeding to the aunt's manor.

She would probably see Hart just once more, at the wedding tomorrow. After her refusal of his second proposal, he'd abruptly left London, not informing anyone where he intended to go or how long he'd be gone. But she didn't think he'd miss Liliana's wedding.

His disappearance should have given her an opportunity to begin hardening her heart to his absence. It hadn't. The only way she found the impending separation bearable was to not think about it at all.

She had years of practice in pushing from her mind things too painful to contemplate.

A knock on the door, followed by the entrance of the butler, pulled her from her gloomy thoughts. 'What is it, Tompkins?'

'A gentleman is waiting in the library for you.'

'Who is it?' she asked, wondering who it could possibly be. The only gentleman recently who'd indicated an interest in her was Hart's friend Lieutenant Tynesley. And he was back in Portugal.

'I think you'll need to see for yourself, ma'am.'

Surely it wasn't one of his army friends with bad news! As alarmed as she was mystified, Claire followed Tompkins to the library, hurried in—and stopped short when she spied Hart standing by the hearth.

His heart thudding with anxiety and anticipation, Hart watched Claire, his darling beloved Claire, walk in.

'W-what…w-why…?' she stuttered.

'I wasn't sure you'd come down if you knew it was me waiting to see you.'

She stiffened. 'I'm not a coward. I wouldn't avoid facing you.'

'No, you're far from a coward. Which is why, before all the excitement tomorrow, I need to give you something—something you certainly deserve.'

'A tongue-lashing for refusing you again?' she asked wryly.

He gave her a soft smile. 'No, I can only applaud your refusal to settle for less than being cherished as you deserve. Another thing you deserve, after working your whole life tending the property of others, is something that belongs to you alone.'

He walked over and handed her a document.

She stared down at the parchment. 'What's this?'

'Look it over.'

She broke the seal and unfolded it. 'The deed to… Highgrave Manor?'

'It's a small property with acreage about the size of Whitley House. You've competently managed property far larger, so I have no doubt you can handle it. Smaller than Steynling, it shouldn't require all your time to keep in order, and the income should be sufficient to allow you to spend the Season in London, if you like, or travel to visit your sister. I've inspected it. There's a fine kitchen garden you can fill with your favourite herbs.'

While she stared at him blankly, as if hearing his words but unable to make sense of them, he continued, 'I've settled a sum on Alex, enough to hire a tutor and provide for his education at Eton, if you choose to send him there, and later at university. I promise to assist him in finding a position when he's of an age to choose one.'

She looked up at him, her expression incredulous. 'You can't do this!'

'I'm a duke, I can do anything, don't you keep telling me? Besides, it's already done. You pressed me some time ago to consult with the estate solicitor, so I was already aware of which properties are entailed, which are mine to dispose of as I choose.'

'But…but I can't possibly accept this!'

He shrugged. 'If you prefer to become a companion to

your brother-in-law's aunt, have your son taken away and consigned to the schoolroom with his cousins, you're certainly free to do that. The property remains yours, whether you live in it or not, and Alex's settlement is already on deposit at the bank.'

'But…why? I'm not your responsibility, and you owe me nothing!'

'I offered my passion—you spurned it. I confessed my love—you didn't believe it. I couldn't think of anything else to offer that might convince you. But you can't disregard this. I want to make life easy for you, lift every burden from your shoulders. I wanted to do that by keeping you at my side as my wife, sharing my life, delighting me with your wit, firing me with your passion, challenging me to be the best man I can be. You've refused to grant me that blessing.

'But if I must live without you, I wanted to at least know that you have every material thing you might need. Though I will be desolate, it will offer some comfort to know you are safe, sharing your life with your beloved son, not dependent for survival on the whims or goodwill of anyone but yourself.'

Taking a shuddering breath, she looked up at him uncertainly. 'Are you trying to force my hand?'

'No force. As I said, this is all done, a fait accompli. Now you never need be dependent again on anyone else. Not even me.'

Still looking uncertain, she said, 'Then…you do love me?'

He took the hand holding the document and kissed it. 'My father used to say of my mother "She's a drap o' my dearest blude". You are all of mine, all my heart and life's blood. I'm not trying to force, cajole or trick you. But if you will accept the truth of my love, accept *me*, I'd be everlastingly thankful.'

* * *

Still shocked and disbelieving, Claire stared from Hart to the document she held in her nerveless fingers. An estate of her own. An income for Alex. A property she could manage for their benefit, not anyone else's. A place where they belonged and from which they could never be cast out.

She swallowed hard, a tear sliding unnoticed down her cheek.

It was if Hart had stared into her soul and seen her deepest fears. Understood her most precious but, she'd thought, impossible dreams. And fulfilled them all.

A soulmate indeed.

His love so selfless, he could offer this priceless gift with the promise that if she preferred, he would hand it over and walk out of her life.

Brushing away the tear, she said, 'So… I truly am first in your heart, before anyone else? Even the girl you wished to fall in love with?'

'You are the only one in my heart. The only one I could ever wish for or imagine loving.'

She'd been disappointed and deceived so often, she could still scarcely believe the words.

But in her hand she held the tangible proof.

As if he sensed her wavering, Hart said, 'Won't you reconsider, my only love?'

Hart, by her side for ever. Teasing, cajoling, delighting with his passion. Sharing moments large and small. Warmth, friendship, perhaps children. A true home.

Loving her and her only.

All she need do to claim what she'd longed for all her life was say 'yes'.

In a flash of brilliant joy, she let go of doubt and uncertainty. 'Maybe I don't mind Scottish sayings so much after all. Yes, *yes*, I'll accept your love—and you.'

With an exultant cry, Hart seized her in his arms. Laughing with sheer elation, she tilted up her chin for his kiss.

Epilogue

$\mathcal{B}$eing a duke did have its advantages, Hart thought, as two days later he waited outside their parish church near Fenniston House, Grosvenor Chapel in Mayfair, for the arrival of the clergyman who would perform the wedding ceremony that would make Claire Hambleden his wife. He'd visited the archbishop's office the very afternoon he won Claire's acceptance, requesting—and receiving—a special licence to allow them to wed immediately.

He'd proceeded from there to track down the vicar of the parish church and persuaded him to perform the service. Not wanting to overshadow the Duchess's great day, with Claire's approval, they'd set the date for the day after Liliana wed Telford.

But in a move that frankly surprised him, once she heard of her sister's impending marriage, the normally self-absorbed Liliana announced she and Telford would delay leaving on their honeymoon so they might be among the small party of witnesses to celebrate their wedding.

How oddly things turned out. He'd experienced the hardship, inconvenience and regret of giving up his army career to assume the burden of an inheritance he'd never wanted. But that inconvenience and that burden led him to Claire, whom he might otherwise never have encountered. Even if he had served in the army until the war's end and gone adventuring as he'd originally planned, life without her now seemed unthinkable.

At the soft sound of the door opening, Hart turned. His heart leapt and joy filled him as Claire slipped in, resplendent in a fashionable blue gown that accented her eyes. Those icy blue eyes that had captured him from the first.

'My beautiful bride,' he murmured, going to her.

Smiling, she put a finger to her lips. 'Don't scold! I know seeing the bride before the wedding is a breach of decorum even more shocking than our unseemly haste in wedding,' she said as Hart pulled her close for a kiss. 'I suppose there's some Scottish saying about it, auguring bad luck for the marriage—but spare me.'

Chuckling as he released her, he said, 'You are my luck. And all of it's good. You are sure, though, you don't want to delay and plan some "grand wedding befitting a duke"? Or be married at your parents' parish church?'

She shook her head. 'A duke is *too* grand for the vulgarity of a large London reception—though we must have a party for all the tenants at Steynling Cross when we return.'

'Still instructing me,' he teased.

She wrinkled her nose at him. 'And my parents are leaving right after the ceremony. When I informed Mother we were to marry,' she continued, her tone turning dry, 'she advised waiting until after they return from Father's campaign trip so I could be wed "properly" from their house.' Shaking her head as if to cast off any negative emotion, she gave him a brilliant smile. 'I would rather be "improper"—with you. You and Alex are all I need. All I will ever need. Are *you* sure you don't want to delay long enough for your mother and sister to come from Scotland?'

'Not another day. I love my family, but I'd rather wed now and introduce you as my wife when we visit on our honeymoon.' The very idea sparked another rush of excitement and delight.

The butler of Fenniston House left the church to announce that their guests were all seated and the vicar awaited them.

Claire turned to him, her face alight and her eyes tender. 'I came to find you because I didn't want to walk in as a bride on my father's arm. We'll spend the rest of our lives together. I want to begin now—walking in on *your* arm. Are you ready, my Hart, to welcome the priest, greet our guests and exchange our vows?'

Hart smiled down at her. 'As equals, partners, lovers?'

'Ooh, I like the sound of that last,' she murmured. 'Thank heavens the guests are few and with Liliana anxious to leave on her honeymoon, the reception will be short. If…if you are still sure you want to do this? With so many other wealthy, well-born—'

Hart pressed his thumb to her lips. 'Hush, dearest. All the wealth I could ever desire will be mine when you promise to be my wife. My greatest status, to be your husband. Besides, how could I bear the burden of being Duke without you at my side?'

Claire clasped his hand. 'Then let us go be wed, my darling.'

* * * * *

*If you enjoyed this story,
keep an eye out for the next book in
Julia Justiss's
Soldiers to Heirs miniseries,
coming soon!*

*While you wait, check out her
Least Likely to Wed miniseries*

A Season of Flirtation
The Wallflower's Last Chance Season
A Season with Her Forbidden Earl

*And why not pick up her
Heirs in Waiting miniseries?*

The Bluestocking Duchess
The Railway Countess
The Explorer Baroness

Harlequin® Reader Service

Enjoyed your book?

Try the perfect subscription for Romance readers and get more great books like this delivered right to your door.

See why over 10+ million readers have tried Harlequin Reader Service.

Start with a Free Welcome Collection with free books and a gift—valued over $20.

Choose any series in print or ebook. See website for details and order today:

TryReaderService.com/subscriptions